Evolution

BALL OF LIGHT, BOOK ONE

AR CHEN

Table of Contents

Foreword by Blaise Corvin

Hello readers! This book is classified as GameLit or RPG GameLit.

You might be curious what RPG GameLit actually is. GameLit, the larger genre umbrella, is any fiction with game mechanics or that takes place in a game. RPG GameLit is a subgenre where stories include some sort of linear progression for characters that is significant to the plot of the story. These types of stories have been extremely popular in Russia and other countries where they are called "LitRPG." They're just now making an impact in the West!

RPG GameLit is usually a funky mix of Fantasy and Sci Fi. The settings can vary, but what most GameLit novels have in common is a world that most gamers can immediately relate to.

***

Alright, so let's get this out of the way: Ball of Light is a very unique story. If I had to describe it past being LitRPG or GameLit, I'd say it's something like a mobile dungeon, or dungeoncore story. Many of the mechanics found in Steve's adventure are staples in stories about sentient dungeons, but as you all are about to see, Ball of Light is completely different.

This book can also be classified as Young Adult. There are some curse words in this story, but the overall plot should be very accessible (and fun) for younger or older readers alike!

Oops. I'm getting ahead of myself, let's back it up a bit.

This is an interesting foreword to write. Ball of Light is the first book I've helped publish that I haven't actually had any part in writing at all. However, I've known AR Chen for years. Buckle in, there's a little bit of GameLit/LitRPG history to share now.

Back in the day (the day being around 2015), when I was an unpublished web serial writer, I shared my work on Royal Road as well as a few other places. While Delvers LLC was on Royal Road ("Royal Road Legends" at the time), I joined a group of authors as a means of self promotion, then made my own.

Let me elaborate.

One of the most challenging aspects of starting out as a web serial writer is finding new readers. Toward this end, I applied to a group for curated authors/stories and was accepted. One member of this group was **Bonnie L. Price,** who has gone on to publish Deck of Souls. The idea behind this group was that readers could follow the link to the group's page from each author's story, then try the stories of other members, knowing that each of them had been accepted into the group on the basis of being unique and well-written.

This was a great idea, but as a GameLit/LitRPG writer, I felt like I could create a new group that would better direct readers to stories like mine.

Thus, the *LitRPG Society* was born.

After starting this group, I recruited a number of authors whose work I enjoyed. Some notable members were **Travis Bagwell, Luke Chmilenko, Jeffrey "Falcon" Logue, Aleron Kong, Outspan Foster,** and yes, **AR Chen.**

As some readers will know, eventually as more member authors had published and we could no longer keep our books on Royal Road due to our contracts with Amazon, I created the LitRPG Society Facebook group. Eventually, this Facebook group was renamed to the GameLit Society, which still exists today.

So let's fast forward to today, shall we?

I've kept in touch with AR Chen, and I've always liked Ball of Light. Now I am honored to help him publish this story! I am sure that you all will have a fun time with Steve, and I really urge you all to connect with the author on Facebook. He isn't as outgoing (or loud) as me, but he told me he will keep readers posted on social media. I am sure we will see many great things from him in the future. He's one to watch.

To this day, I don't think I've ever seen a story quite like Ball of Light before.

***

I really had a lot of fun helping AR Chen produce this book. Normally I'd put a bunch of links in this area to help people find my work and my social media. However, this is not my book. Instead, I suggest you visit the author's note at the end and connect with him on social media. :)

It's never a bad idea to help out an artists whose work we've enjoyed. If you liked this book, please remember to leave a review.

I hope you all have as much time with Steve as I did when I first read this story a few years ago!

-BC

Chapter 1

"Wake up, Steve!" a female voice shouted. "We have to start now!"

Steve awoke with a massive headache, wondering why an unfamiliar voice was yelling at him, and feeling too dazed to comply. The world was a swirl of bright colors, but as his vision resolved, he found himself in a forest of some sort. He was having difficulty focusing on any one thing, as everything was too vivid.

He didn't remember how he got here; in fact, his mind was something of a blank slate. Steve wasn't sure how he felt about that, or anything really.

Then, he sensed something. Right next to him was a thin long creature, two feet long and dark brown. Steve disapproved of creatures with so many legs on principle. *What are these things called again?* Steve felt that he should've known what it was.

"Come on, Steve!" the Voice pestered. "You're falling behind."

This time he was feeling a bit better and decided to get up as requested.

Only, he didn't actually stand up, just sort of floated up from the ground. As Steve realized this, he was startled to full consciousness and instantly shot up five feet in the air, looking in all directions simultaneously. Steve couldn't really put a finger on it, but this felt wrong. He wasn't sure what wasn't right; there was just something at the back of his mind.

He once again turned his attention to the forest surrounding him, this time noticing the many colorful rocks on the ground in the little clearing where he hovered and some blue trees not too far off. The trees ranged in height from three to twenty feet tall or more.

Steve realized what was wrong. The Voice urging him on was nearby, but he didn't see anything besides the…bug, yeah that's what this kind of creature was called.

A talking bug wasn't the strangest thing about his situation, so he asked it, "Hey, what's going on?"

The bug just stood there, unmoving as it replied, "Well…you're in a new place now, Steve. I can tell you a bit about the situation, but you'll need to do something for me, head towards that red rock over there."

With an effort of will, Steve found he was able to hover in the direction indicated. He kept his vision focused on the bug as he moved and it began to explain.

"This is a world filled with danger and opportunity. I'm not too sure why you were brought here, but your memories are sealed by Ancient-class magic. Here you will have the opportunity to be anything you want to be, but at an equivalent cost. To my knowledge, it seems like there were several others as well," the distinctly female voice of the bug continued as it slowly walked along behind him.

"Others?"

"I am sorry, but I don't know much about that. I can tell you the rules, though."

"There are rules?" Steve felt like he existed in a constant state of confusion.

"Yes, I have been given a set of rules for you for the first countdown, they are as follows:

1) Don't die.

2) Don't wander outside of your ten-mile radius before the countdown ends.

3) Don't evolve before the countdown ends.

4) Don't kill before the countdown ends.

If you fail to obey these rules, there will be consequences."

Steve was confused. He understood the rule part, but nothing about the countdown part.

Steve would have frowned if he could feel his face. "What's this about the countdown?" he asked the bug, which had closed half the distance between them.

"If you focus your mind on the word 'countdown', it'll pop up for you!" the many-legged bug happily answered, clearly pleased that Steve was paying attention.

Steve focused his mind for a bit and found the countdown. It currently read:

4 Days, 23 Hours, 20 Minutes, 10 Seconds

It tracked the seconds to four decimal places, all but the tenths blurring past far too quickly to be readable, which was interesting to watch, though sort of useless. Steve reached the rock still feeling disoriented, like he was having trouble adjusting to his new body.

Steve tried to frown, but nothing happened, as he had no face. This threw his thoughts into confusion; hadn't he always been a normal ball of light?

He floated down to collect himself, coming to rest on top of the red rock the bug had led him to. Having no idea how to proceed from here, he asked what seemed like the obvious question, "What do I do now?"

"Good, you're in the sunlight now…um, I guess you can start considering your options!" the bug replied, her voice merry. "I'll send you a mental list."

Instantly, a list appeared in his mind's eye, similar to the way he'd seen the countdown. He didn't have a name for the language he was seeing, and didn't even recognize the alphabet, which only made it stranger that he somehow knew exactly what it said.

Page One:

1) Goblin

2) Elf

3) Undead

4) Troll

5) Ogre

6) Slime

7) Kobold

8) Naga

9) Turtle

10) Human

He mentally turned the page, seeing even more options, and a bunch of long explanations next to each of the entries, but now didn't seem like the time to go through all of that. Just a bit ago the bug had been in such a hurry to get him moving; why would it now want him to read all this? Something else was nagging at him still, but Steve couldn't quite place his thought on it.

His mind was still slightly hazy, but he really did feel much better than when he'd first woken up. Now he could feel energy coursing through his body, warming and strengthening him.

Suddenly a thought struck him; the bug didn't seem to volunteer much so he'd better keep the conversation going if he wanted to figure out what was going on. "What are you?" he asked the bug, which by now had nearly reached where he was sitting.

"I'm your helper! Unfortunately, my memory has more holes than Swiss cheese. Although, what is Swiss cheese, and why did I think of that comparison? Hmm, that seems odd…" The bug's voice had started off strong, but trailed off. "I also don't know too much about this place at the moment, but I can assure you I can help…"

The insect's voice had sounded like it was right beside him, or maybe even in his mind this entire time. Steve wasn't sure how that worked, but the bug seemed trustworthy, so he decided not to worry about it—which was easy to do with the ever-increasing, pleasant warmth suffusing his body.

"I originally told you to move closer to this rock because the sunlight is more direct in this area than where you started. Is it helping?" the bug asked hesitantly.

"I'm feeling a lot better now, thank you," Steve replied. He was feeling better by the minute, and now he knew why. Feeling grateful, he turned his focus to the red sun shining down upon him.

Wait, a red sun? It seemed so tiny, surrounded by fluffy white clouds in a deep-blue sky. Both the size and the color felt wrong, but he wasn't sure what would have seemed right.

"Um…Steve?" the bug called for his attention in a concerned voice. "You might want to move away from that bug."

Steve turned his focus back to the bug. He felt confused. "You mean that isn't you?" he asked. With it so close, and no longer sure of its intent, he noticed that it wasn't an insect at all; it had what seemed like a hundred legs, and more concerningly, two huge, glistening pincers.

Then, the bug jumped him.

***

A few moments later, Steve was sure his thoughts were clearing, as he started feeling distinctly concerned. "This doesn't seem good? Why is this happening to me?"

Wiggle wiggle wiggle.

"Well, your body is slowly adjusting to the new climate," the

Voice helpfully answered. "It's normal to feel fatigued at first, then recover your energy over time…I think."

"That's well and good…but can you tell me why this thing is inside me?" Steve rephrased the question. He couldn't see inside of himself; his luminescence was far too bright, but he could vaguely feel the intruder moving around inside him. It was a disturbing sensation, and yet for some reason, not as concerning as he felt it should be.

"Ah…Oh! I remember now. This is an arthropod common to this region, I think it's called a centipede." The Voice seemed happy about reclaiming some of its memory. "I think it likes you!"

"I…I really don't think that's the case," Steve stated.

At that moment, the pleasant warming sensation accelerated significantly. "Hold on, I'm beginning to feel something, I feel…great!" Steve exclaimed. "It must have something to do with this centipede!"

There was no reply from the Voice this time. Steve felt that this was a bit odd, so he phrased it as a question. "Does this feeling have something to do with this centipede inside of me?" he asked.

"Yes! I believe you are currently absorbing its energy, fueling yourself as a light being," the Voice continued in a lecturing tone. "Energy has many uses in this world!"

Abruptly, the large centipede writhed in apparent panic, and forced its way out of his body. Thankfully it wasn't painful, just an awkward sensation. Once free of his body, the centipede charged off into the forest, moving far more quickly than before.

"So, that just happened," remarked Steve. The voice didn't say anything. After a moment, he mentally sighed and asked, "What should I call you, voice?"

"You can call me Bonnie!"

"Okay, what do you need to tell me now, Bonnie? The bug is gone, but I have no clue what I should do next and time matters, right?"

"Oh, right! I think you should be learning to control your energy." Bonnie sounded a bit unsure of herself, but still cheerful. "Try it, Steve! Visualize your inner energy pool, and use it to blast a small Shock at that tree right there."

Steve focused on the nearest tree and tried to harness the inner sense of warmth he was feeling, which he assumed was his 'inner energy pool,' but nothing happened.

After a few minutes of unproductive effort Steve asked, "Nothing is happening, what am I doing wrong?"

"Try visualizing your energy as a fog, shape that fog with your thoughts, into a small lightning bolt!" Bonnie directed.

Steve followed Bonnie's directions. After another few minutes, he produced a lightning bolt that arced out, struck the tree, and left a smoldering crater in its trunk.

When he realized he'd succeeded, a wave of enthusiasm washed through Steve, as he stared at the smoke rising from the glowing embers. That was followed by a wave of fatigue, and the realization that the energy expenditure had significantly dimmed his radiance. Judging by the way he was feeling, Steve estimated he'd just expended about twice what he'd absorbed from that centipede.

***

Five minutes later, Steve was feeling somewhat restored by the sunlight he had absorbed and decided to ask, "So…what should I do now?"

"I'm sorry, I'm not able to discuss that with you," Bonnie replied apologetically, but firmly. "I am here to provide you with basic information, but am not allowed to direct you, or even influence your decisions!"

Steve's thoughts were still in a jumble, as if he was missing something, other than the obvious loss of all his memories prior to waking up here. His initial stupor upon waking in this colorful world had thankfully faded, but things still didn't add up, so he examined what he did know.

He was a light being, though something about that still didn't seem right. He had Bonnie, who was some sort of assistant, and he could shoot out lightning from his body. At that thought, he looked back to the tree, which was now enveloped in a cloud of smoke that stretched skyward. He checked the countdown timer once more, just because he could. It read:

4 Days 23 Hours 3 Minutes 55 Seconds

One of the few things that seemed clear was that this timer was important, so he decided to ask Bonnie, "What does this timer do?"

"The timer counts down to your first evolution!" Bonnie answered excitedly. Steve briefly wondered if she got bored, having nothing to do but wait for him to ask her a question. Before he could ask, Bonnie continued, "Make sure you understand all your evolution choices and collect enough energy for the big moment!"

Steve thought about this and checked the list once more in his head. Once again, he only skimmed the entries, starting on the second page this time.

Page 2:

11) Beast-man

12) Vampire

13) Dragon

14) Orc

15) Dwarf

The list seemed to go on for at least several more pages, but none of it meant anything to Steve so he tried to gather more information. "Does each evolution require different amounts of energy?"

"Yes! Some evolutions are more powerful than others, so the base energy necessary for the change will be greater!" Bonnie paused, then helpfully offered, "I can list them out in terms of most to least energy required if you would like!"

"Please do," Steve agreed, and immediately saw the reorganized list, which now read:

1) ???

2) ???

3) ???

4) Dragon

5) Undead

6) Elf

7) Slime

8) Turtle

9) Goblin

10) Vampire

"I can't read the first three choices," Steve stated. "What does it mean?" As he asked, the smoldering embers became tongues of flame.

Not particularly concerned, Steve turned his attention back to the list.

"Um, they're hidden, but I think the cost means they must be better than a Dragon!" Bonnie exclaimed, stating the obvious.

"Well, I suppose I should focus on gathering energy then." Steve thought of something. "By the way, why are you helping me?"

Before Bonnie could reply, she was cut off by a shout.

"It's over here!" an unfamiliar voice called from somewhere on the other side of the smoke cloud which surrounded the burning tree.

Chapter 2

"It's over here!" Ash turned and called back to his group. Then he hastily chanted a basic water spell to put out the small fire, which was licking its way up the bark of the tree before him. The water, collected from the atmosphere, doused the small flames. Breathing heavily from the run, he thanked the gods that he'd arrived in time to prevent it from spreading. Just as he was preparing to head back, he noticed the tree before him was blue. Maybe it was diseased?

Turning to really examine his surroundings, he found himself in a wonderland. A multitude of the trees around him were various shades of blue. He'd never even seen a single blue tree before, in all his nearly fifteen years, but that was actually the most mundane aspect of the scene before him. There, in the center of clearing he stood at the edge of, was a hovering globe of light and… "Wait, are those Crystals?" Ash breathed in disbelief. His thoughts raced. Crystals. Glowing mass of light. Blue trees. It was all adding up.

"Azra! Loop! Come take a look!" Ash turned around and called for his companions, before turning back to watch over the strange scene. He was aware that the glowing yellow orb of light in the clearing might be dangerous.

"What is it? What do we need to do?" Azra asked, then went silent and wide-eyed as she took in the scene. As usual, Ash's sister looked very put together, like she'd just left the house, rather than walked half the morning. She was younger by almost a year, newly fourteen, and a good head shorter than Ash.

Azra's red hair was pinned to the side with her trademark flower, which was blue today, matching her clothing. Her dress was modest, but with the hem still high enough to properly explore the wilderness. Azra could be a bit hot-headed, but she was still practical, and certainly didn't enjoy mending tears, nor getting caught on things.

"Is that a god or something?" Ash turned, to see that Loop had also caught up. His friend's brown, shaggy hair had sticks and leaves in it, and his simple tan smock had a half-dozen fresh green scuffs, as if he'd hit every branch he passed on the way here. Despite being almost two years older than Ash, Loop was a few inches shorter, and always seemed to be colliding with things, including the ground, or getting into trouble.

Ash sighed. "Well, I've never met one before so I wouldn't know." Of their little group, Ash knew he was the most responsible and level-headed, but it got tiring sometimes. He kept on observing the light globe, while trying to keep out of sight behind a tree. "It doesn't seem like it—"

"Ash! We need to do something!" Azra demanded, cutting Ash off. When he looked over, she was preparing her ice summon spell under her breath. Her hands were glowing. "It could be a threat to the village. We need to—"

"No, we don't!" Ash told her emphatically. He was the leader, and she was acting without direction. Last time she'd done that, they had nearly been gored by a wild boar, and this thing could be much more dangerous. "Stop that, Azra! Just give me a moment to think." He glared at her a moment, before she caught his eye and the glow around her hands faded away.

The glowing light ball had to be a magical entity, right? So Azra casting a spell would likely alert it to their location and attacking would be certain to anger it. They needed to proceed with caution. Ash massaged his forehead, as he tried to remember what the Elder had told him about gods, but he just couldn't.

Ash felt out of his depth—whatever he did here might affect the lives of everyone in the village. There was no guarantee that the light ball would still be here if he went back to consult the Elder, but he was nervous making such an important decision on his own; they weren't equipped to deal with something like this.

On the one hand, if this light were a magical construct formed by some conjuror, they might still be around, and could be a rogue mage much stronger than their party of three. On the other hand, it could be a blessing to the village. Only one thing was certain: this was no natural phenomenon—it could be terrible, wonderful, or both. He was only sixteen, what was he supposed to do if Loop was right and this was a god! Finally, he had an idea.

"Loop, run back to the village. Look for the Elder, tell him we saw something in the forest," Ash said quickly. He was in a cold sweat now, sneaking looks back to the glowing light in the clearing. Though it was afternoon, with the sun shining brightly and illuminating the clearing, the orb was clearly visible. "We'll stay here."

They were close, but it hadn't noticed them yet. Or maybe it had but didn't care.

"Ash. I have an idea," Azra said. Ash looked at his sister again curiously; she had apparently grown calmer while Ash worked himself up. Before he could ask about her idea, she shocked him by marching into the clearing.

4 Days 23 Hours 0 Minutes 0 Seconds.

Out of nowhere, Steve was hit with a wave of euphoria. He felt confident and powerful. None of his earlier concerns mattered in the face of this glorious feeling, so he tuned out everything and just basked in it.

"Steve, there is a human here," Bonnie interrupted his bliss.

Grudgingly, Steve turned his focus back to reality. *Hmm? It seems like my presence has attracted visitors!* he thought, as he watched a human use water magic to extinguish the fire he'd started. After a while, he was joined by two others. They spoke amongst themselves and it seemed like they thought he didn't notice them, as they peeked around the tree.

After a while, one determinedly marched towards him, followed reluctantly by a second one. When they were near, they knelt and seemed to intently study the dirt. As he examined the prostrate humans, wondering what they were doing, he realized they must be expecting him to do something and spoke, "Rise, good people!" Steve didn't really know what he was saying and didn't really care. Being magnanimous seemed to be coming naturally with the way he felt now.

The two human youths shared a glance before slowly rising, while keeping their eyes on the ground. Finally, the smaller one asked a question. "Please forgive our ignorance, mighty one, may we know which god we have found ourselves in the presence of?"

"My name is Steve!" Steve exclaimed, confirming to himself with the pronouncement that Steve was his name, as it felt right, even though he still couldn't remember how or when that name had been bestowed upon him. Hearing himself called a god made him wonder, was he a god? He wasn't sure what exactly being a god meant, but from what the short one had said, it was clear they must be strong. The term didn't resonate with him like his name did, but he did feel powerful, so maybe—looking back at the short one, a concept formed in his mind, *girl*— yes, maybe this girl was correct.

"Oh mighty god Steve, I, on behalf of my village, beseech you to bless us with your presence!" the other human, who seemed to be a *boy* asked, then paused, as if trying to remember something. Steve waited patiently, trying to appear humble in all his shining magnificence. "Uh, please come meet with our elder," he clarified.

"I think we should take this opportunity, Steve." Bonnie's voice had a crafty tone, which was new. "We could learn a lot from this village."

"I will come with you!" Steve said confidently. This wonderful feeling seemed to have something to do with the arrival of these people, so surely being near more people would be even better. "Lead the way, good people!"

It was at this moment that another human boy hesitantly walked out of the trees and the three began whispering. After a few moments of hushed but fierce conversation, the smaller one, the girl, looked back, stealing a glance just below where Steve was hovering. She asked, "May we take one of your Elemental Crystals back to the village?"

The new boy immediately stammered, "P-please, she meant no offen—"

"It's completely fine! You may even have two!" Steve interrupted the nervous human, impressed with his own generosity.

At this point, Steve was completely overcome with his newfound feeling. The rush of confidence kept growing every time he made a decision, and the quicker he made them, the better he felt. He almost worried he would lose himself, but that concern was quickly swept aside just as all his earlier ones had been.

The first boy and girl moved forward hesitantly, but eventually stooped down to collect the two rocks they'd been allowed to take. They chose one red and one blue rock, neither of which seemed too big or heavy. The new boy fidgeted in place, seeming not to know what to do with his hands, as he watched the other two. When the three humans were standing together again, they shared one more look.

"Oh mighty god Steve, follow me," said the tallest boy. "My name's Ash." Then he pointed to the girl next to him. "This is my younger sister, Azra. That messy one over there is Loop. Please, follow me."

With that, Ash turned and put action to his words, heading towards the thicker part of the forest. The other two youths followed, with the one called Loop now holding the two rocks in his arms.

Steve took one last look at where he'd awoken, then followed Ash. As he began moving, he floated up to head height and easily matched their pace. This was far faster than he'd moved before, and he felt momentarily proud of the accomplishment, before that feeling was also subsumed by the mania he was experiencing.

When they were into the forest proper, Steve noticed that the trees and rocks abruptly looked completely different. The trees were green, and in place of the variously colored rocks, there was only a grayish-white. At first, he wondered what was going on, then finally was able to reason out that he had been in a special place before, one where the environment had had different colors. When he figured this out, he experienced a burst of satisfaction, feeling incredibly clever.

The four of them moved at a leisurely speed. Steve discovered that he didn't have any trouble with the terrain, adding to his overall good mood. He became so engrossed in examining their surroundings, he hardly noticed that the humans kept talking to him. As they walked, Ash, Loop, and Azra took turns carrying the stones. Carrying them seemed to cause the humans some difficulty. Despite being significantly smaller than others that had been in Steve's clearing, they were still apparently quite heavy. Occasionally, Azra would sneak a peek at Steve, thinking he wouldn't notice.

He noticed.

Steve once again checked the countdown. It now read:

4 Days 22 Hours 40 Minutes 3 Seconds

He felt that there was something more to the countdown, but without any new information, the thought didn't hold his attention long.

The four beings walked and floated a while longer, before they arrived at the point that the forest gave way to a plain. The plain was filled with blue grass that grew to the youths' waists. After looking around a moment, Ash led them to a weathered-looking path of gray stone which cut a gash through the ocean of grass. Ash started down it, cradling the red rock in his arms. His clothes were soaked with sweat at this point and he looked exhausted.

"Eh…I really thought it would be more fun than this," Bonnie complained. "We've been doing nothing but wandering through this boring forest."

Steve was taken aback by this, having quite enjoyed the journey so far. He decided not to even acknowledge the comment as he continued taking in everything, turning his focus on anything that caught his attention.

A while later, Ash pointed forward. "Up ahead is our very own Niti Village!" He sounded excited at first, but then coughed and said, "Uh, we're just a simple farming village."

Steve noted what the boy said but didn't respond. He decided to float far above the uniform grass, moving higher until he could see the entirety of the village in the distance. As the group grew closer, he was able to see that while simple, it did look fairly large. Its buildings and animals looked strange to Steve, but again he didn't know what would feel normal.

In the immediate vicinity of the town, a number of animals grazed, and there were more still within pens near some of the homes. Beyond the grazing animals, there was something large and blue, which sparkled in the sunlight—with a moment's concentration, he realized it was a pond. He tried to drink in all the sights at once, but even with his omnidirectional vision, he could only study one thing at a time. The people he saw seemed similar to the three he had first met. When he noticed that a group of people had gathered together near the entrance, looking his way, he observed them with interest.

"What are all these people?" Steve inquired of his guide.

"They are the humble residents of Niti Village," Ash replied deferentially.

The group kept moving until they arrived at the village entrance. A wooden pole with a larger block of wood on top had been pushed into the ground, with characters that Steve didn't recognized carved into it. *So, this place is called Niti,* Steve thought.

As they entered the village, Steve noticed that almost all the people were wearing dark, pointed hats. As they noticed him, they stopped their conversations and bowed low towards him. It seemed like a respectful gesture, which pleased Steve, even if he didn't understand why they were doing it.

As he thought on the matter, he remembered that the boy named Ash had talked a little about the gods of the world while they were walking. He'd said that the texts in the village taught that gods could take on whatever form they wished and were the highest form of existence in Zeth, this world. Gods held the power to change the fate of lower-level creatures like humans. None of this had really meant anything to him before, but now he realized that the villagers must really believe he was one of these gods.

Now that he understood a little more about his situation, he felt even more reluctant to ask questions. Steve worried that admitting to his lack of memories, or ignorance of something the villagers might think a god should know, would cause them to lose faith in him. He wasn't certain that he was a god, but Steve was definitely enjoying their belief that he was.

As he examined the bowing people, Steve thought about the journey to the village. *How far had they traveled to get here from the clearing?* Maybe a few miles, he decided. He had no idea how he'd calculated that, but it felt right.

To the side, Ash suddenly said, "I'm sorry, uh, god Steve, but I must leave you now to check in with the Elder. Please wait a moment."

When Ash walked away, the bowing villagers seemed to take that as a sign and began to disperse to their own tasks. Most of them avoided looking directly at him, but Steve found himself liking the attitudes of these pointy-hatted people. He noticed every time one of them would turn to face his direction, studying his magnificence, and Steve wondered if their expression was worshipful. He wasn't sure but decided to believe it was. Steve floated proudly, trying his best to give off a regal air.

In his peripheral unfocused view, he saw Azra follow Ash to a pointy-hatted villager and a smaller human. Focusing on the man, he noted strange symbols on the hat the man wore, but Steve didn't think too much on it. They would come back to his godliness soon— at least, Ash had said they would. Ash, Azra, and the man spoke in hushed tones, too quiet for Steve to make out, then returned to where he still hovered.

"Esteemed god Steve," the older man began. "I am the village chief, known as Leffer. We welcome your presence in our humble village."

"Hello, Leffer!" Steve said, grandiosely. "I am in need of a place to stay for a few days. Is Niti Village willing to accommodate me?"

"Of course, Great One," Leffer answered. "We will see to your lodgings right away. We thank you for blessing our village with Elemental Crystals of fire and water. These resources will not go to waste." The Elder turned to Ash and issued a command. "Lead god Steve to the guest house."

Ash nodded in acknowledgement and then said, "Please follow me, Great One."

Happy that the villagers were being so accommodating, Steve followed Ash's lead. The boy pointed out and named many buildings in the village as they passed, but the names meant very little to Steve, so he found it easy to tune them out. His thoughts wandered to himself, and he ultimately concluded that his form must be quite pleasing to the eye, given the frequent glances of the humans in his direction. Contemplating his circumstances, he decided that though he had no idea where he was, or why he was here, he was quite satisfied with the course of today's events.

Steve followed Ash to a small building constructed with thick earthen walls. Although it looked quite small and simple from the outside, the inside was surprisingly cozy.

When Ash was done with the tour, he apologized for the simple accommodations, but assured Steve that it was the nicest guest house in the village. He finished by saying, "If you need anything, god Steve, feel free to come to me about it."

"Ask him for a chicken!" Bonnie suggested. "You'll need to absorb lots of energy if you're going to be ready for your evolution. You get diminishing returns from just absorbing light."

"I require a chicken for my glorious being." Steve was certain this was a polite and appropriate way to phrase his request.

"Uh. Of course," Ash replied. The boy had seemed shocked for a moment, but then hurried away with purpose. Steve watched him leave through the cloth-covered entrance as he let his thoughts wander once again.

I'm pretty great, aren't I? Steve thought. On a whim, he tried to project the thought to Bonnie.

"Eh…sure," she replied.

That had sounded sarcastic, but he was a magnanimous god, so he let it go. *If only everyone could be as great as me,* Steve pleasantly thought. There was no reply this time.

Moments later, Ash hurried back through the cloth-covered entrance with a small creature in his hands. Almost immediately upon entry, it began squawking and thrashing. Steve assumed that this was the chicken that he had requested.

"Wha—" Ash exclaimed as he tried to keep his hold on the chicken. With a frown, he flicked it on the head and it went still. He adjusted his grip on the chicken and brought it over to where Steve was floating. "Here it is, god Steve. Sorry for the delay!"

"It's fine, really no trouble at all," Steve replied, putting his merciful nature on full display. "Thank you, Ash."

"Uh, what would you like me to do with this?" Ash lifted the chicken slightly for emphasis.

"Just put it down there, that's fine."

Ash quickly complied, and spoke as he backed away, "Well, if you need anything else, you can find me at the village center." He then turned on his heel and exited quickly enough that the curtain which served as a door was left fluttering in his wake. Steve liked this human already; he was very efficient and respectful towards his greatness.

"What do I do with this chicken?" Steve asked Bonnie, only now realizing how it may have looked to the humans for him to be conversing with an unseen partner. Surely it only enhanced his divine allure.

"The rules don't allow you to kill, but I can guide you in how to intentionally siphon energy from a living being, as you did instinctually to the centipede that entered your body in the clearing," Bonnie answered readily, though seeming to sound a little less enthusiastic than before. She continued, "Focus on the chicken and visualize its energy in the same way you did your own energy when you shot the lightning bolt. Then, picture the energy flowing towards you. Just don't take too much or you'll risk killing it!"

Steve did as instructed. He figured it would be easy, so he focused on the chicken and its energy. Slowly, but surely, he saw the energy flow towards him in his mind's eye. As the tendril of vitality reached and entered his body, he felt a heady rush of elation. Even the way he'd felt since meeting the humans was insignificant in comparison. He needed *more*!

"Steve——I think you're taking a bit too much!" Bonnie warned. "Steve, can you hear me? Steve?"

Can't be bad if it feels this good, right? Steve justified his actions to himself. Latching onto the sensation, Steve kept going, drawing more of the cloud into himself. The chicken had been calm before, but suddenly squawked loudly. It flapped its wings in desperation, which sent feathers around the room, as it ran in panicked circles. Then it fell over as its legs kicked spasmodically.

The feeling built until it was a mind-numbing bliss. His glowing body felt ever warmer, but never unpleasant. Soon the flow of energy began to ebb away, and the chicken's struggles became ever weaker. As the last shred of energy entered Steve's body, the chicken struggled no more.

Bonnie's voice suddenly bored into Steve's mind, her tone inhumanly dispassionate. "Due to disobeying the rules, consequences will be applied."

Steve felt a tingle, and everything went dark.

Chapter 3

4 Days 21 Hours 0 Minutes 0 Seconds

"Steve…your turn," someone nearby nagged. "Are you going to make a move yet or what?"

Steve shook off his daydream, feeling confused. He was in the Grand Library, surrounded by other kids his age, all paired off and playing a board game.

"Come on, Steve, you know you can't win this time," the voice bragged. "I've got your rook and queen off the board already."

He glanced at the person talking, a short, thin-lipped young man with sharp eyes and a nervous smile. With a slight frown, Steve turned his attention to the game. As he studied the board, he recalled the name Xander—that was his opponent's name. Steve always played this ancient board game with his good friend Xander, during lunchtime in the chess club.

What a weird daydream, Steve thought to himself as he got his mind back into the game. After a moment of thought, he moved his bishop to check the enemy king.

Earlier he had sacrificed his queen and rook in order to get to this position. He only had two knights and a single bishop left, but the enemy king was out of position. Xander had castled earlier, which was often a good way to get the king into a more defendable position.

However, Steve had fully expected and even wanted this reaction to his advance; Xander was right where Steve wanted him. Steve's analytical skills and sense of strategy had been honed over years of playing this game competitively. Multiple chess championships had earned him a high rating within the chess community. By this point, Steve liked to think he had mastered most of the many elements that went into playing chess at a high level. At the very least, he knew all of his strategic strengths and weaknesses.

"Checkmate," Steve pronounced a few moves later, as he leaned back and stretched in his chair. When he checked the time, he realized the game had lasted for a good portion of the hour.

"Agh—what the heck, how do you do this, man?" Xander shook his head in defeat. Steve had to give Xander credit; he hadn't played badly at all, just not well enough to win.

Steve tried to explain it to Xander. "Dude, you made a blunder about turn ten where you castled instead of pushing. Your loss of momentum left you wide open to my 'pawn storm' on your queen side. People think that going first as White is an advantage, and it is, but it also means you are given the chance to make the first mistake. If you—" Steve trailed off, midsentence. He couldn't shake that weird daydream he'd had. Even now, it felt like it had been real; he'd never had that kind of experience before. Maybe he would need to go to the hospital; his head felt funny.

Of course, he wouldn't speak a word of it to Xander, lest he wanted to be made fun of for years to come. They'd call him "Kooky Steve," or something like that. He was confident that Xander would think of something.

Trying to settle his mind on reality, he tried to think of what he had for lunch, but he drew a blank. He thought of his classes, but again nothing. As frightening as being unable to remember what he'd been doing just before coming here was, worse was the definite sense that he had a memory, but something was preventing him from accessing it.

As soon as he put that thought into words, he knew it was true and felt a chill creeping up his back. He turned his head, glancing from person to person. Some of them still held pieces in their hands, but none were playing. They were all staring at him. Silence filled the room.

Was this even chess club? Had they always been looking at him? Steve couldn't remember.

Has it always been like this? Steve wondered, as he silently looked across the Grand Library. Goosebumps tingled across his body. He vividly felt multiple realizations and fears cross his mind at once, like an emotional relay race.

As Steve turned back to Xander to ask what was happening, he heard a mechanical, and vaguely female voice in his mind. "Congratulations," it droned. "You are the first to break the rules within three hours of starting."

Steve remained silent, concerned about what kind of punishment he would receive for his transgression, and unnerved as everyone in the room continued to stare at him, unblinking. He knew that 'daydream' had seemed too real.

"You have been granted a skill due to your audacity!" the Voice continued. "For your boldness in defying the rules, you shall receive: Greater Mind, a passive skill which will allow you to resist mind control and mind-influencing effects to some extent."

His surroundings blurred, then winked out of existence.

***

Steve awoke again in a flash of heat. His omnidirectional vision was back, and now that he had experienced what it was like seeing with eyes, he realized how unusual this was. Was being in that room, playing that game, one of his memories from before? He couldn't be sure.

Steve focused in on the dead chicken, lying nearby in the beam of sunlight shining in through a window. To think, all this had started because he couldn't resist draining that bird. Steve tried to access more of his memories but had little luck in doing so. Even some of the detail of what he'd just experienced was starting to fade, but what he did remember most clearly was the voice telling him he had gained an ability.

"Greater Mind," was it? Steve thought to himself. *A reward for being adventurous? Or bold? What does that mean?* He remembered Bonnie and projected a thought at her. *I have a Greater Mind skill now?*

"Yes." Bonnie's reply was monotone. Something was different about her right now...whatever she was. Steve couldn't pinpoint what was going on, though he had a theory, or maybe as he had no evidence, it would be more accurate to call it a hunch.

So, it seems like now I've recovered some of my reasoning ability, some of my old analytical skill from before I was in this form. I could be skeptical that the me in the vision was…me, but I think I'm right. Steve pondered further, remembering everything that had happened since he'd awakened in the clearing. *I don't think the entire change is related to that chicken. The last time I absorbed energy from something, I didn't have weird visions and didn't change.* He thought some more. *Maybe it's related to the countdown.*

He checked the countdown again.

<4 Days 20 Hours 40 Minutes 33 Seconds>

After carefully doing some math in his head, he thought he might be on to something. *It seems like my mind underwent change at around four days and twenty-one hours, since I think I started at five days. The last big change was when those humans arrived, I'd thought it was because of them, but it was at four days and twenty-three hours. Could this be a simple pattern?* he wondered. Working on a gut feeling, which was strange without a gut, he did some more math. *If my hypothesis is correct, I should expect a new change when the countdown reaches 4 Days 18 Hours 0 Minutes 0 Seconds. Yeah, I'll wait and see if anything happens then, I guess.*

Bonnie announced, "Steve, you are eligible to learn new skills now that your energy level has risen." The voice was Bonnie's, but she also definitely still sounded weird.

She continued, "What would you like to learn? You have a

choice—" At this point, her voice suddenly cut off. Then it came back into his mind, "—lowing message."

"Please—carefully—" Her voice cut out again, then after one more blip, it was gone entirely.

Two spells came to the forefront of Steve's mind immediately.

***

Blink – Flash instantly to a nearby point

Teleport – Channel you and three nearby willing beings to another place in memory

***

Well, this is a problem, Steve mused. *I have no idea what to pick, and very little information to base a decision on.*

Whatever was going on with Bonnie, she apparently wasn't going to be helping him with this. Steve had tried willing a few questions to her, but there was no response.

He stared at his two choices, or what he assumed to be his two spell choices, for some time. Finally, he thought, *Well, Blink then.* He'd reasoned that Blink seemed more versatile and practical than Teleport, though he couldn't put the reason into words. It seemed like it had something to do with that game he remembered playing in his previous life.

After he'd made the decision, information to execute the Blink spell instantly flowed into his mind. Now he knew that by expending the right amount of energy, he would Blink to a nearby location. Thankfully, its operation was just as simple as it had sounded in the description.

Steve tried to use Blink in the guest house. He cast the spell, focusing on a spot about six feet from his current location. Nothing happened.

"Uh…" Steve said aloud, confused.

Bonnie's voice suddenly filled his mind again. Her tone had reverted to normal: chipper and upbeat. "Remember, Steve, your evolution path will be determined by what spells you learn, energy usage, and your innate disposition!"

"Okay," Steve replied. That wasn't very helpful in this situation; was she even paying attention to what he was doing? Well, that was the least of his questions regarding her, there was also who or what she was, and why she was here to help him. She'd seemed to respond mostly to direct questions but was now blurting out information, seemingly at random. As he thought on that, he realized how strange his own behavior was prior to his vision. What made him feel so euphoric, why had he been so confident or even arrogant?

He paused to center his thoughts, circling back to what he knew. His goal right now was to evolve into something worthwhile, as powerful as possible. Bonnie had said that he was the first one to break the rules, meaning that there must be others, and she'd dropped other hints about this before, too. For the time being, he was going to assume that he was in a competition of some sort. There was so much he didn't know, so many things he hadn't bothered to ask in his earlier state of megalomania, but if his thought that this was a competition was correct, he couldn't afford to spend much of his limited time asking what might be pointless questions.

For the time being, nothing really made sense. Why was he a ball of light now, if he had been human before? What had changed him and why? Even the "consequence" applied for killing the chicken seemed disconnected from much of the guidance he'd received so far. From his perspective, he'd been rewarded for violating the rules.

Projecting his thoughts, he asked, *Hey Bonnie, can you bring up the evolution paths listed that are best-suited to me?* Mentally communicating with her was becoming nearly second nature at this point; the process seemed to include visualizing a space in his mind as Bonnie, then projecting his thoughts there.

"Sorry, I can't do that, but I can show you the list so you can browse it yourself!" Bonnie replied. That was strange. Steve could've sworn Bonnie had done such things for him before.

How do I unlock the three question-mark evolutions at the top? Steve mentally asked. He remembered there had been three unknown evolutions at the top of his list, which had been followed by Dragon. *Give me a description of the rest of the top 10, too.*

Even as he formed the question, he realized that exploring his options might take a while. He quickly checked his mental countdown timer again, to make sure he had enough time to prepare for his next change, or vision.

4 Days 20 Hours 2 Minutes 30 Seconds

Bonnie replied, "The three evolutions at the top will be unlocked after completing specific unknown tasks!" This was the most Steve had ever conversed with her and Bonnie seemed pleased by the attention. After a slight pause, she reported, "Okay, you should be able to see it now."

1) ??? – End Evolution – Undetermined

a) Initial Power – Medium

b) Energy Gain – Easy

c) Energy Consolidation – Hard

d) Innate Benefits – Copycat

2) ??? – End Evolution – Undetermined

a) Initial Power – High

b) Energy Gain – Medium

c) Energy Consolidation – Easy

d) Innate Benefits – Resistant Skin

3) ??? – End Evolution – Undetermined

a) Initial Power – High

b) Energy Gain – Difficult

c) Energy Consolidation – Medium

d) Innate Benefits – Worship

4) Dragon – End Evolution – Dragon God

a) Initial Power – High

b) Energy Gain – Difficult

c) Energy Consolidation – Difficult

d) Innate Benefits – Dragon Race

5) Undead – End Evolution – Undead Emperor

a) Initial Power – Low

b) Energy Gain – Easy

c) Energy Consolidation – Easy

d) Innate Benefits – Blight

6) Elf – End Evolution – Undetermined

a) Initial Power – Low

b) Energy Gain – Medium

c) Energy Consolidation – Easy

d) Innate Benefits – Leadership

7) Slime – End Evolutions – Undetermined

a) Initial Power – Medium

b) Energy Gain – Easy

c) Energy Consolidation – Hard

d) Innate Benefits – Indestructible Body

8) Turtle – End Evolutions – Undetermined

a) Initial Power – Low

b) Energy Gain – Easy

c) Energy Consolidation – Hard

d) Innate Benefits – Time

9) Goblin – End Evolutions – Undetermined

a) Initial Power – High

b) Energy Gain – Easy

c) Energy Consolidation – Easy

d) Innate Benefits – Goblin Clan

10) Human – End Evolution – Undetermined

a) Initial Power – Low

b) Energy Gain – Undetermined

c) Energy Consolidation – Undetermined

d) Innate Benefits – Tenacity

Well, that's all the information I can get for now, I guess. It's not enough to make any decisions, but I also won't need to for a while yet, Steve analyzed. He focused his attention out the window of the guest hut, seeing that dusk was falling, the sun already half hidden below the horizon.

Steve came to a decision, sighed and said aloud, "Time to practice Blink…again." He'd reasoned that he needed to have an escape mechanism for dangerous situations. It was likely that he would be tested in the future, since this was a game of sorts. Actually making the spell work seemed to still be a problem, though. Why wasn't he able to cast Blink?

"Energy level," Bonnie piped up. Steve noticed that she was speaking up at increasingly random times. "Got to make sure you have enough energy."

And she couldn't say so earlier? Steve felt that this was a bit unfair. He hadn't considered the idea of a way to measure energy level and thus, hadn't asked about it. "How do I see my energy levels?" He waited patiently for a response.

A minute passed. Steve was confused. Was Bonnie gone?

He considered asking again, but decided against it; he would figure it out himself. There was no time to waste. He tried to check his energy level the same way he approached mentally communicating with Bonnie. Steve quickly made a space for the idea of "energy" in his mind, and then focused his attention on it.

Current Energy – 6

Max Energy – 25

It had worked! He saw the two numbers just as when he checked the countdown.

He examined the numbers and pondered for a moment. There were two ways of obtaining energy that Steve had encountered thus far: absorbing living creatures and soaking up direct sunlight. It seemed like the chicken he'd killed earlier had given him a lot of energy. Though, seeing this numerical representation begged the question: What would happen if the energy count went to zero? There was still far too much he didn't understand about the world and the system.

Despite the likelihood that he was in a life-and-death situation, Steve realized that he was enjoying himself. If Steve could grin, he would have. His mind raced as he considered all the possibilities. Everything he'd seen or done so far was so fresh and wonderful.

Now he knew that he would have to gather energy if he wanted to practice the Blink spell. It was dangerous to rely on the villagers. They worshipped him as a god of some sort, but he didn't know them well enough to predict what they would do, or what they may want in return for the favors they were doing for him. He had to be cautious.

It seemed like the boy Ash had wanted elemental crystals. Perhaps they were a valuable currency in this world? He mentally added that question to his growing list of things he didn't know. The one thing that was clear to him was that, to obtain more bargaining power and more control over his situation, he needed to increase his repertoire of powers.

He floated outside; the sun had set, his own body the lone light in the now dark village.

Chapter 4

Whew! This is mentally taxing, Steve thought to himself. He was in the middle of absorbing the energy of a rabbit which lay disabled on the ground before him. He'd already consumed several small creatures in this way. He'd stun them with his Shock skill, then drain them to death. It seemed that there were no additional consequences for killing after the first incident. Each rabbit creature he killed gave him ten full energy points.

But... Why is he just staring at me? Steve wondered. Ash had shown him to a field with small creatures for him to absorb. The human now stood just a dozen feet away, unmoving. *Maybe he needs energy as well? It might be selfish for me to take all the rabbits.*

"Hey, Ash. Do you also need to absorb, as well?" Steve called out, focusing his gaze on the boy. "Don't hold back on my account."

"I, uh. Humans don't absorb," Ash stammered and shuffled his wooden stick back and forth between his hands, as he looked everywhere but at Steve. "Please, continue. Don't mind me."

"Alright," Steve replied. *If humans don't absorb, how do they survive?* He didn't really have time to worry about that now, but made a mental note to find out later.

They'd exited the village the same way they arrived earlier in the day, then left the path to wander through the grass just beyond the walls. Ash had said that going any further would be 'dangerous.' Apparently, wild animals and 'monsters' came out at night. Steve was dubious of this claim, not having seen anything of the sort himself made it hard to believe.

The light shining from his body illuminated a small area around him nearly as brightly as the afternoon sun, so seeing was no issue at all. On the other hand, Steve was sure that anything out there would also see him and come to investigate. But what would Ash gain by lying to him? Another question Steve decided was best to keep to himself.

As he drifted along, hovering just above the tall grass, Steve saw an animal dart forth from its hiding place. It was fast, but Steve was faster. He readied a Shock spell, then fired when he had it back in his sight. The lightning arced from his body and into the rabbit. The small creature went into, well, shock. Another ten points of energy for him.

It was getting easier for him to cast the Shock spell, and he noted that the cost of the spell had also gone down with more use. It used to be five energy per Shock, now it was only about three. The spell wasn't very strong though; he doubted it would be very effective on a large creature. With that thought, Steve began to wonder if he could make it more deadly. That and a half dozen other thoughts crowded his mind, as he searched for his next target.

As he continued forward, Steve noticed Ash looking back and forth, as if he was searching for something. *Maybe he really is concerned about being out here?* he mused. Another few minutes passed fruitlessly as Steve failed to find any more animals, despite his omnidirectional vision and vigilant searching.

"Can I take these rabbits back? The village could use them," Ash suddenly spoke.

"Certainly, if it will aid the village, I am happy to gift them to you," Steve said pragmatically. The corpses of the rabbits were useless to him, but he did want to build up his reputation with the humans. He watched as Ash collected up the bodies, removed a leather thong from a pouch, tied them together by their feet, and finally tied the cluster of bodies to his wooden stick.

"Please continue, I will be back soon, god Steve," Ash informed him. The boy stumbled over something as he walked off into the darkness, the jostling caused a rabbit to slip free of the binding, falling to the ground with a soft thud. Ash muttered something in apparent irritation, but Steve couldn't make out what was said. Steve watched as Ash bent to pick up what he had dropped and lost two other rabbits in the process. Ash sighed, knelt, untied the remaining rabbits and spent a few minutes tying them more securely. Steve watched the human in silent fascination.

Once he was alone, Steve continued his search, but there seemed to be no creatures around. Soon he grew bored and checked the timer once again, keeping a bit of his attention on his surroundings.

4 Days 19 Hours 15 minutes 23 Seconds

Maybe it was time to practice Blink.

The best way Steve had found to cast spells, was to visualize each spell as a separate space in his mind. That was also the only method he knew, but that was beside the point.

He envisioned all he knew about casting Blink in a corner of his mind, losing track of his surroundings other than his intended destination, as he turned his focus inward. He imagined himself appearing at that point in an instant, then pushed his energy into the thought. There was a strong pull on the core of his being for an instant, then the spell was complete.

Examining his surroundings, he could tell he was a half dozen feet from where he started. Steve then summoned up his mental note of current and maximum energy.

Current Energy – 25

Max Energy – 50

In the course of this short hunt, he had doubled the maximum size of his energy pool and more than quadrupled his current energy. When he'd started, he had expected to only need to drain a few rabbits to max out his energy, but not only had he missed a few times with his Shock, it turned out that as he hunted, his capacity had increased as he used his magic. Steve spent a moment calculating—with the cost of casting Shock factored in, he would be near maximum energy after three more rabbits.

Storing plenty of energy seemed like a good idea. He still wasn't sure what would happen if he reached zero, and certainly didn't want to find out in the middle of a fight against a monster. That was, if Ash had been telling the truth about the possibility of encountering one out here.

Steve spotted the gray furry ears of another rabbit, just barely within the range of his illumination. As he silently moved towards it, he saw the rabbit was chewing on something. Somehow it felt appropriate that it got a last meal, though he was a little surprised to see that rabbits were so ferocious. Watching the cute little animal taking large bites out of another creature was unsettling, even to him.

Steve shot a disabling Shock towards the rabbit, which was instantly paralyzed, its fur of its hind leg darkened by the arc. He smoothly drifted over to envelop it with his body, having found this was the quickest way to absorb the energy. This time, he kept track of his changing energy levels, seeing that once again his maximum energy had increased.

Current Energy – 22

Max Energy – 52

He was also getting better at the Shock spell; the difference between the first shock he'd cast on the tree and this one was clear. He could now control the power to some extent and the accuracy was vastly improved.

As he drained the rabbit, he found himself staring at another creature that had appeared as it entered the edge of his light. Steve turned all his focus to studying this interloper. It was a large, four-legged, dark grey beast. It was obviously several times more massive than a human, though even if it weren't crouched low, it probably wouldn't be as tall as one. Steve was impressed by the way it silently made its way towards him, as he continued to absorb the rabbit's energy.

"Can it hurt me?" Steve wondered out loud, half hoping that Bonnie would be listening and answer him. "My body is made of light so…"

As the beast drew near, its lips peeled back to reveal gleaming white teeth. Steve understood this was a sign of hostile intent, even though he had no idea what to call the creature. It seemed like it was looking for a fight, and presumably thought that he hadn't noticed its approach. But he had, his omnidirectional vision making it nearly impossible for something to sneak up on him.

Steve finished absorbing the rabbit, then prepared himself to face the beast by readying his Shock spell. Having done that, he tried to envision and prepare a second copy of the spell, and was able to do so, but found that three wasn't possible, at least for now.

Suddenly, the beast took two swift steps then launched itself forward, full force. Steve was caught off guard by the speed of the leap but reacted by unleashing one of his Shock spells. The bolt struck it directly in the chest, though the creature's momentum meant that it continued along its trajectory towards Steve, jaws spread wide. Not wanting to find out the hard way that he could be harmed by such an attack, he quickly shot up out of its reach. He considered moving in to absorb its energy, but he had no idea if he could drain this new being.

The beast shook its head from side to side, clearly not paralyzed as the rabbits had been, but seeming dazed. Steve didn't allow it any time to recover. He shot his other Shock spell at it; this one scored a direct hit to the top of its head. The large quadruped growled loudly, then charged him once again.

It was too fast. Before he could react, the beast had jumped and swiped its forepaw through his body. Steve felt his energy pool shudder as his yellow light wavered; he'd lost some energy to that attack. *I guess this is where Blink comes into play,* Steve thought. *Shock isn't working.*

The beast landed and rapidly spun to begin its next assault. Before it could, Steve Blinked out.

***

"We've known this so-called 'god' for only a few hours," Amon said resolutely. He was speaking to a number of the other villagers who had convened for an emergency evening meeting in the Elder's house. "We have absolutely no records of this god, no myths, legends, nothing. I, for one, don't believe that he's a god!"

"While that may be true, we also must consider this being's power," Leffer countered. "It is likely that Steve is stronger than I am. Magical beings are generally more powerful than humans."

"He could be an Astral," Vim, the village's general merchant, commented with a grimace. His forearms rested on the table before him and Lee, his assistant, stood next to him.

Amon had opened his mouth to speak but became lost in contemplation of this possibility.

"Well, if that's the case...assuming it is, we have to consider whether it's Cania's Astral or Zufrid's Astral. Of course, we must also consider which demigod Astral Steve is under," a reedy voice rang out across the table. It was the village librarian, Timmun. "Make no mistake, there is no way we can go against the gods. Let him stay until he—"

"No, that's just a wild theory. I say we make Steve leave. Whatever this thing is, it has no place among humans," Yoleman interrupted. The burly blacksmith stood with his arms folded across his chest, leaning back against the wall.

Amon glanced at Yoleman in consideration. Tradition did dictate that they pay respect to godly beings, even those of diluted bloodlines. Though, if Steve wasn't a godly being, then the only sensible course of action was to defend the village. The chance that Steve was a benevolent being, interested in the good of Niti was...low. They needed to oust Steve before anything bad happened.

"I say we make him leave, just like Yoleman said, then take the

Crystals in the field," Leeroy interjected into the slight lull in the conversation. Amon glared at the village Elder's son. Theft was below the dignity of Niti Village, even if they were in dire straits.

"We need to make the most of this opportunity," Leeroy went on, completely ignoring Amon's ire. "Let's send men out right now, we know where the Elemental Crystals are. It's a quick two miles from here, my son Lemoy can lead the way. Jenkins, what say you?" Leeroy turned to a nearby man who had the glint of greed in his eyes.

This was trouble, Amon couldn't condone this plan. Jenkins and Leeroy were close friends, even inseparable, since childhood. Unfortunately, they were both scoundrels as far as Amon was concerned. He looked to Leffer with a frown; the Elder needed to step in right now to stop this plan in its tracks. Leeroy might be an important member of the L clan, but he didn't have final say; in fact, he barely had any authority. The village prided itself on merit-based leadership, in addition to the Empire's tradition of the strongest clan ruling.

Leffer was sprawled in his chair, one hand on his face and the other on the table, obviously deep in thought. As the village Elder, he would have the final say in any decision of this magnitude. The fate of Niti was on the line.

"We have little to nothing to lose from 'finding' and claiming a stock of Elemental Crystals. So long as we report it to the Empire and pay the taxes they will demand, all will be fine. Even angering one rogue magician would be a minor concern, compared with what we stand to gain. These Elemental Crystals could help train future wizards and witches in our village!" Jenkins was working himself into a frenzy with his own words. "Obviously this 'Steve' apparition is just a conjuration."

Amon surveyed the men in the room. Jenkins would blindly support Leeroy. He believed Yoleman was too honorable to go along with such a vile plan. As for Vim, well, Amon couldn't tell what he was thinking. The ability to mask thoughts and emotions was a necessity for any merchant.

As he turned to examine the remainder of the men, the sound of the door opening drew everyone's attention to the entrance. Ash stumbled in, clearly off-balance. He carried his staff in both hands, with several large rabbits tied to it. Amon was impressed to see that they were all clean kills.

"Ash, you took down all these rabbits by yourself? I'm proud of you, son." Amon stood with a grin. Between their savagery and speed, this was no simple task. "The citizens of Niti will eat well because of this...but going out at night, alone was a big risk." He frowned at the realization.

"Nicely done," Yoleman grunted from where he stood. The rest of the men held their peace and looked at Ash expectantly. They all knew that Leffer had sent the boy to investigate Steve.

"Um." Ash looked around the silent room, a little unnerved at being the center of attention. Amon could see he was struggling to bear the weight of so many rabbits. "This wasn't me."

Leffer stood so quickly that his chair nearly tipped over. "We'll let Steve stay," he pronounced. "I doubt any of us could have done that so quickly, and certainly not this cleanly. Did you see what he used?"

"I think it was lightning elemental magic. But he just used it to stun them, he said he was 'absorbing' them," Ash replied. "Asked me if I wanted some, too."

Intriguing, Amon thought as he took a closer look at the dead rabbits. *A lightning-based spell, delivered with pin-point accuracy to the hind leg of every one.*

Amon racked his brain for any myths relating to Light-based lifeforms on Zeth. "It could be a light elemental. Or an Astral, playing around," Amon mused out loud. "Or a ghost?"

"Astral was my guess as well," Leffer replied, looking at Vim. The Elder then turned to look at Amon. "We, as citizens of the Empire, must not interfere with any upper-echelon beings. We all know that."

"Yes, but a lesser light elemental could be taken to a city and traded away," Vim spoke immediately after Leffer. The merchant leaned back in his chair, interlacing his fingers behind his head. "I can investigate."

Ash mumbled something under his breath and shuffled across the dining room, towards the kitchen with the rabbits. "Lily, Ash has meat for the stew," Leffer called out. When Ash was out of sight, Amon turned his attention back to the conversation.

"What do we do then?" Yoleman pressed, always the man of action.

"Well, Yole, we still haven't figured out whether Steve is an Astral or not, from Cania or Zufrid. I would think Cania, since you know, light. But it is peculiar that he uses lightning, which is a destructive force. I'm afraid I don't possess enough information to come to an informed conclusion. Perhaps it is best that we continue to call him a god for now? If he *is* a god, it would only be proper, and if he is not, I doubt it is too far off. Even the least powerful of elementals have god-blood in them," Timmun analyzed. The village librarian was too scholarly to be useful in many situations, but this was one of the times that his wealth of lore was a true asset.

"Uh, where's Lily?" Ash called out from the kitchen, once again disrupting the conversation.

"Wasn't Lily in the kitchen? I saw her go in there before we started the meeting. Could she have gone out the back door?" Amon asked.

"Did anyone see Lily leave?" Leffer asked. When everyone in the room indicated they hadn't, the Elder sighed. Amon understood his frustration. While Lily wasn't physically unwell, her mind...wasn't what it used to be. She had become forgetful, clumsy, and generally disoriented as of late.

"Go investigate, Lee," said Vim. His Beast-man assistant bowed his furry head and hurried across the room toward the kitchen at the command. It was well-known that the greatest of the Beast-men's senses was their greater natural affinity for detecting mana.

Amon followed Lee out of the room. Perhaps Lily had wandered off unnoticed, though he considered that improbable. How could a clumsy old woman slip past a room full of men on high alert? He quickly considered the possibility of an enemy attack.

Mottor and Ekem were the only two nearby villages and they'd had no direct contact with either for a long time, making both unlikely. Though Amon wouldn't put it past either of them, Mottor was the somewhat more likely candidate, as it was believed they had been sending spies and scouts into Niti's territory over the last few months. It was even rumored that they had been in contact with rogue magicians.

As they arrived in the kitchen, Ash stood near the cookfire looking around. The rabbits lay in a haphazard pile on a nearby table and Lily, as Ash had said, was nowhere to be seen. "Lily isn't here," Amon called back to the rest of the group, then watched Lee as he sniffed the air.

The Beast-man's ears were perked up, nose lowered and head moving side to side. Lee then opened his mouth and drew in a lungful of air across his tongue. "There's something here," he said. "It's faint, though. Nothing recent."

"Go back for now and attend to our guest, Ash. There's nothing for you to do here, Lily probably just wandered off," Amon told him.

Ash nodded and left quietly. Amon understood why Leffer would want Ash in particular to watch Steve, even though he didn't like it very much. Ash was the best mage under fifteen that they had. Being a talented mage showed he was competent and disciplined, while still being considered a child meant that he couldn't be held responsible, if he were to somehow offend Steve.

"Seems like she must've walked out the back door, since there's no recent mana residue," Amon told Lee, shrugging as he took one last look around the room. Nothing seemed out of place. The Beast-man nodded and they both returned to the meeting.

Lily would turn up eventually.

Chapter 5

"This is a bad idea, Ash," Azra warned, moving to bodily block him. "We should *not* be doing this. Ask the Elder for permission first or at least tell him!" she insisted.

Ash stepped around her and continued towards Steve once more. The village Elder would likely do nothing because of stupid traditions, and he knew that Loop's father would be up to no good. Ash was aware of the clan's declining position as he grew up and now he desperately wanted to contribute to the village. After all, it was almost his Name Day, only a few more days until he would be fifteen.

"I have to help somehow, I must ask, at least once. The god Steve didn't seem to be concerned by tradition or above giving assistance. After all, he freely gave us those two precious Crystals," Ash voiced his reasoning to his sister. "We need this. The god's presence in our village is a blessing in itself; I can feel it."

Seeing that he wouldn't be dissuaded, Azra followed along silently. Power meant authority and while Ash was already powerful, his power would spike on his Name Day, where he would become an adult and full-fledged mage of the village. Ash was undeniably a special case among the children of Niti; his innate power was probably comparable to the children of the capital. Though his sister was also powerful and Ash had heard about female heroes, mages, and the like in legends, unlocking the potential in girls was unfortunately impossible for Niti.

When they reached Steve's residence, Ash impatiently knocked on the wall next to the cloth which served as a door. After waiting a while, they called out for Steve. When there was still no response, they entered, assuming Steve must still be out hunting.

They were shocked by what they saw. Feathers were scattered everywhere, and a dead chicken lay on the floor. It looked like a chaotic struggle had taken place inside the residence. Ash couldn't help but frown at the sight, as he remembered bringing a chicken to Steve earlier in the afternoon. Though he didn't know what would happen to it, he definitely hadn't expected the god to torture a mere chicken.

There was total silence in the guest house for a while, as they took in the sight.

"Zufrid in disguise?" Azra asked, breaking the grim hush by speaking the god of destruction's name.

***

Steve had Blinked nearly one hundred feet from where he had been battling the beast and quickly ducked behind a nearby section of wall. He was glad now that he'd heeded Ash's advice not to wander too far from the city. His sudden disappearance from the fight seemed to have confused the creature, as Steve heard a frustrated growl from that direction as he checked his numbers.

After using Blink, he had plenty of energy left, which was good news. Steve had long since realized that everything he did consumed his energy. Even moving constantly drained him, though very slowly. The countdown currently read:

4 Days 19 Hours 10 Minutes 30 Seconds

Suddenly feeling uninterested in hunting any more tonight, Steve floated through town and soon ended up back at his guest house, only to discover that someone had been in it. The chicken was gone, but after inspecting for a few minutes, he decided that the coast was clear; the house was empty. Steve was a bit confused as to why someone would have wanted to take the chicken, but it was fine. He decided to go talk to the Nitians, after coming to the conclusion they must have been coming to check on him.

Steve thought a moment about where he should look, before he remembered there had been a relatively large building near the village center, probably for meetings. As he headed there, he worked on sorting out his priorities. He needed to gather information about this new world, in order to survive long enough to evolve. Even if there hadn't been a rule against dying, Steve wasn't interested in risking it. Getting lucky once didn't mean he would get lucky twice, obviously.

I guess I should work with their assumption that I'm a god, Steve thought to himself. *Their reverence for me could be useful. At the very least, it's probably better than telling them the truth: that I'm an amnesiac light being, who sometimes has visions and can only do a little magic.*

Steve mentally prepared a strategy for the upcoming conversation and assessed his energy. He had enough for two Shocks and one Blink, if necessary. He wasn't expecting any trouble and knew he had some degree of invulnerability to physical attacks, but what worried him the most were magical attacks. If even that young human could use magic, surely there were others. Even though he hadn't been struck by magic himself, he knew it could do a lot of damage. He had confirmed that multiple times while hunting rabbits. He imagined a magical attack would drain his energy in a similar fashion to the way the beast's physical attacks had, but more effectively, and he really didn't want to find out what happened if it reached zero.

Deciding that he was as ready as he could be, he called up the list and spent a few minutes looking at the new spell options available to him at his increased energy level.

He soon arrived in front of what he guessed to be the town hall. Luckily, like the guest house, there was only a curtain covering the entrance, so he was able to enter without a problem. As soon as he was inside, he noticed a few things. The first was that boy Ash, the short girl Azra, and the Elder, all seated around a table. The second was the two older-looking humans who stood behind the Elder, carrying long wooden sticks.

The room was spacious, seeming larger than Steve had guessed from the exterior. It was somewhat sparsely furnished, but still gave off a feeling of grandeur. The architectural skill and craftsmanship that went into the construction of the building and its contents seemed superb, though once again, Steve couldn't remember much to compare it to. He could only recall a single room from that vision of his prior life and had only the guest house where he was staying now for comparison in this world.

"Greetings, god Steve," the Elder began in a stately, formal tone.

"I imagine that you must have questions or concerns weighing on your mind, as you've come here so late." The Elder hesitated a moment then continued, "Shall we begin?"

***

Mere minutes earlier...

"Elder. I have something I need to report." Ash hurried through the cloth-covered entrance, panting slightly. He'd rushed all the way from the guest house, even going so far as to use a small wind-spell to help him along, believing his report too urgent to be delayed even slightly. "Steve might be from Zufrid's side."

Leffer was still seated where he'd been when Ash departed earlier. Behind him, in their ceremonial positions, were his Right and Left. Going all the way back to the founding of the Empire a millennium ago, it had been tradition for every leader to have a Right and a Left. These were their most trusted companions, friends, and usually fighters or mages. The Left happened to be Ash's father, Amon, while the Right was Leffer's closest friend, Joffrey. These two were the most accomplished magic users in the village, likely even comparable to the Lefts and Rights of higher-tier towns. Though Ash couldn't be sure, he thought they were probably four-star mages.

Aside from his initial outburst, Ash wasn't sure how to proceed. He could tell the village leaders were currently forming plans for Niti.

The village's economy had been on the decline for many years, mostly thanks to their rival, Mottor, but exacerbated by a few other nearby villages. They'd somehow fallen behind their neighbors, and it was Leffer's job to make sure that trend didn't continue. With the rapid expansion of nearby villages and their rival's aggression, the future seemed bleak; this was becoming a matter of survival.

Then, Steve had appeared. Leffer had immediately come up with a plan to persuade Steve to help them, but the other important figures in the village had been resistant, at least until Ash's earlier interruption where he had demonstrated Steve's generosity.

"Really? Then please report." Leffer immediately turned his attention on Ash while holding up a hand to silence the others in the room.

Leffer would be personally overseeing Ash's Naming ceremony in a few days' time. He'd trusted Ash to find evidence to back up his hope that Steve was a benevolent force. Even though Ash was doing nothing but reporting on what he'd found, he felt terrible to deliver news that might crush all their hopes.

Then Leffer said something that truly made Ash's heart sink. "It might change our plans entirely."

***

Steve focused his attention on the men behind the Elder. He

could see the whole of the room in an instant with his omnidirectional gaze, but only by focusing could he see the finer details. On second inspection, these men didn't appear to be that old at all; it was only their white hair that gave off the initial impression of age.

"Sure, I'd like that. You're right, there are some things I would like to discuss." Steve gave Leffer the chance to start it off. He wanted to know where they stood before he got to what had brought him here.

"We live in dangerous times, as I'm sure you well know. The Empire is threatened by two nations on either side and as a result, the villages are all growing their strength to help in the coming war effort. These two men are my Left and Right, my most trusted advisors. You've met my grandson, Loop, as well as Ash and Azra." He gestured toward Ash and Azra as he introduced them.

"With the formalities out of the way, I'll get straight to the point. We wish to know which Greater God you, of the gods like you, are in service to." The Elder was in full diplomat mode; he phrased the question in a completely inoffensive manner, but left it open enough that Steve may volunteer even more information than was directly requested.

Steve unfocused his gaze as he considered this request for a moment. The villagers seemed unable to look directly at his radiance for more than a moment, but seemed to be making an effort to avoid appearing rude by looking elsewhere. This left them staring towards the empty floor below where he hovered, which created the awkward feeling that they were afraid to look directly at him. Though, if they believed he was a god, perhaps there was an element of trepidation to their behavior as well.

"Well, earlier today, I woke up in a field of Elemental Crystals," Steve began. "Most of my memories seem to be sealed at the moment, though they are slowly returning. At this moment, I am unable to tell you which Greater God I serve since…I simply can't remember anything like that." Steve hadn't planned to be even this honest, but realized that this half-truth suited his plans. Mentioning the Elemental Crystals which they clearly desired only strengthened his hand in this conversation.

"How many Elemental—" Joffrey began.

"Well, as you have lost your memories, we formally invite you to stay in Niti while you recover." Leffer immediately cut in by holding up his hand as he re-extended his invitation.

But even this fragment of a sentence had been enough for Steve. This confirmed his belief that the Elemental Crystals were items of great value to these people. This was good news as he had intended to pay for more information about this world using the Crystals that he had left in the forest. Of course, he also hoped to get more than information in the deal; after all, there were a lot of what he'd once thought of as just 'colorful rocks' in that clearing.

"Thank you, that is a generous offer, but I don't plan on staying too long. How about I trade some of my Elemental Crystals for information and the assistance of several men, when I want to venture out to explore the area. Though, I won't take them beyond say…ten miles from here," Steve counteroffered. If he was going to be confined to this place for a while, he might as well explore it. There was a beast which had already harmed him lurking around the village; he didn't want to go out again without bodyguards, not if he could help it.

"Done." Leffer looked ecstatic. "These Elemental Crystals will be a great boon to the village. We appreciate your generous contribution to the future of Niti. Whether we sell them or use them to empower our children, you can rest assured that they will be put to good use. I am glad we reached an understanding so easily and will strive to aid you as best as we are able, god Steve."

At that moment, a panicked-looking woman burst through the entrance. In her haste, she tore the curtain over the doorway free and began shouting out her message before it even fell to the floor.

"Elder! Loop, his father, and around twenty other men are gone!" Her voice rose as she spoke, till she sounded near hysterical on the last word.

Steve heard all this. Hesitating for just a moment, he came to a decision and Blinked out.

***

"Sard," Leffer accidentally let out, as Steve disappeared. Leeroy and Jenkins had fucked everything up. He hadn't meant to curse, especially in front of Ash and Azra, but he couldn't help it.

Nearby, Ash's and his sister's eyes widened in surprise. This was the first time they had ever heard the Elder use such coarse language and they were shocked by it.

Amon began to wonder exactly how much of his memories the god had recovered. He had obviously just used Blink, which was a high-tier space manipulation magic. The mana cost of such a spell was already high and to use it without proper preparation…well, safe to say if he'd wanted to use the same spell in the same situation he'd just seen, the cost would have been astronomical.

Joffrey, on the Elder's other side, wondered if his brother Jenkins knew what he was doing. Knowing Jenkins, probably not. His brother had been greedy and cocky ever since they were kids and hadn't improved at all with age. He sighed inwardly; gods that knew high-level magic were most often exceptionally powerful. Even he could only cast Blink if he did everything perfectly and even then, only if it were a lucky day. Offending such a divine being was foolish and should only be done as an absolute last resort, if their demands were beyond all reason. Somehow his idiot brother had apparently done so when this god had just agreed to give them a treasure for practically nothing.

"Gather the casters and a few warriors, we must depart immediately." Leffer barked his command at the occupants of the room, who had been stunned into silence by the sudden turn of events. "I'll give you three minutes to assemble everyone you can. Ash and Azra, you're with me, guide us to the clearing where the Crystals are. We can't risk offending the god Steve any more than I fear we already have."

As soon as Leffer finished speaking, his Left and Right hustled out of the building to gather the troops, while Ash and Azra moved to stand beside him. As they followed him outside, Ash began to reiterate the directions to the clearing. Being well into night by now, it was difficult to see anything as they stepped out of the brightly lit room into the dark town center. It was generally a bad idea to go anywhere in the dark, and this was especially true around Niti Village.

Chapter 6

Steve moved as quickly as he was able; the uneven forest terrain was no obstacle to his levitation, which allowed him to travel faster than the most experienced ranger. He had only been this way once, going the opposite direction and hadn't been paying much attention, but he felt confident he was on the right path as he noted the fresh wagon tracks ahead of him.

They had tried to steal his Crystals. To be fair, he didn't know if the Crystals were his to begin with, but they certainly didn't belong to the villagers. Steve still wasn't sure of their exact value, but he was sure of one thing: If he was to survive, he needed a form of currency.

Without something to trade, he would be reduced to relying on his personal strength. That would be a problem, because battling his way through everything in the vicinity sounded like a great way to advertise his presence to every being in the region. Considering his luck so far, he didn't believe for one second that they would all be friendly. Also, as he had learned from fighting the beast earlier, any battle that wasn't a one-sided victory for him would end up draining his energy reserves. Steve couldn't afford that right now; he needed to build up his energy levels in preparation for whatever was coming when the countdown reached zero. At that thought, he checked the time remaining again.

4 Days 18 Hours 30 Minutes 20 Seconds

Damnit. If I don't finish this fast, I'll probably fall unconscious in front of those guys, Steve thought to himself. *I'll need to be as intimidating as possible, right from the start.* In a few moments, he had thought up a plan, but he needed to make a detour first.

***

"Hey, Leeroy! Where should we put this?" Jenkins grinned as he and another man held up a huge green rock.

The men were in high spirits, already imagining the money, power, and glory this night would bring to both the Nitians as a whole, and especially themselves. It was no exaggeration to say that these Crystals would be the start of a new era for the village. With this kind of wealth, it was entirely possible they could reverse their long misfortune and grow into a prosperous town.

That wasn't even considering the trees; Elemental Bark was an essential component of many potions and magical staffs. Wizards would flock to serve their village or pay the exorbitant price for some of the wood from these blue trees. The wealth concentrated in this clearing was frankly astounding. Lemoy had certainly done them a huge service this time.

"Anywhere on that wagon." Leeroy gestured. "I think it can bear the weight." He then turned to Lemoy, who had anxiety mixed with guilt written plainly on his face. "You've done us a great service, my boy," Leeroy said proudly, clapping his son on the back. "We'll make you a full member of the Squad after this. As well as making sure you receive some benefits from these Crystals, of course." If there was one aspect of leadership Leeroy was an expert in, it was rewarding loyalty. After all, that was key in gathering subordinates under your banner.

His small faction within the village was known as the Squad of Scoundrels; it had started with four key members: Leeroy, Jenkins, and two other men. The others had left the village long ago due to dismal prospects. The two men had said their goodbyes and promised to return; they never did, though nobody had expected them to anyway.

Lemoy, unlike the others, was filled with guilt and more than a little fear. He had never done anything like this and thus never felt this way before. Part of him still didn't want to believe that they had gone directly against the Elder's orders.

On one hand, he knew what a benefit these resources would be to Niti. Further, there was his loyalty to his father; the man had raised him and never really asked anything of him in return. This was the only thing he had asked for Loop to accomplish, if he couldn't even oblige this request…

On the other hand, they were stealing from a god! Okay, maybe not a god, but even so, the powers behind Steve or even Steve himself might be powerful enough to take them all down. This was an incredibly risky operation. They were almost done, but until they were, it was all Loop could do to keep his hands from visibly shaking.

Suddenly, there was a flash of light from among the trees that struck one of the men's legs. He cried out loudly and fell to the ground with a moan. Everyone froze; nobody dared make a sound, other than the injured man, whose piteous moans dominated the otherwise silent clearing.

***

The thing was, everything Steve did cost energy. So the most important aspect of his plan was to harvest as much energy as possible before confronting these thieves. He had accomplished this by finding small animals and large insects nearby.

Most of that energy had been expended acquiring a new spell in the hope that he could win this 'fight' without ever really fighting. Once he had done that and made sure that he had some energy in reserve, the men had been easy to find. They were working by lantern light, making themselves beacons in the night, and hopefully at least partially masking Steve's luminescence as he snuck up.

When he was in position, Steve focused in on a guy carrying a Crystal, striking him in the leg with a Shock spell from twenty feet away.

***

Sard! Jenkins thought the moment his guy went down. *There is a hidden mage! We are sarded.*

Mages filled something of a specialist role on the battlefield. The pros of having magical support far outweighed the cons, however. They could cause devastating damage if let loose on an enemy group. However, they required more care and supplies than the average warrior, in addition to being easily overwhelmed, if caught unprepared. One way around this glaring weakness was to hide them. Having a few hidden mages in a forest or mountain battle would put immense pressure on the enemy and likely turn the battle in their favor if left unchecked.

In short, Jenkins was terrified of magic. Having been a poor student, especially when it came to such matters, the only thing that had stuck was how dangerous a mage was.

Knowing it was their only hope, he was about to order the men to run towards the area where the spell came from. There was a small window of opportunity while the mage gathered the mana and performed the chant to cast another spell; they had to hope they could take advantage of it. Of course, if there were more than one caster hiding, they were doomed anyway.

Before Jenkins could move, or even issue a command, he felt an immense magical energy in the air, or rather, it felt like something was sucking the energy out of the atmosphere itself. It was an unfortunately familiar feeling. When he'd been a teenager, the air had filled with energy like this once. Back then, the previous Left had cast a massive area-of-effect earthquake spell at the cost of his life, which saved the entire village. Jenkins immediately knew they had no hope; they were at the mercy of this unseen foe.

Then, a voice rang out; it sounded just like a certain god they had recently met.

***

"If you don't want to die where you stand," Steve began flatly, "put down anything you're carrying and lie down on the ground. If you want to try your luck, just know that I have no qualms with destroying a few lesser creatures that have offended me. Though I need not have, I give you this warning now, as a sign of my mercy."

A few of the men looked like they wanted to say something but didn't dare in the face of such a threat. Steve watched as they carefully put down the Crystals they were carrying and lay prone on the ground. Leeroy and Jenkins beat everyone else to it, immediately dropping to sprawl in the dirt. The man who had been shocked was still moaning, though it had mostly died down as he curled into a fetal position and clutched his charred leg. It looked like a nasty injury; it was almost enough to make Steve pity the man.

Almost.

As the last man lay down, Steve prepared to withdraw his presence from the vicinity. Lesser Area Energy Drain hadn't seemed like much when he first came across it in the list of spells, earlier that day. It was right next to incredibly powerful-looking fire or ice bombardment spells that had a massive area of effect. They had been tempting at first glance, but the cost was too high.

One cast would have left him with negative energy, something that he still feared would be very harmful, if not fatal, so they weren't suitable for his current purposes. Also, the utility of such spells wasn't that great. Sure, one cast would destroy everything, but what would that accomplish? If he lost rather than gained energy from his battles, wasn't it a waste of time? Especially in this case, it was better to instill fear, rather than cause massive casualties.

With this Lesser Area Energy Drain spell, after spending a little bit to get the effect started, he could intimidate enemies and gain energy! As he'd expected, just extending his magical control over an area made it so that most lesser creatures were too afraid to move.

Steve watched his energy go up some more, quite satisfied with this result already. His max energy had also improved a few times over the last minute. Deciding they'd had enough, Steve let go of his drain on all of them. Really, there was no reason to continue, as he'd finally reached his max energy for the first time. Excitedly he read:

Current Energy - 70

Max Energy - 70

How much for the human evolution? Steve wondered, mentally communicating with Bonnie. It was only the tenth-most powerful evolution listed, so he figured that it couldn't be that expensive.

"If you paid up front, 20,000 energy should do it. Of course, it would be better to have more as any excess will allow you to start out stronger after you evolve," Bonnie replied. "Energy cost is dependent on your current skills and compatibility, of course. So you can expect it to change from time to time."

Steve was shocked. He had expected the price to be steep, but to this much, he could only react one way. *What?*

***

Leffer and Ash led the way to the clearing. They brought along the Left and Right, five other casters, and two other warriors. Fearing the worst, they traveled as fast as they dared, only to find everyone on the ground and a familiar ball of light floating above them all in the middle of the clearing. Near the two large wagons, they saw one man clutching his leg as he rocked back and forth in apparent misery.

What happened here? was the thought on everyone's mind as they came to a halt.

***

Steve pondered his options for what to do with these would-be thieves for a few minutes before he spotted several lanterns headed toward the clearing.

Well, it's not like I could hold them here forever. If they came any later, I'd have had to think of an excuse to let them go. Steve was well-aware that if all these men attacked at once, his only option would be to outrun them in the forest.

He turned his focus to the man on the ground, who was still occasionally whimpering and wondered if he should just put him out of his misery. Steve decided against it, on the basis that it might put his relations with the other villagers at risk, and he really didn't stand to gain anything from it. The villagers might turn against a vengeful god, especially if they cared for that man and he had no way to tell if that were the case. On the other hand, if he played the part of a powerful but merciful god for the people of Niti, he should be able to enlist their aid in achieving his goal of evolution. The steep price of 20,000 energy Bonnie had quoted to him seemed to be well out of his reach if he didn't get some kind of help.

4 Days 18 Hours 0 Minutes 0 Seconds

As if a light flashed in his mind, Steve addressed the villagers lying on the ground to offer them a deal. "I shall grant you a chance to repent and be forgiven. Serve me for the next five days and it shall be as if these unpleasant events never happened." There was no response, and Steve assumed they may still be too frightened to speak.

Steve then turned his focus to the Crystals; two hours ago when his intellect returned, he had realized that they must be energy sources as well and this fact was probably what made them valuable to the humans. He needed some way to evaluate how much energy they contained, even though he probably wouldn't be able to make any use of them at the moment. He had just witnessed the depth of the humans' desire for the Crystals, but there was no time like the present to determine their true value for himself, before he made any more, possibly foolish bargains.

Bonnie, help me scan these Crystals' energy contents as I direct my focus at each one, Steve commanded, then started with the largest Crystal he saw.

"One thousand energy and will also give an attribute," Bonnie replied. Steve wondered what attributes were but set that aside for now.

Steve shifted his focus quickly between all the stones. All of them came up short of the 1,000 of the first Crystal, with the lowest being 50. The wealth of energy in this clearing was substantial, though Steve knew it wouldn't be enough.

Bonnie. Same thing with the trees, alright? Steve requested once more, then focused his attention on a single part of the tree, the trunk.

"Fifty." Bonnie gave a single number. Steve shifted his vision to the top of the tree and all around it whilst searching for the numbers. All of them were well below 50, each large batch of leaves combining to make 1 energy.

By then the village Elder had arrived, coming to stand quietly before him. Turning his full attention to the Elder, the man's deference and respect was clear. Steve decided it was time to capitalize on that.

"I had struck a bargain to give some of these Crystals to you in good faith, but now I see that generosity was misplaced and must reconsider," Steve began. "However, I will still not deal with you unfairly. I've recently regained some of my old memories, which have allowed me to formulate a clearer strategy. In return for some of these Crystals, I want full command of this village for one week. Of course, I won't do anything to harm the village or its people. I just need a base and assistance to begin my preparations. I will also require a lot of livestock and criminals."

Steve felt that this was a good enough deal for both parties involved. If they agreed, he would have a stronger foothold in this world to help prepare for his evolution. He would have a safe place to stay and a military force at his disposal. All that in addition to the energy he would gain.

Leffer was hesitant, this sounded like a good deal; in fact it was *too* good, there must be a catch. A god would never offer to give something of greater value than what they received in a trade. There had to be some hidden downside for the village that he just wasn't seeing; the Crystals really were too valuable. Who would ever pay even a single Crystal to hire a village for a week? Hell, he could have asked for two weeks of work with no problem. Any work they had to set aside could be made up later, but Crystals? There would be no way to acquire them if Steve took them and left.

"Is that the whole of the deal?" Leffer asked.

"Of course not. I want to see how you handle the beast I encountered near the village first, before deciding if you're worth what I'll be paying," Steve said nonchalantly.

"Alright then, that won't be a…Wait a moment, what kind of 'beast' are you talking about?" Leffer inquired. When Steve had described it, Leffer's eyes went wide. "That sounds like a dire wolf! There are have been no dire wolves sighted in these parts for thirty years." Realizing that such a dangerous creature would be a serious threat, and most of the fighters were here in this clearing, he quickly began to issue commands. "We must return to defend the village immediately! If there is a dire wolf nearby, then lives are at stake.

"Leeroy, Jenkins! I'm assigning you and the men who followed you to be god Steve's personal attendants for the next few days. If you do well, the penalty for acting in defiance of my commands will not be as severe." After saying this, he signaled to his Left and Right and the Elder's group set out.

Leffer had no use for thieves in his village and hoped that with the newfound competency he'd just displayed, Steve might save him the trouble of dealing with them and reform the so-called 'Squad of

Scoundrels' for him. At the very least, it seemed Steve had the means to force their compliance, and anything the god did to them couldn't be held against the Elder.

Steve turned to his new servants and commanded them to load every Crystal they could find onto the wagons. Seeing that the man with the scorched leg couldn't rise, he asked that someone treat him, and someone who apparently knew a little healing magic stepped forward to do so. All the while, Steve hovered above them doing his best to appear ominous and illuminating the clearing while they worked.

I hadn't even realized some of them might have magic, now I'm even less certain I could have won in open combat, Steve thought. *It took so much focus to maintain Lesser Area Energy Drain over this whole clearing…Combine that with what it would have cost to cast so many consecutive Shocks and I think I might've failed. Luckily, intimidation was so effective and the Elder arrived soon after.*

Bonnie, pull up current descriptions and energy costs of the top twenty evolutions, in terms of overall power level, Steve commanded.

Chapter 7

"Let's run through the plan one more time, alright?" a man with a mask obscuring his face said. He and the two men he was speaking to, all had the same dual markings on the back of their black clothes.

"What's there to talk about, Remley?" one of them replied. "We just control the dire wolves and send them in the direction of the village. We watch what happens and we leave. That's it." The third man nodded but remained silent. They all understood the plan, but it was customary to review immediately before putting it into action.

"Lord Mottor won't tolerate any mistakes because of carelessness," Remley hissed. "Let's run through the specifics once more."

"It's a good idea, the payment is too good to risk losing. Actually, it makes me wonder if there's anything we might've missed when we surveyed the village yesterday," the silent one spoke this time. "A whole Crystal…just for this?"

"Overthinking won't accomplish anything. If you're both dead set on wasting our time, let's just get this review over with, get out of here and get paid," the second one said impatiently.

"Alright, let's start from the beginning," Remley said.

***

Steve viewed the top twenty list, sorted by their current overall power. Though he understood that gaining new skills and improving his aptitudes and possibly even his actions would alter which race was ultimately the best option, when it was time for evolution. As if to illustrate that point, the current list already looked different than the last time.

1) ??? - ???

2) ??? - ???

3) Vampire – Cost: 15,000 Energy. End evolution is the Legendary Vampire or Undetermined. Evolution starts out extremely low-powered. Will receive help from the current Vampire clan.

4) Dragon – Cost: 50,000 Energy. End evolution is the Dragon God. Evolution starts out medium-powered but gaining energy and consolidating it is difficult. Will receive help from the current

Dragon race.

5) ??? – ???

6) Undead – Cost: 45,000 Energy. End evolution is the Undead Emperor. Evolution starts out low-powered, however amassing undead is easy. Gaining power is easy, however keeping it might prove difficult. Almost all other races will join forces against you if your nature is discovered.

7) Elf – Cost: 20,000 Energy. End evolution is the Greater Elven Magister. Evolution starts out low-powered. Gaining energy is medium difficulty while keeping energy is easy. Races will tend to trust you, making interacting with most of them easy.

8) Slime – Cost: 15,000 Energy. End evolution is Undetermined. Evolution starts out medium-powered. Gaining power is easy, just absorb! Monster-class being, other beings will want to hunt you.

9) Turtle – Cost: 100,000 Energy. End evolutions are the World Turtle or Undetermined. Evolution starts out low-powered. Gaining power is easy, just eat! Monster-class being, however, other beings will help you.

10) Goblin – Cost: 25,000 Energy. End evolutions are Greater Goblin King, Greater Goblin Magister, or Undetermined. Evolution starts out with a clan. The growth of the Goblin Clan will determine your evolution path.

11) Human – Cost: 20,000 Energy. End evolution is Undetermined. Evolution starts out extremely low-powered. Evolution path will be determined by training.

12) Beast-man – Cost: 10,000 Energy. End evolution is the Beast King. Evolution starts out high-powered. Evolution path will be determined by choices.

13) Dwarf – Cost: 8,500 Energy. End evolutions are the Dwarven Magister or Undetermined. Evolution starts out medium-powered. Evolution path will be determined by lifestyle. Can absorb minerals to increase strength.

14) Orc – 7,500 Energy. End evolutions are Orc General or Undetermined. Evolution starts out high-powered. Evolution path will be determined by leadership ability. Will receive the help of all Orc tribes.

15) Troll – 5,000 Energy. End evolution is Undetermined. Evolution starts out high-powered. Evolution path will be determined by leadership ability. Will receive the help of all Troll tribes.

16) Naga – 3,500 Energy. End evolution is Undetermined. Evolution starts out high-powered in bodies of water and low-powered on land. Evolution path will be determined by choices. Will receive help from the oceans and seas.

17) Ogre – 1,000 Energy. End evolution is Ogre King. Evolution starts out extremely high-powered. Evolution path is determined by power level. Will receive assistance from the current Ogre clan.

18) Kobold – 1,500 Energy. End evolution is Undetermined. Evolution starts out medium-powered. Evolution path is determined by lifestyle. Will not receive assistance from any race until special conditions are met.

19) Treant – 1,000 Energy. End evolution is Undetermined. Evolution starts out low-powered. Evolution path is determined by spells learned. Will not receive assistance from any race until special conditions are met.

20) Rock Being – 0 Energy. End evolution is Undetermined. Evolution starts out with low power. Evolution path is determined by lifestyle. Will receive assistance from the Greater Rock Forefathers.

Steve noted that Vampire had shot up toward the top of the list in terms of power. He had learned Lesser Area Energy Drain, which seemed like a spell suited to Vampires, so it made sense that the Vampire evolution's overall rating had gone up.

The thing was, Steve wanted the very best. Vampire was only sitting at number three right now because of his recent decisions. In order to meet his future objectives, he needed the best evolution possible. He couldn't even be sure that learning Lesser Area Energy

Drain had caused much of an increase to the Vampire evolution's relative power, as opposed to making the question-marked option's rating go down, because it was incompatible with the spells he had learned.

He idly watched Loop as he thought. The poor kid looked worn out from hauling Crystals to the wagons. It had only been a few hours since Ash, Loop, and Azra first found him in that clearing, but the three youngsters' paths had already diverged. Loop had made a bad choice, but Steve didn't really blame him. There were apparently many adults in the village who were a bad influence on him.

Steve thought of what kinds of things he could do to unlock those first two evolutions. He didn't really have any brilliant insight, but he did have a lot of time left. He checked the countdown again:

4 Days 17 Hours 50 Minutes 20 Seconds

I have almost 4 hours until the next change, Steve thought. *I need to have the village under my control by then.*

He watched as the last of the Crystals were loaded into the wagons. Then, a few of the men got onto the wagons and began getting them turned back towards town. Still, nobody had made any attempt to speak to him.

Just when he was beginning to think that they were too afraid to even communicate, Leeroy turned to Steve, eyes downcast. "We got everything loaded just fine, god Steve." His tone was meek, devoid of the force from before. Even if he could defy Steve without being killed, that would only ensure that he was banished. Leeroy knew his father, Leffer, well. If he fucked this situation up even more, he could forget about coming back to the village. A life of banditry at best, or even dying alone in the wilderness would be all he had to look forward to. "We're ready to go."

"Alright, let's set out," Steve responded brusquely.

Steve took one look back at the blue trees; they would have to come back for those later. He had to exploit all of his resources to the utmost, but if he were too greedy, too hasty, he might do himself more harm than good. If he absorbed the largest Crystal in the clearing, he imagined he may just blow up in a flash of heat. Perhaps if he absorbed the energy from one of the blue trees, Treant, which was currently at number nineteen on the list, may suddenly became his most-suited evolution. Steve needed more information and time to analyze his situation. There was no reason to take such big risks, just yet.

***

Ash followed the Elder in their frenzied dash back to the village. His father Amon, the Left, had cast a wind spell to help them all run faster. It was a pleasant feeling, running with the wind at his back, assisting him. His father's spellwork was still somewhat better than he could manage, but Ash expected that to change after his awakening. After all, the powers manifested in childhood were only a fraction of what they could be after their Naming ceremony.

The Elder would soon personally Name him, bringing out his full potential. Ash couldn't deny that he was excited, this was the biggest milestone of his life. He was even a bit nervous because although he knew that he was the best of their village's younger generation, he still feared some kind of complication. After all, he'd always heard his Elder say that there are very few sure things in this world.

In moments, they were out of the region of the Elemental Bark trees and onto one of the better paths through the forest. There they could truly move as fast as possible, the Right adding his own speed-enhancing spell to Amon's efforts. They had already prepared for the possibility that they would need to use these spells earlier, picking up the catalysts from their homes before they set out. The appropriate catalysts could be used to instant-cast spells when the proper technique was used.

The group arrived at the village in record time. There were no dire wolves, or any other threat to be seen. The village was quiet, the sun long gone, and most residents probably preparing to sleep. The village, lit by two moons high in the sky, was a beautiful sight. Most of the buildings were also illuminated by one or more lanterns, set along the main paths, for any villagers that may have responsibilities that kept them out past dusk. Seeing this all from his current vantage, Ash felt the village was already a small town. Why it was still called a village, he had never understood. Maybe it was some kind of Empire regulation; he'd need to ask the Elder about it later.

In spite of the apparent peace, Ash knew they were far from safe. Dire wolves didn't travel alone—if god Steve had encountered one nearby, then there had to be more. The last time the village had suffered a dire wolf attack, the previous Left had sacrificed himself to ensure the safety of his fellow Nitians. He had intentionally overspent his mana and concentration to case a massive earthquake spell near the village entrance, just before the wolves could get in. Then Ash's father had taken over for the deceased Left, hence the age difference between the Elder and his Right, and his Left.

Of course, the weak, fleshy bodies of human beings as a race were only capable of so much. They were incapable of withstanding too much mana running through them. Maintaining enough energy to stay alive was even more of an issue—go too long without eating or drinking and humans would drop dead. If a human managed to survive until the age of sixty, let alone seventy, they were better off than most. They were a race with massive, inherent weakness, that had still somehow managed to build up an Empire in what the other races considered the middle of nowhere.

The Empire's predominant race was human, meaning that almost all those who held power, whether political or magical, were human. It was a more distributed system than many other nations, where the whole country was ruled by an elite, powerful being and their immediate family. Niti Village was situated somewhere in the East of a normally peaceful country called Turkey. Being a minor, far-off village, they held almost no power in the Empire and knew their place in the food chain. Ash's hope was that once his latent potential was unlocked, he would be able to change that within his lifetime.

***

At Leffer's signal, the Left and Right fanned out with their men and began searching around the village. They would collect volunteers they could count on from some of the houses as they passed. Most men would jump at the opportunity to be useful to the Elder. His word was law here, as the most powerful being in Niti. Although, Steve's arrival had called that title into question.

If he were to fight Steve now, based on what he had seen, Steve would definitely lose—very badly in fact. Leffer apparently had decades more experience wielding magic than him and was a skilled warrior to boot. However, one did not survive that many years and eventually become the Elder of a large village, without realizing the risk of acting immediately. If he were to make a move against Steve, he needed to wait for the right opportunity.

If Steve did turn out to be a god-class being, then even fifty Leffers working together at the maximum output couldn't hope to stop him. If they offended a god, the village may be destroyed, perhaps even nearby villages as well, if his wrath was great enough. To make it even worse, the Empire would never come to their defense but instead send offerings to appease the god and make amends for the village's wrongdoings. Leffer couldn't allow that to happen.

That was the other half of the reason that he had no qualms leaving his son, Leeroy, to any fate less than death for what he had done. Although it did pain him personally, that outcome was still far better than hurting the whole village.

While Steve appeared weak, there was also evidence which seemed to indicate he was some sort of being of power, even if not a god, as well. Ash had reported that Steve had drained a chicken and later the rabbits of their *energy*, not mana. There was an important distinction; draining mana was something that any mage with a bit of training could do to a target that didn't resist. An ordinary animal wouldn't have much mana, but would easily survive the process of having it drained away.

But that wasn't what happened. From examining the bodies and hearing Ash's description of what happened to the rabbits, Steve had used something akin to a Greater Energy Drain to literally suck the life energy out of the animals. This was something on the level of High Magisters in the capital. It was impossible for any mage's construct to do this, no matter how skilled the mage. Thus the only safe assumption was that Steve was the real deal. An honest to gods god had appeared within their village.

***

Steve arrived back in the village with his group of attendants. He ordered them to drop off the wagons near his residence, then go help the Elder in the search for dire wolves. It would be a serious impediment to his plans if the village were destroyed by beasts.

"Bonnie, can you give me any hints that could lead to unlocking the question-marked evolutions?" Steve asked directly. He knew Bonnie was unlikely to volunteer any such information as nearly all the important things he'd learned from her were the result of direct questioning.

"Nope! Good luck with that, though," Bonnie replied, cheerfully as ever.

Well, I guess everything has calmed down now, Steve thought. *I think I should focus on understanding my energy and spells. I'm going to absorb some of those Crystals sooner or later, so I could get started now.*

Steve's current energy level was still near max, so he shot a few Shocks onto the ground just to make room to absorb more. *I will first check the effects of one red Crystal,* Steve thought as he hovered above one of the smallest Crystals on the wagon and started slowly absorbing from it. *I'm pretty sure red means fire-attribute, which could be good news for some of my evolution paths. It'll probably re-arrange the whole list.*

The Crystal's deep-red hue slowly faded to a lighter shade, then began to flicker between that and grey. Soon, the Crystal had no color at all, appearing to be nothing but an ordinary rock.

My energy level has gone up so much from that one Crystal! Steve thought. The effects really were amazing. He had started with around 30 in Current Energy and 70 Max Energy. Now he had been brought up to 80 in Current Energy and 90 Max Energy. His use of spells had expanded his max energy while the Crystal replenished him.

Steve then checked his evolution paths again. The power ranking hadn't changed, but the energy required for each evolution had moved around a bit. As there were no major changes, Steve wasn't concerned at all. Even if there had been, he hadn't figured out a way to guide his evolution path and lower the cost of evolving into the things he was most interested in.

Whatever he evolved into, he needed to make sure he would retain his Blink skill. It was too important to his strategy; he could lose Shock—it was just a mild attack—but Blink was his instantaneous travel. With it, he could survive most situations easily, if not avoid them altogether.

Steve turned his focus back to the Crystals covetously. He hesitated about consuming them to increase his energy levels for a split second, before he made up his mind. *It'll be fine as long as I leave the few I promised as payment...right?*

***

A few hours of work later, the next change hit:

4 Days 14 Hours 0 Minutes 0 Seconds

Steve's vision swam and he blacked out for a split second. When he came to, he was in a room. Feeling the comfortable mattress beneath himself, he realized it was a darkened bedroom. He stirred and tried to sit up but found his arm pinned beneath something.

My bedroom? What am I doing here? Steve thought. *This is so weir—*

"Steve! What are you doing?" a soft, distinctly female voice asked him in the darkness.

"Uh..." Steve couldn't find the words, his mind going blank. Then memories came flooding back; this was his girlfriend. "I..." He was suddenly overcome with emotion. The girl lying with him on his bed startled as he suddenly grabbed her in an awkward, desperate embrace.

"Hey...hey! What are you doing, Steve?" she exclaimed. "How can you already want another round? That would be our third tonight...you shouldn't be ready again that quickly! Though, I have to say, the attention is flattering."

What was her name? Steve tried desperately to think as they cuddled together. He remembered everything, her face, her laughter, all the things that he loved about her. As his recollections continued, he found a fool's grin spreading across his face. He basked in the moment, as he remembered all that they had shared together.

Steve then remembered the other world: his new, dangerous life as a ball of light. His thoughts gradually darkened as he hugged her closer. Why had he been taken away from this and brought there? What had happened to her when he was taken away? He couldn't remember anything apart from memories of his time with Xander and this girl.

The feeling of warm breath on his bare skin snapped him out of his dark musing. Her body was warming up, and his was starting to respond. He didn't know how long this vision would last, nor did he care.

In that moment, the two of them were the only reality.

Chapter 8

"Remley, what the fuck is that!" the normally mute member of the trio spat out in surprise. "How the fuck did it get there?" They had just checked last night with their Looking Mirror and seen no complications. Today, the three stared open-mouthed as they made a final check, which should have been a mere formality before they launched the attack.

"I don't know, Ronnie! I swear to the fucking gods it wasn't there yesterday, I double checked." Remley was as shocked as any of them. "Reagan, can you identify it?"

"Sure thing, boss! Looks like a ball of light floating in mid-fucking-air. Good enough for you? How the fuck did you actually expect me to ID something like that?" Reagan spat sarcastically. Deep down, he was still bitter that Remley had authority over him. "I've never seen something like that, I don't think anyone has. Look at the way it moves, it can even cast spells! What the fuck?"

"Hold on, it's going somewhere," Ronnie stated. "Please, be quiet. I'm going to clarify the picture."

With a quick spell, he zoomed the Looking Mirror in and saw Steve drawing the energy out of a Crystal which sat… In a wagon *full* of Elemental Crystals.

"Holy shit! Are those—" Reagan began.

"We must notify the Mottor clan immediately," Remley commanded sharply. "They're going to want to know about this."

***

Steve drifted into the guest house as he silently brooded; even his earlier elation at absorbing so much energy had been obliterated. A dark cloud had descended and blackened his mood.

4 Days 9 Hours 0 Minutes 0 Seconds

Even when the countdown hit, he didn't react and barely even noticed. *What's the point? I'll never see her again…* Steve thought to himself as his mind spiraled down into increasing self-pity. *Why am I trying so hard? We're in completely different worlds right now. I don't even know if she's still alive! Fuck! I still don't even remember her name!*

He had spent hours now, trying to dredge up her name from his memory, but there wasn't even a hint or vague impression there.

Why couldn't he find it?

Steve just floated, wallowing in his misfortune. He wanted her back so much! When he asked Bonnie if there was any way he could return to his world, she'd glibly replied, "No can do!"

The two of them had been everything to one another. They were going to live long, happy lives together. Why? Why had whoever brought him here set it up like this? It was like they had dangled everything that made life worth living in front of him, then snatched it away so they could laugh at him. What was the fucking point!

The red sun slowly climbed into the morning sky. Steve noticed in passing, but didn't care. There was no point to any of this. He ran through his memories, over and over, obsessing about what could have been.

Only when he heard a knock on the guest house wall did he finally rouse from his daydream. Steve slowly and groggily floated through the curtain to find Ash outside, in apparent high spirits and raring to go at the break of dawn.

"God Steve! The Elder is ready to discuss terms with you and has prepared the prisoners and livestock you requested. We gathered all that we could spare. Are you ready to go?" Ash asked.

"Alright, that's fine," Steve replied halfheartedly and began to follow the boy. Then, he recalled something.

Bonnie had said that he wasn't the only one of his kind. Maybe with assistance from the others, he would have some hope of getting home. Steve knew that it was a long shot, but it was the first possible solution that had occurred to him, so he couldn't help latching on to this shred of hope.

In order to make contact with those other light beings, he needed to evolve. Becoming powerful would put him in a better position when it was time to bargain with those others. If he didn't, he wouldn't stand a chance. There was no way he was going to stay in Niti forever.

Steve suddenly cursed himself for the wasted hours. He could have been absorbing Crystals and refining his skill in magic. Every time he cast his abilities, he could feel that his mental state was becoming sharper and the effort of casting was less taxing. Magic was apparently like a muscle. When it was used, it became stronger.

***

Leffer was out of bed an hour ago, before the sun had even risen, despite having gone to sleep late last night. He'd taken the time to set up some sentry traps in key locations around the village. These traps would alert him if anyone or anything approached the outskirts of the village. He didn't like starting his day with so little rest, but it had to be this way. There was always so much to do, especially today, when he needed to negotiate terms with a god. If Steve didn't ask for too much, that would be great, but even if god Steve demanded a lot of assistance from the village, they would have to endure it. After all, they really needed those Elemental Crystals, and were lucky he was even offering to bargain, rather than just taking what he wanted by force. As for Leeroy and his grandson, Lemoy, he might have to ask the god for leniency. Not so much for Leeroy—the man was hopeless—but for Lemoy, or Loop, as the kids called him.

Gods know where kids get these strange nicknames nowadays, Leffer chuckled to himself. Then he sighed. "Ah, I remember when Joffrey and I were kids."

Leffer had reviewed all the books he had on gods and goddesses again when he got up. Nothing on any Light God named Steve, not even a mention of any divine being by that name. Well, the world was always changing and the books were older than he was, anyway.

Looking through the window, he saw Ash and Steve approaching and went out to meet them. "Good morning, god Steve," Leffer began. "Shall we head to the village hall now?"

Steve agreed and they set off; Leffer's residence wasn't far from the place anyway. When they arrived, they found the Left and Right awaiting them, having already taken their places. The two were in the middle of reviewing their responsibilities for the day. All complaints, arguments, and requests were handled either directly by them or their subordinates. This aspect of their roles took a lot of pressure off the Elder, allowing him to better fulfill his role as the ultimate authority and face of Niti.

As they all got settled in, the Left handed the Elder a slip of paper. On it was an accounting of the prisoners and animals the village could readily spare. If they let Steve have more than the numbers listed, it would be a hardship for the village. After all, humans must eat. Leffer looked at the sheet and nodded his agreement, as Ash approached and whispered something in his ear.

"I'd like to gift you the Squad of Scoundrels, that's what we call the twenty men that tried to steal your Crystals, god Steve," Leffer offered. "We'll also trade you what livestock we can spare and prisoners for Crystals, at a fair rate of course. I understand that you are currently in need of energy. The Crystals are yours, of course, but draining their energy devalues them."

"What about the trees?" Steve asked shrewdly. It looked like they had hoped he would just forget about them.

The Elder winced as he replied, "You mean the Elemental Bark?"

"Exactly. How about this, you give me the livestock and prisoners as I need over the next couple of days, and in return I'll trade some of the Elemental Bark from my clearing and a few Crystals to you.

You're right that I need energy, but I could easily absorb what I need from the Crystals I have," Steve bluffed. In reality, he had 10,000 energy worth of Crystals, at the very most. That wasn't nearly enough to accomplish his goals. What he really needed was the villagers' help to harvest all of the trees, and together they would contain much more.

"My memories have continued to return and I believe they will continue to do so over these next few days. I will also need details on this village and its surroundings. Serve me well, and I'll reward you fairly." Steve was banking on the idea that the Elder wouldn't be too greedy. From what he had seen so far, he was still regarded as some kind of supreme being, but if those three men acted together to subdue him, he doubted he was a match for them. Once again, Steve cursed himself for falling into despair and wasting so much time last night. With his prior changes, his mind had grown sharper, but with that last memory, and the change after that, all he'd gained was dolor.

"We have a deal," the Elder replied, seeming unwilling to push his luck against a god any further. Steve wondered if his caution was due to the reputation of the gods on this world, or perhaps some past trauma.

Over the next twenty minutes, Steve and Leffer worked out the details of the agreement. The Left and Right dutifully recorded everything, while Ash just kind of stood there awkwardly. It was decided that after this, Ash would help Steve deal with the villagers and later on they would gather up men to carry out the tasks.

Bonnie, countdown please, Steve requested. He needed to be ready for the next vision, as it seemed there was one with every other interval that passed.

Bonnie instantly and cheerfully replied, "Four days, eight hours, twenty-five minutes and thirty seconds." Though she was less and less talkative recently, it still seemed he could count on her to brightly reply to his direct requests.

***

The first thing Steve did after the meeting with the Elder was to evaluate what he'd gained. The livestock they'd given him were mostly strange creatures they called 'pigs.' They were large, slow, noisy, and fat. They were a shade of pink almost reminiscent of humans, but it was hard to tell, as they were covered in muck and their own waste. When he scanned them, he saw that each contained 50 energy. Steve decided to not absorb them just yet; he needed to confirm some things with Ash, about their world first. The pigs were left in their sties for now, where they continued to wallow in filth.

Steve now had the Squad of Scoundrels as well as another 50 prisoners, which brought his current workforce to 70 people.

Addressing them, he said, "You guys are mine for the next five days. Serve me well, and I'll see what I can do for you. However, if you are lazy, negligent, or decide to run…Well, let's just say you guys are the perfect targets and I need the practice, anyway." Steve did his best to be clear on this point, as he needed their labor, and didn't want to waste it by making an example of someone. Steve continued, "I think I'll refer to you guys as Workforce One and Two. Leeroy! You're in charge of the Squad of Scoundrels. Now, for Workforce Two, Loop! I'm putting you in charge of these prisoners. If you see them shirking, feel free to tell me."

Steve chose Loop to oversee the prisoners because for one, it didn't allow any of the prisoners to have power. Two, it let Loop have an opportunity to redeem himself. Steve didn't feel like it was Loop's fault that he got into this position. The first time they had met, Loop had been quite polite and hadn't seemed at all like a ruffian. As for the Squad of Scoundrels, Leeroy was the only reasonable choice. He was already the leader and Steve doubted he could do anything other than make trouble by trying to put someone else in charge.

Everyone stared at the ground beneath Steve, not daring to contradict him or complain. Against other villagers, they might be able to argue or bargain for better treatment. But against a god? They were lucky he didn't just harvest them for their energy. The only useful attribute these guys possessed in Steve's eyes was their ability to perform hard labor. If they refused or tried to undermine him, Steve wouldn't hesitate to drain them.

Steve commanded them to gather up the axes, wagons, and other supplies that the Elder had provided. Once that was done, they started out toward the forest. Steve made sure they were all single file so that he could spot any stragglers easily. He had omnidirectional vision, after all.

Turning his attention to Ash, he decided it was finally time to get a few questions answered about the world. "As you know, my memories haven't yet fully returned," Steve began. "I require a lot of information about this world."

"Of course, god Steve. I'll answer to the best of my ability," Ash replied. As the son of the current Left and future hope of the village, the boy was better educated, knew more, and had a deeper insight into matters regarding the Empire and the world.

"What are the known races of this world? What is the current state of the world?" Steve began his questioning.

Up ahead, in his omnidirectional vision, Steve saw some of the prisoners whispering to each other. They had shackles on their legs but had their arms were free. They were gesturing to each other but

Loop hadn't noticed. The kid was too busy staring at the surroundings instead of paying attention to his job.

"We are currently located in the Empire, if you want to know exactly where, you'll have to consult a detailed map. The Empire is controlled by the Human race, with the Emperor being the overall ruler. His imperial clan dictates what happens within the Empire and international relations. As for the other races, there are just too many, I don't even know them all." Ash didn't really know where to begin with such an overbroad question.

Not wanting to seem useless to Steve, Ash continued telling him everything that came to mind. "We're located in a small country within the Empire named Turkey. To the North of the Empire is the Satanland, which is ruled by Satan, aside from that we have very little information about that place, truthfully. It is said that the Satan of Satanland is tens of times more powerful than any human alive. To our West is the Great Ocean, Lovoth. There you can find all sorts of powerful aquatic races, including the Great Turtles and Naga, or so I've read in my texts. Most of this I can't be too sure of, since I've never been very far out of Niti before."

It was then, that the prisoners, deeply engrossed in their conversations, began to slow down. Finally, even Loop noticed, despite his daydreaming. He weakly shouted at them to stop talking but was ignored. The kid didn't know how to exercise power at all.

Ash took a breath and continued, "In the vast East, there lies Mudda, which is a land composed of various Beast-man tribes vying for control. What lies beyond Mudda, we don't know. Our Empire's spies have never made it that far, or so it is written in Empire texts." Ash was smart enough to not believe everything the Empire told him. Obviously, they weren't going to make their secrets public.

"To the South of the Empire lies the Great Desert. It's a dangerous place, which has claimed the lives of many travelers and adventurers. The Empire won't release any information about that place, leaving it even more of a mystery than the East. Aside from those places, there are the Sky Islands that float around somewhere but I really don't know anything about those places, sorry. I'm afraid that everything I know is either from stories or Empire texts, I don't have much firsthand knowledge, god Steve." Ash ended his long explanation, knowing that he hadn't really told Steve much useful information.

"Thank you, it's fine." Steve would double check with the Elder later, anyway.

After he replied to Ash, a group of prisoners broke off from the group. The rest of the party stopped and stared, as five prisoners ran away as fast as their ankle chains could allow. Ash immediately started chanting, but Steve was faster.

He shot four Shock spells, in extremely rapid succession, having had his focused vision of these prisoners the whole time. As soon as they started moving, he was already prepared to shoot them down. The last prisoner saw what had happened to his friends and immediately stopped running; he knelt on the ground and begged for mercy.

The whole group was silent as Steve floated toward the fools.

Chapter 9

"It's not like I didn't warn you," Steve declared. Prisoners, by definition, were people who had previously committed crimes serious enough to justify incarceration. They weren't exactly the cream of the crop in either intellect or morals, so he had expected this, even if he'd hoped to avoid it. These were useless, desperate law-breakers, or most of them were, anyway. "I did warn you. Right?"

He focused his attention at the four prisoners moaning on the ground. Their legs were in even worse condition than the last man he'd used Shock on, as they wore only flimsy prisoner's garb rather than the sturdy clothing of a working man. The material of their outfits was so charred it looked like he'd nearly set them on fire. Steve turned his attention to the one prisoner on his knees begging him for forgiveness. He was babbling something about repenting for angering the 'divine' being. These men's will to resist was clearly broken.

Steve called Loop over and addressed him. "Hey, kid. Loop, right? This is your fault, you know? This is what happens when you're unable to control your men. Now they're useless. What do you have to say about this?" Steve accused. He needed Loop be useful to him.

"I...uh...uhm," Loop stuttered and stumbled over words as he went pale. He was clearly scared out of his mind. To him, Steve had blasted the men instantly with Divine Lightning the moment they had stepped out of line. Any kid watching this feat would be afraid. Well, except for one. "I'm sorry! Sorry! It won't happen again. I swear on the gods!"

***

Ash, on the other hand, was terrified for a different reason.

Auto-cast...my gods. That's insanely high-level magic. Holy gods, that's fucking crazy! Ash's mind was spinning, this was incredible. Then he had a more coherent thought, *Maybe I should ask him to teach me...after my Naming ceremony.*

***

Leeroy and Jenkins felt sick watching the exchange. It confirmed just how wise their previous decision to not resist Steve had been.

They shuddered at the thought of what could have happened to them. What Steve had just done, casting multiple spells that quickly, with precision, was unheard of.

"Well, now these prisoners are useless. Will you carry them back and waste my time? What do we do here, Loop?" Steve asked his stunned observer. The kid was fixated on the men moaning on the uneven forest floor. Steve was really getting annoyed; no one had even passed out. The tools they had carried were on the ground, back where they first started running.

"Uh…do we split the force to take them back? Send a runner to request for help from the village?" Loop had finally realized the importance of the situation he was in, as the impression he made on the god mattered. What Steve reported to the Elder would likely affect the course of his future. He racked his brain for solutions.

"No. We don't," Steve said slowly and calmly. "Try again."

Two of the grounded men were crying at this point. To them, a god had just smote them with divine retribution. They were repenting where they lay on the ground, looking like pathetic, miserable creatures.

Loop now understood. He had a different look in his eyes as he turned around and met the pleading gaze of each of the men. Then, he handed down their death sentence. "My god, here are five perfect offerings to aid in your rise in this world," Loop said with manic fervor. "May these lesser beings be of use to you."

"Good," was the only reply.

***

None of the prisoners talked after that; they all walked a little bit faster and didn't dare step out of line. Not just the prisoners, the Squad of Scoundrels was the same.

Steve was down to 65 total in his Workforce, but it was fine. Steve just needed to harvest the trees within four days. If it really went too slowly, he'd just request more help from Leffer, anyway. The most important part of this operation was to confirm the effects of absorbing Elemental Bark. He had access to enough energy; he just needed to unlock the best evolutions. Absolutely nothing would stop him from achieving his goals.

As they walked, Steve didn't stop questioning Ash. The kid had a whole new respect for him, now that he had shown some of his magical prowess. There was a fanatical shine in Ash's eyes when he stared below Steve.

"Tell me more about these Sky Islands," Steve said. "How do they work? How did they get there?"

"Well…to be honest, the Empire doesn't tell its citizens much. The legends claim that there are Angels up there that control the

Islands. Other godly beings, such as yourself, as well. I was hoping when you recover your memories, that you could tell me about the world." Ash tried to be helpful, even as he failed to contain his growing excitement.

So Celestial beings such as Angels might exist. Also, there was a Demon race that was seemingly powerful but not included in his evolution choices. Steve quickly ran through the list again. No mention of Demons, though they could be the question-mark evolutions. Steve once again wondered how to unlock them; there had to be something he was missing.

"It's fine. When I recover my memories, then I'll be sure to tell you, if I know." Steve was straightforward in this exchange. Ash had provided him with adequate information about the world already. "What is the most powerful race that you know of in this world?"

Ash had to think about this one. "It's too close to make a clear judgement between the Satan and the old Dragon race, but I'll say it's the Dragon race," Ash decided. "Dragons haven't been seen by us for hundreds of years, or so the Empire says. They were rumored to have been extremely large and terrifying at their peak, capable of almost all magic and practically indestructible. The only issue was, as I heard, their energy consumption was also extremely high. This led the race to extinction, or at least near extinction, as whenever they needed to consume food, they would also expend a lot of energy to acquire it."

It wasn't the answer Steve was looking for. He already knew about Dragons and their power level. They were high up on his list, no matter what he did. Although, if Dragons weren't the most powerful even back when he hadn't learned spells, what was?

Steve was still deep in thought when they arrived at the clearing.

***

Remley, Ronnie, and Reagan were back at Lord Mottor's residence. In the Empire, when someone controlled at least two large-sized villages, they gained the title of Lord. It had taken them the whole night to ride back on their horses, but this news couldn't wait.

The morning air was fresh and invigorating, but after their late-night ride they were completely beat. Hopefully it would be worth it, Lord Mottor would definitely want to hear this, and he was generous with the pay for things he wanted. Only time would tell how much they gained from this information.

"Hey! We come bearing urgent news!" Remley shouted when they arrived at the residence. The village guards had quickly let them in earlier, seeing their insignia on their clothing. The dual markings meant that they were some level of magician.

The residence guards called for the Lord and let them in, albeit a bit reluctantly. They also knew that the Lord had hired them himself. While it was great that the Lord could take control of two villages, the methods he was rumored to have used were terrible.

"What is it?" Lord Mottor demanded of the three rogue magicians he'd hired, who were sitting opposite him on his comfortable chairs. They were supposed to be out, keeping an eye on his next conquest, Niti.

It was going to be his greatest conquest yet, but he had to do it right. He couldn't go in with his main forces; it would attract too much backlash. Their strength would be depleted by 'random attacks' from dangerous wildlife. Then, when they were desperate, he would offer his aid and take them under his wing. The plan was foolproof, so long as the rogue magicians did their jobs.

"Sir. We've spotted a ball-of-light being in Niti Village. It seems like a magical race of some sort, though we can't identify it. Could be from the Eastern lands, for all I know..." Remley trailed off as Lord Mottor frowned. Remley got ahold of himself and got back on track. "This sort of news isn't unheard of, I know. Magical beings sometimes do travel to our part of the world. But what was remarkable, is that it had a stash of Crystals!"

"How many?" Lord Mottor asked immediately, leaning forward in his seat. Crystals were serious business.

"Two wagonloads," Reagan replied immediately, knowing the importance of delivering good news to a superior. "We rushed back as soon as we could to report."

They had been forced to return in person due to Lord Mottor's devious and cautious nature. In the event that they were captured or killed, he wanted no evidence that could lead back to him. A rune, symbol, or tool could all be used to communicate over long distances, but were also easily traced. If Lord Mottor were caught in the act, he would instantly be deprived of his position, and even staying alive would become extremely difficult.

"Hmm…" Lord Mottor had to think about this. Two wagons full of Elemental Crystals. If they were all of the lowest quality, then it wouldn't be worth attacking immediately. "What quality?"

"I was only able to observe them through the Looking Mirror, but it looked like at least mid-grade Crystal. The color was there," Ronnie offered helpfully.

Lord Mottor's eyes now gleamed. This opportunity was too good to pass up. Even if those were small wagons, mid-grade Crystals were exceptionally valuable. The Capital would pay extremely well, especially the rich mages and nobility.

"We'll have to speed up our plans. Drastically. I want an army marching towards Niti by tomorrow." Lord Mottor had made up his mind. "Don't worry, men. I'll reward you with a couple villagers of your choosing for this information."

It was time for war.

***

Steve continued to check his countdown every fifteen minutes. He wanted to be ready for the next vision.

4 Days 5 Hours 20 Minutes 23 Seconds

They had been harvesting for a few hours now. The prisoners and the Squad of Scoundrels were working quite diligently. They already had a full wagonload of Elemental Bark.

Might as well start training and absorbing now, Steve thought. *Bonnie! Can you tell me about any changes to the list as I absorb?*

"Sure!" Bonnie replied ecstatically. Recently, Steve had been ignoring her and now was certain she had become bored. Then Steve began absorbing the Elemental Bark. He started on one with 50 energy, continuing until its blue hue turned gray. It was just a normal piece of lumber now.

Bonnie, no changes? Steve wondered. There had to be something, right?

"Treant evolution overtook Kobold," Bonnie replied happily. "Also, there were minor changes to energy costs. The energy costs of the top ten evolutions, aside from Elf and Slime, went up."

Damn, that's bad. I shouldn't absorb any more. Steve's thought process was simple: if he wanted to have a good evolution, he should only do things that benefited the top five evolutions in terms of cost. After all, Bonnie had said that any excess energy he had left went towards fueling his evolution, making him stronger. Although, if that were the case, it might be better to become a Treant, with all this Elemental Bark lying around. He was sure that if he absorbed enough…

No, if he were unable to unlock the question-mark evolutions, he would still be better off becoming a Vampire. All he had to do was suck up energy from living beings, it seemed. It had to be impressively powerful, being ranked above even Dragon, currently. *Although, I should probably find out what a Vampire is, first,* Steve thought. *That would be wise.*

He went over to Ash and talked with the boy for a little. Steve explained that he had the word Vampire lurking around in his 'memories' and wanted to know more about them. Ash turned out to be a font of information on the subject, having grown up hearing stories of heroes, monsters, and other beings. Vampires were one type of these other beings, definitely not heroes, though not quite monsters.

"They say that Vampires are descended from a Monster God

fusing its energy with a Demonic God. Nobody knows for sure, honestly, but their creation was a disaster. At some point before the Empire existed, it's said that there was a time where the only beings in power were Vampires. My Grandmother was an excellent and accurate storyteller, she told me that blood magic was extremely powerful. Some Vampires could destroy a blooded being with nothing but a look. The Legendary Vampire, George, was known and feared by many titles back then."

Ash paused for a bit to catch his breath. He loved Vampire stories as a child and had even wanted to be like George when he grew up.

"George was like a god. He united and reigned over all the Vampire clans as one and controlled this whole continent. They say, even if one wasn't a Blooded creature, his power was so great that he could still take your life at a glance. There are uncountable legends written about him, though I can't tell you exactly which ones are true."

Ash had gotten a little carried away, but suddenly remembered who he was talking to and his tone became a lot more serious.

"He was called the King-Slayer, Conqueror of the Great Ocean Lovoth, and so much more. All the races had to bow down before him. Finally, when his power began to wane, they say that he was betrayed by his clan. They were power hungry and seized the opportunity to make an army of magic-immune Golems to attack him while he was resting. After that, there were no new tales of George, so it is believed that he died to the treacherous attack."

"What happened to the Vampire clan?" Steve asked. He was considering becoming one of them, after all.

"They tried to hold onto their power, and they succeeded for a time. Eventually, with no true champion to guide them, internal struggles and greed seized the nobility, and before they realized it, they had fallen. Large marked golems, made by an unknown Archmage, pushed them back and into their capital. After a siege, the last Vampire there committed suicide. It's unknown whether or not any Vampires remain in existence…but one thing is for certain—"

Ash was slightly out of breath, having said all that in one go. He looked around the clearing, saw that the Workforces were still working, and finished his thought.

"If aVampires are ever seen again, every single race on this continent will unite to destroy them completely."

And with that chilling pronouncement, Steve no longer had any interest in becoming a Vampire.

***

After a while of waiting around watching the workers' progress, Steve's countdown hit:

4 Days 3 Hours 0 Minutes 0 Seconds

This time he was prepared when his vision swam, as he was launched into a flashback.

***

Steve opened his eyes. This time, he had fixated his mind on the idea that he should examine his old body, so that was the first thing he did. Steve needed to make sure he got as much information as possible out of this vision. He seemed like a 20-year-old male and was wearing a black skin-tight suit.

When he shifted his gaze upwards, he saw some sort of three-dimensional screen. *Oh, it's a hologram.* Steve turned around, assessing the spacious room. He now felt strange without his omnidirectional vision. *What is this place? Where am I?* With that question, memories came flooding back to him, all at once.

This is a lecture hall? Young adults go here to learn? Steve was astounded by the revelation.

He felt a tap on his shoulder and turned to find it was Xander. His friend was mischievously grinning, like he had just seen something funny. Or was about to. "Hey, it's going to happen any moment now," Xander told Steve in a whisper. What was going to happen? The young adults filing into the room were all taking their seats. Standing in the middle of the room, near the hologram, was the professor, an older, stern-looking man.

"What's goin—" Before Steve could finish, the hologram flashed brilliantly, attracting everyone's attention. Everyone in the room looked to see what was going on… And then it started.

"Oh! Michael! Mmmmmhhhhh," a loud female voice moaned. It came from the hologram, which now was a 3-D figure of a naked man and woman, crammed together in a small shower.

More memories flooded back. Xander roared with laughter and as the memories settled into place, Steve joined in as well. He remembered it all.

Earlier that day, they had hacked into the school's computer system. They had thought it would be hilarious to replace the current lesson with some of Xander's porn. And it was.

The whole room was in an uproar. Some students were gawking at the hologram, some seemed embarrassed, but most were laughing. The professor took one look at the hologram and immediately dialed for help on his smartwatch. Where before he had just seemed stern, now he looked angry, furious even.

Steve couldn't stop laughing. This was the funniest stunt they had pulled all year. He started slapping Xander's back as the two of them continued to watch Michael and that random female porn star copulate. By now, the girl somehow had a blindfold on. They were still in the fucking shower!

They laughed until they had tears in their eyes and when he was finally able to catch his breath, Steve turned to his friend. "I didn't know you were like that, Xander. What the fuck kind of porn is this?" he asked jokingly.

They looked at each other and dissolved into hysterics again.

Chapter 10

Steve was still chuckling to himself when he regained consciousness, but slowly came down from his laughter high.

He remembered Xander very clearly now. The guy was seriously hilarious, absolutely dependable and loyal. Xander was his man if he wanted to do anything fun. He remembered a few good times. Now Steve wondered who he missed and wanted to know about more; it would be a tough call between the girl and Xander.

Also, he got a good amount of information about his previous world in this last flashback. He had been overwhelmed with memory for the latter half of it, but in the first half, he had remembered to learn all he could.

Apparently, Steve was a human from a technologically advanced planet. They hadn't yet ventured out to create colonies in space, but it was the new, emerging frontier. All the cadets would learn in lecture halls—like the one he'd been in—in the mornings, then receive hands-on training in the afternoon. Most of the cadets there had similar dreams to him—to set up their own space colony and be the founding leaders on a new planet.

Steve picked up on a noise nearby and quickly turned his attention to the workers. They were working slower now; it seemed like they were running low on energy. It seemed mistakes were also being made, the sound of a prisoner's dropped axe was what had caught Steve's metaphorical ears. Maybe they needed to break for food; however, that wasn't Steve's call to make. Well, ultimately it was, but he had assigned people specifically for situations like these. There was no way that Steve was going to concern himself with everything that these workers needed over the next few days. Nope. That sort of thing was Loop and Leeroy's responsibility.

Thinking of Loop and Leeroy, he turned his focus toward them. Loop was glancing from the ground below Steve to the workers and back, deep in contemplation. Leeroy, on the other hand, was still guiding his workers. The Squad of Scoundrels probably ate better than the prisoners, as they were better off physically. They could work for longer without fear of their body deteriorating. Loop seemed to have finally come to a decision and walked toward Steve.

"God Steve! We have finished loading three wagons though it is now just past lunchtime. I think we should break to eat back in the village. We could see if the Left or Right could spare some time to watch these workmen. You don't have to waste your time watching over us." Loop had finally spotted the issue and immediately offered a solution. He was learning fast; Steve had wanted to do this anyway.

"Sure. Good job," Steve replied affably. His time with Xander hadn't faded from his mind and seemed to be buoying his mood.

"Pack it up, everybody! We're going back to the village for lunch!" Steve announced. They had harvested enough lumber today anyway. He'd leave the rest to the Elder; it was terribly boring work and it seemed that it wasn't useful to his evolution, anyway. Unless he wanted to become a Treant, of course.

The group's trip back to the village was uneventful. Steve successfully passed on his duties of babysitting the workmen and waited for Ash to eat his lunch. The two of them talked some more, while Ash was eating. He learned that Ash's Naming ceremony would be in two days and also found out a little bit about their village culture.

Everyone had pointed hats that they wore specifically to meetings to easily identify themselves as part of whichever family. Families were made clear by their shared first letter. The language they used was different from Steve's language, but somehow, he could still understand it. It was like the translation software from his old world but ingrained in his mind. Bonnie, on the other hand, was like an AI program that was maybe a little faulty.

So, the house of J had Joffrey, Jenkins, and the rest of the family. The same rule applied for the house of A, which had Azra, Ash, Amon, and the rest. Loop, Leeroy, and Leffer were all part of the same family, basically three generations of L-family men. Women married into a family, as their society was largely a patriarchal one.

It was a little bit different for Naming ceremonies, however. Ash would get a title that he would attach to his name, sort of like a surname in Steve's old world. The title would be based on the Name-giver, the person conducting the ceremony.

Usually, it was customary to base it on an element that the person had high affinity for. Ash's last name wouldn't be random; it would be Blaze, Aqua, or something related to the elements. Most likely pertaining to water since that's what he excelled at.

After lunch, Steve wanted a tour of the area around the village. Ash drove a wagon filled with smaller Crystals for Steve to absorb and practice his magic while they went. It was peaceful. They didn't see many creatures, and the animals that they saw weren't aggressive at all. Or maybe they were intimidated into pacifism by a ball of light firing lightning all over the place. A lot of animals and even people would be terrified by that.

Hmm...Maybe I'm the reason we aren't seeing much, Steve thought to himself, then cast another Shock spell at a nearby rock. The rock exploded. *It seems like my spells are getting even stronger. I have so much better control as well!*

For most of the time, Ash just stared at the things Steve destroyed. For one, the casual destruction of nature was terrible. More importantly though, the god casually destroying things and absorbing Crystals was just an unbelievable sight. Ash finally couldn't hold back anymore, after hours of traveling. "Please! Teach me your magic!"

"No can do!" Steve replied cheerily, just like Bonnie. She was really starting to rub off on him.

"I'll do anything to be your disciple!" came the instant, desperate reply. "Please."

Steve reconsidered. If Ash would do *anything* for a chance to learn magic from him, then it might be worth accepting the offer. "I'll give it some thought, kid," Steve replied seriously. If he ever learned how to easily teach his way of magic to someone, he would be able to amass a sizeable force in a short time.

The two talked until it was late afternoon. Steve found that Ash was relatively smart for a human kid. He understood the connections between historical events and could think for himself. Even though his innate magical talent was high, he still worked hard. That was what separated him from the rest of the kids his age.

Steve had seen at the academy just how mediocrity was bred. If a cadet started out as a genius but then just lazed around and did nothing, sooner or later he'd just be average. If it went on like that, he'd eventually fall below the average.

He felt that Ash, with his talent paired to a good work ethic, had potential. Steve didn't know what he wanted to do after evolving but having Ash as one of his companions didn't seem too bad. After Ash's naming ceremony, he'd see how powerful the kid could become. If it wasn't too much trouble, Steve would try to take him along for the journey.

While they rolled along, Steve perused his current top seven evolution options. He figured there was no point in looking at anything below that. With that in mind, he had a list that looked like this:

1) ??? - ???

2) ??? - ???

3) Vampire – Cost: 12,500 Energy. End evolutions are the Legendary Vampire or Undetermined. Evolution starts out extremely

low-powered. Will receive help from the current Vampire clan.

4) Dragon – Cost: 55,000 Energy. End evolution is the Dragon God. Evolution starts out medium-powered but gaining energy and consolidating it is difficult. Will receive help from the current Dragon race.

5) ??? - ???

6) Undead – Cost: 47,500 Energy. End evolution is the Undead Emperor. Evolution starts out low-powered, however amassing undead is easy. Gaining power is easy, however keeping it might prove difficult. Almost all other races will join forces against you, if your nature is discovered.

7) Elf – Cost: 15,000 Energy. End evolution is the Greater Elven Magister. Evolution starts out low-powered. Gaining energy is medium difficulty while keeping energy is easy. Races will tend to trust you, making interacting with most of them easy.

Absorbing those prisoners and that piece of Bark really messed up his Energy costs. He found that values for Vampire and Elf went down, but the rest of the values went up. There were no changes to the descriptions.

Steve was confused. Based on what Ash had told him about Vampires, shouldn't there be something in the description that said all races would hunt him down? If the last Vampire truly committed suicide back then in their capital, why did it say that he could receive help from the current Vampire clan?

There must be a Vampire clan left in this world, Steve thought. *That's the only explanation.* Steve was curious about the clan. Maybe when he grew more powerful, he would pay them a visit to learn more.

He then guessed at the first, second, and fifth spots. A Demon evolution could be a potential for the number 5 spot. Ash had said a Dragon was more powerful than a Satan, though only marginally. A Godling or God being could be number one or two. That still left one more option unknown. Steve hoped he could solve this mystery.

Steve heard a rustle from a nearby bush and saw a tan-colored creature, standing on four legs. "What's that one? It's not afraid of us." Steve was a bit confused. He had been shooting lightning and absorbing Crystals this entire time.

"Oh! It's a stag. Those creatures somehow aren't afraid of anything," Ash explained. "Legends say that they're the animals that the gods themselves have blessed. I don't believe it, though. They seem pretty dumb to not run from you."

"Hmm." Steve went back to browsing his evolution potentials. He needed to properly analyze these options with Ash before learning more spells. If he learned the wrong one, the consequences might be disastrous. If Rock Being suddenly became his top evolution, he might as well just give up all his hopes. Though, Rock Being did sound interesting.

"Have you ever heard of a Rock Being or a Rock Forefather?" Steve asked Ash. The kid had heard a lot of tales, so who knew, maybe he would know about this.

"Sorry, I haven't." Ash was straightforward in the things that he didn't know. One of his most promising traits. "What's a Rock Being?"

"Ah, it's fine," Steve replied. He then explained a little more. "Just another one of those random bits of memory."

Steve checked the countdown again. They had been walking several hours now. It had been just over a day since he first came to in this world. The timer read:

3 Days 23 Hours 5 Minutes 20 Seconds

In just three hours, he would acquire yet another feeling from his last life.

The two of them continued around the outskirts of the village. They encountered rocky terrain, but it was mostly forest land. Apparently, there was a small lake not too far from the village in the opposite direction. Steve wanted to go there tomorrow.

Steve then checked his Current and Maximum Energy levels. He hadn't consumed a Crystal large enough to make his attributes change, but the energy levels were growing. It now read:

Current Energy – 449

Max Energy – 770

This didn't mean that he could cast the Shock spell two hundred times in a row, however. After about ten times in a row, he would start feeling a little lightheaded. There seemed to be a cooldown period between when the spell was first cast and when he could cast it again without any negative effects.

It was the same with Blink as well. Though the spells were entirely different, the cooldown period was there. If he ignored the cooldown period and continuously cast spells, aside from the hit his mental concentration would take, his energy would also be depleted more rapidly.

Checks and balances, Steve repeated a saying from his old world in his mind, though he didn't know where it came from.

***

Hours before…

Lord Mottor glanced at his army trailing behind him. Well, it wasn't really an army yet. Gathering his men would take some time, as they needed to be rounded up from both of the villages he controlled. Plus, he needed to figure out what that ball of light was.

That was where his advance party came in. Not having directly attacked another village before, he thought it would be wise to test out their defenses. If it was a god-class existence, like in the legends, then at least he would only lose the twenty men that he was sacrificing rather than his entire force, or even his own life.

The advance party consisted of two ten-man squads; each of them was led by an experienced rogue magician. They were to act as new banditry around the area and terrorize the village. The rogue magicians had communication devices with them this time. How else was he going to find out what that ball of light was?

The Capital wouldn't stand for outright slaughter, but if he was able to overwhelm some of the men using the forces of both his villages, while silencing the rest by taking their families as hostages...who would ever know? Even if some of them made the long journey to the capital, it wouldn't matter, so long as he hadn't done anything bad enough to justify the effort it would take to come after him. But if his main assault with all his men failed, he might as well start digging his own grave as he would be at the Nitians' mercy. That's why the information was so critical.

Lord Mottor let the R family men have a bit of fun in the village brothels that day. They were tired out, and they needed some rest. It didn't sound right, village brothels, but the reason why they weren't called a town yet was because of the Empire's specific regulations. You needed to have a Bronze Key to be known as a town, and such a key could only be purchased at an extremely high price from the Capital. Even though each of his villages were around the size of small towns, not having the title of town was unfortunately detrimental to their economy and power.

His bandits, on the other hand, rode all day so they could arrive in Niti around evening time, Once there, they would coordinate a small assault on the village. Niti was their rival village, so it wasn't hard to find men willing to attack it. A long time ago, someone pissed off someone else and boom, a rivalry. It didn't make sense anymore, as nobody even remembered what had started it, but demonizing each other up to this day finally led to something.

Lord Mottor refined his plans all day, waiting for the signal from his communication device. They were expensive things, made from Crystals that he imported from the Capital. Expensive, but useful. If he didn't have them, taking over the two villages he currently owned would've been far more difficult.

"Sir, we've arrived," one of the squads reported in.

"Good. After you harass Niti Village, immediately report in," Lord Mottor commanded.

The main force would be ready to start marching tomorrow

morning, after all preparations were complete and he had the information he needed.

Lord Mottor really coveted the town title. He could purchase it, and so much more, with the acquisition of those Crystals. He'd seen them with his own eyes; the recordings of the Looking Mirror couldn't lie. Or at least to do so, was well beyond the capabilities of those magicians. They were only two-star, after all.

***

Steve had wandered all over the place with Ash that afternoon. After that one animal they found, he had floated through a bunch of forest and a smaller rocky area. By dinner, the two found themselves back in Niti.

Steve finally felt like he had enough information to work with. After a day of questioning Ash, he felt that he should improve his power a bit, or at least add something new to his arsenal. If it meant something going awry with the energy costs of his evolution options, then so be it. Having spent the whole day collecting and analyzing information, he was ready to go.

Right now, Vampire doesn't seem bad, even though they were hunted, but I should open up other options. Hmmm, Steve thought. *Dragons were known for their fire magic mostly, so maybe I could try learning a fire-related spell to try and lower that evolution's energy cost.*

He checked his countdown again. This time should be a random feeling. It read:

3 Days 20 Hours 2 Minutes 2 Seconds

Two minutes until countdown hit.

Suddenly, he heard screams and shouts from the village outskirts. He immediately went towards the commotion to find out what was going on. If it was too dangerous, he could always Blink out.

"Special Event. Successfully defending the village will unlock ??? evolution." Bonnie was back to a robotic, monotonous voice. It was like an AI, rather than a sentient being, was speaking. This had only happened once before, when Steve had broken the killing rule.

That was a reward too great to pass up, which made his course of action clear. He was going to defend his village!

Chapter 11

The two ten-man squads had split up, one on the right side and the other on the left. The rogue magicians were both hiding nearby. They had started it out with a massive wind spell to cause panic. Then they sent their men in with sacks on their backs. They were to quickly pillage anything of value they could from the village outskirts and then make a swift retreat, using the darkness for cover.

The rogue magician leading squad one was known as Tenk. He had been forced to go rogue when he had gotten himself kicked out of his house. Usually, a magician is a blessing for the house, but in this case, Tenk had been a serial rapist when he was younger. Because he had abused his power, the village Elder banished him, years ago.

His partner was a guy named Fom. He was a young-looking but reticent man. Fom was also a one-star rogue magician, like him.

Tenk didn't know much about Fom's past, other than that he was abandoned as a child and found himself in odd jobs. He also didn't care enough to learn more.

The raid initially seemed to be going well, but they hadn't expected the ball of light to act so fast. They had known that the magical being was somewhat nearby, but the thing was suddenly in midair above the men. It immediately unleashed five lightning shocks in a rapid volley, followed by a spell that sucked the energy out of the air. That was high-level magic, but Tenk could have replicated it…if he prepared for a couple days beforehand. Maybe.

This was ridiculous! "Fom! We have to protect our men!" Tenk knew that without their men, they had no chance of making it back. It was only safe traveling through the wilds in the first place because they had numbers; without them, they would succumb to the wilderness even if they escaped successfully.

Fom had nodded his confirmation and began to chant his biggest spell. It took a good fifteen seconds to complete, during which time, that light being took out another three of their men. This was a nightmare. How was it this strong? Why could it fire consecutive lightning spells like that!?

They had lost almost half of their force in the span of ten seconds. The men who were still on their feet broke and fled in every direction. They were rightfully scared out of their minds.

Tenk had only one thing on his mind; he needed to kill that thing. He had to curb their losses and find somewhere they could recuperate. It wasn't supposed to go down like this, they had made sure that the Elder was on the other side of the village.

He released his spell; it was a decent one he had nicknamed Flame Lance. The jet of flame was wide where it left his outstretched hands, but it became thinner and faster as the outer flames dissipated into the atmosphere.

The light being had just shot lightning at another one of his fleeing men—good, it was distracted. Now he was sure that he would hit it. Once it was damaged, they could take it down for sure. It was two against one. In a magical fight, even a two-star magician couldn't take them both on at once.

Fom was still chanting his spell off to the right. The pressure was building in the air as he clasped his hands in a weird way in front of him. The guy was a decent mage; maybe he would rank up to two stars soon.

The spear of fire streaked across the sky toward the ball of light. However, in that moment before impact, the ball of light vanished.

Holy shit, so that's how he got there in the first place! Tenk thought. Then he shouted, "Fom! He's using Blink!"

What the fuck was this? How was it casting without chanting? How could it possibly have so much mana? Tenk had so many questions as he turned to run away. He could care less about Fom right now; anything that could use Blink instantly was no joke. He must be facing a god! Come to think of it, Lord Mottor had said there was a slight risk in this mission.

Fuck! He fucking tricked me. Tenk was furious. If he had known about the actual dangers of this mission, he never would have gone through with it. If he lived through today, he would go straight to the capital and tell them all about Lord Mottor's atrocities! The fair people of the Capital would be sickened, and Lord Mottor would get what was coming to him.

Fom finished his spell and stone tore from the ground to create a prison where the light being had just disappeared from. It was a good spell under normal circumstances, though completely useless now.

Both magicians were sweating bullets now. The fear combined with rapid depletion of their mana had caught up with them. Tenk had just rounded the corner of a building, when he saw the flash of a lightning spell coming right at him out of the corner of his eye. The light being was there!

Tenk really had no chance. Mages could erect barriers, but unless one knew where the spell was coming from and what type of spell it was going to be…Well, in a situation like this, there was almost nothing a mage could do. He felt a searing heat in his right leg; it felt like the limb had been burned away. The pain was unbelievable, almost as bad as his Naming ceremony.

"Fuck! Fom! Do something!" Tenk screamed. Fom began chanting again while holding up his trembling fingers toward the ball of light.

Then there was some sort of blindingly bright light, as if it had cast Flash or something similar. Even though they hadn't been looking at the ball of light, due to its uncomfortable brightness, the pulse of light completely robbed them of their vision.

Fom's chant immediately cut off and he dropped his head into his hands, obviously in a lot of mental pain. Of course, Tenk couldn't see this, as he writhed around on the ground, blinded and screaming.

Then, they felt it happen. There was heavy magic in the air, that same spell they'd seen used on their men earlier. It was sucking the energy out of them! Being magicians, they could tell what was going on. The remaining dregs of mana in their bodies were being forcibly drained out.

Tenk's mana pool ran dry first; when it was gone, he started feeling weaker. At this point, he was no longer worried about his wounded right leg. The feeling of weakness had spread through his body and began to subsume his mind. His vision was starting to return, but it didn't matter.

Nothing mattered anymore as Tenk fell unconscious.

***

Steve was staring at the listing changes.

What the fuck? was the only thought going through his mind. *How...*

He was back in the village center, with the Elder and his people. They were incredibly noisy, but Steve tuned out the background noise, as he couldn't be bothered. He just kept on staring at the newest changes to the list in his mind:

1) ??? - ???

2) Deity – Cost: 150,000 Energy. End evolution is Undetermined. Evolution starts out extremely high-powered. Will be hunted by all Celestial beings.

3) Vampire – Cost: 10,000 Energy. End evolutions are the Legendary Vampire or Undetermined. Evolution starts out extremely low-powered. Will receive help from the current Vampire clan.

4) Dragon – Cost: 65,000 Energy. End evolution is the Dragon God. Evolution starts out medium-powered but gaining energy and consolidating it is difficult. Will receive help from the current

Dragon race.

5) Undead – Cost: 40,000 Energy. End evolution is the Undead Emperor. Evolution starts out low-powered, however amassing undead is easy. Gaining power is easy, however keeping it might prove difficult. Almost all other races will join forces against you if your nature is discovered.

6) ??? – ???

7) Elf – Cost: 20,000 Energy. End evolution is the Greater Elven Magister. Evolution starts out low-powered. Gaining energy is medium difficulty while keeping energy is easy. Races will tend to trust you, making interacting with most of them easy.

It seemed like defending the village had been a bad idea. Most costs went up by a few thousand while Vampire and Undead costs fell a bit. Undead and one of the question-mark entries actually swapped places, becoming fifth and sixth respectively. All that to unlock an evolution that cost way too much.

Steve thought back on what had happened. As he had seen the area that was being attacked, he suddenly felt a rage build inside of him. He was angry that these lowly humans dared attack his starting village.

He surveyed the area and decided to surprise attack before the enemy could come up with any countermeasures. Steve had mentally prepared his Blink spell along with three Shock spells. That was the limit of what he could currently do in a single moment.

He'd Blinked into the fight and Shocked three enemies in the legs. Followed by using his Shock spell twice more to cripple two others before he needed to wait for the cooldown.

Steve had been in complete mental focus, taking in all the visual information around him. After shocking a few more enemies as they fled, he'd Blinked to dodge a dangerous spell coming at him. Steve hadn't taken a hit from magic before, and he didn't plan to, it might've been disastrous. Just because he was angry, that didn't mean he'd become stupid. Steve had hidden behind a building to wait out the danger. After an earth spell burst from the ground where he'd been, the two mages who were trying to run away ran straight into him instead.

First, he sent one mage tumbling to the ground with a Shock-crippled leg. The other mage had begun to cast something, so he turned up his light to max power to blind everything around him. It took a lot of energy, but it was worth it. With the second mage's casting disrupted, the fight was over.

Soon afterward, the Left and Right appeared with their men. They rounded up the stragglers and found Steve draining the two mages in cold blood. They were helpless and incapacitated on the ground, but Steve wouldn't stop.

The energy he sucked out of them was delicious. He killed the crippled one first. It felt good, so much better than the other living things he had taken life from. Maybe it was because these two were magicians.

"Stop! God Steve! We need this one!" Ash had shouted, running towards him. "Please!"

And now he found himself next to the Elder trying to figure out why his evolution had become that much more difficult now. His rage was simmering down now. Steve found that taking it out on those bandits really helped.

Then he noticed something: the magician he hadn't killed was speaking into a Crystal on his wrist. Something about it being okay to send the main force? Maybe he should be paying better attention now. He could mull over the new listings later.

"Yes, we are fine. Mission was a success, though we lost one of our men. The light being killed him with a lightning spell, then ran away," the magician said as he held up the communication device to his ear, under the careful supervision of the Elder and his men. "Oh, yeah, Tenk is here, but he was exhausted and passed out. To be honest, I'm just about to fall asleep myself. Go ahead with the initial plan, we'll be expecting you." When the Crystal blinked out, the magician looked visibly relieved.

"God Steve, we thank you for aiding the village. Even though we would have repelled this attack ourselves, we may have suffered casualties and the enemy advance party would have gotten away. If that had happened, we wouldn't have discovered that the Mottor clan are sending their forces to take your Crystals," Leffer said, facing Steve. "Now that we have this warning, we could defeat Mottor's forces even without your presence here. We'll be ready for their attack."

They all bowed.

"You're welcome," Steve stated simply. His rage had subsided and he was taking a real liking to the Elder. "What will you do with him?"

Leffer suddenly looked a bit sheepish. "In exchange for betraying his employer, I offered to let him be your subordinate. He jumped at the chance. I tried to ask, but you seemed preoccupied at that moment," Leffer explained.

Everyone in the room suddenly held their breath. They had been shocked to see Ash shouting at god Steve earlier and now Leffer was making bargains on his behalf. Even though they had been around Steve for about a day, they still found such behavior astonishing.

They all let out a collective sigh at Steve's response of, "No problem."

Steve liked Leffer's thought process. He could use a capable subordinate, especially if things with Ash didn't work out. The boy had strong ties to the village and it may be hard to convince him to leave. Though, he had offered to do anything if Steve would teach him...

But that was getting ahead of himself; he would decide after the kid's Naming ceremony. For now, he had to decide what to do with the taciturn magician he had found himself in command of.

***

This isn't fair! Azra thought. Ash was only slightly more talented than her, but she was treated completely different. They wouldn't let her be Steve's guide or even go with them. She was fourteen already and Steve didn't even seem that dangerous!

"It's too dangerous," Azra mockingly mimicked her father. "You could get hurt."

She practically spat the last word. It had been the same her entire life. Good girls weren't supposed to go out to have adventures; they weren't allowed to spend their time with the gods. Good girls were to stay at home, practice sewing, and learn how to be a good homemaker. There wasn't even a need for that anymore; they could do it with magic!

If she could learn to become at least a great Royal Mage, all the village's troubles would be over. She heard that the Archmages in the capital were so wealthy that even their servants lived in luxury. Good mages were always in high demand in the Empire, as not many humans had the necessary talent. Sure, most could learn magic and practice it. But without talent, it would be a hundred times harder.

"Now Ash will get even further ahead of me," Azra hissed bitterly. "God Steve may have already taught him Blink or something."

It was common knowledge that five-star mages or higher could relatively easily cast Blink, at least if they knew how. The four-stars and below weren't counted as good mages.

While there were always exceptions, the ranking system usually went like this:

One-star – Able to cast basic attack spells and one defense spell. Spells take a long time to cast but are still effective. Can use basic utility spells.

Two-star – Able to cast basic attack spells and two defense spells. Able to cast one buff spell or the equivalent. Spells are somewhat faster than one-star. Can use basic utility spells.

Three-star – Able to cast basic attack spells and three defense spells. Able to cast three buff spells and one debuff spell, or the equivalent. Cast times reduced to moderate, unless complex. Can use medium-level utility spells.

Four-star – Able to cast medium attack spells and four defense spells. Also able to cast five buff spells and three debuff spells, or equivalent. Spell casting should be fast and mana-efficient. Can use medium-level utility spells.

Azra knew the first four ranks very well. She was already a two-star mage, having learned and trained since childhood. She loved magic, a lot. Girls just rarely had the opportunity to learn it in their patriarchy. Niti Village was a bit too conservative in her opinion; she was only able to learn magic because she was Ash's sister. He was always seen as the golden child, while she was only able to leech off him.

Finally, they had found a good enough excuse to keep her away. Ash was the guide to a god, descended from the sky itself. What if Steve really didn't accept her being there? She wasn't sure if she could handle it. That was the only reason she didn't complain too much about this.

If a god directly told her she was unnecessary, she would probably break down. The only man who ever supported her drive for power was the village Elder. Not even the village Left, Amon—her own father—did. Even then, the Elder probably just wanted more mages for the power of the village.

As for Ash, she got the sense that he had mixed feelings about his sister learning magic. For one, magic was a dangerous path. It was somewhat safer if you trained in it from childhood, but still, the backlash of a failed spell could make one an idiot for life. Even if you had the talent, this was still a very real risk with potentially terrible consequences. Also, being a mage was miserable for those who didn't truly love and thrive on magic.

Spending hours and hours on anything that one hated was torture. Practicing magic was like school for some of the village children. They despised going and would much rather help on their parents' farms or learn to be a warrior. These children would never excel in magic, but that was completely fine. Not everyone could be a great scholar or mage; that much was obvious.

Azra walked aimlessly around the village, the dusk suiting her dark mood. Then, she heard the screams. She ran as quickly as possible toward the sounds and there, she saw her god.

Shining brightly in the twilight sky, he used his divine lightning to strike down the bandits that had attacked. Then she noticed the rogue mage conjuring up a powerful spell, just as he finished. She wanted to shout out to god Steve, to warn him of the incoming danger, but the spell was too fast. Just as the spell was about to strike him, she gasped. He was no longer there.

It was a Blink! He instantly cast Blink! Azra was shocked. This meant that Steve's status was higher than a six-star mage. She had seen him cast the spell once before, but she assumed it was prepared beforehand. Auto-casting, or casting instantly, was extremely difficult.

She watched in silent fascination as Steve took down those one-star magicians like it was nothing. Luckily, she had heard the Left arrive on the scene and when she'd looked his way, she was spared the blinding that her father and his men received along with the mages. Azra turned back to watch as Steve drained one of the magicians of all mana and energy. She was enthralled.

She found her god early the next morning at his residence. Ash was inseparable from Steve since yesterday but was thankfully still asleep inside on the bed, since the god had no use for it. The mage from yesterday was there, too. The guy was sleeping on a mattress they had brought in for him.

While she poked around, the god Steve seemed to take no notice of her. He was currently consuming a Crystal and practicing his magic. He seemed completely engrossed in what he was doing; she wouldn't disturb his practice. Azra knew how hard it was for great mages to find peace and quiet long enough to train. The greater one's power became, the more people would start asking for favors or help.

Magic was a double-edged sword. The more you practiced it, the stronger you became. You would think that because you were stronger, you would be safer. But the stronger you became, the more dangers you had to brave—it never got easier. This was the saying taught to every child who aspired to become a mage in Niti. Some immediately gave up after hearing it, choosing instead to pursue a more mundane path in their life. Others, like Ash and Azra, felt that this was the challenge of their lifetime.

The world of magic she'd dreamed of was sitting right there. Floating right there! Sitting on a rock to wait was one of the hardest things she'd ever done.

***

Steve noticed a girl approach as he worked to expand his energy pool. She poked around his residence, then sat on a rock. He remembered that she was Ash's sister, Azra. Other than that, the girl hadn't really made an impression on him.

But she was staring at him. Well, nobody really stared straight at him, since he was made of light, but her gaze was locked on the space below him. He tried to ignore it, but that was one of the negative aspects to having omnidirectional vision. No matter what he focused on, he still noticed her staring in his peripherals. It was more than a little bit annoying.

He glanced at his current numbers:

Current Energy – 1,151

Max Energy – 3,565

He was getting there. Steve had trained all night long, from after the meeting ended until now. He would cast until his energy was mostly drained; it was difficult training, but it expanded his energy pool quickly. Every now and then he would go absorb a Crystal or take energy from the pigs. They would make loud squeals of protest every time he took from them, but it was a necessity; Steve didn't feel sorry at all. They were a great energy source since there were so many pigs. Later, as his energy pool grew further, he would require better ones—the fatter the better, it seemed.

It had been over twenty minutes and she was still sitting on the rock. *Isn't that uncomfortable?* Steve wondered. *Why is she just sitting there like a statue?*

Steve wanted to use all of today to expand his energy pool and further his ability in magic. Every time he had a training session like this, his abilities increased noticeably. If he didn't expand his max energy pool significantly, he would have trouble even becoming a Vampire. If no other events occurred by the end of the day, he would risk learning another spell.

Finally, Ash came out of the residence, rubbing the sleep from his eyes. "What are we doing today, god Steve?" he asked. Then he saw his sister sitting on the rock. "Azra! What are you doing here?"

"Same thing as you, Ash. I'm here to serve the god Steve," Azra replied directly.

"But that's my job!" Ash was confused. Who had sent her here? He couldn't explain everything in front of god Steve.

"It should be fine if you both serve me. Ash, could you check up on the Workforces and make sure they're getting ready? I want them sent out again, after breakfast," Steve tasked Ash. "Also, find Loop and tell him it's the same deal today."

Steve just wanted to train his magic today; he really didn't have much time left for anything else if he was going to have any hope of a good evolution. Steve checked his countdown again. It read:

3 Days 13 Hours 30 Minutes 23 Seconds

In about an hour and a half, he would get another vision from his past; he was hoping to find out more about his old world. He remembered his girlfriend, his best friend, and a bit of his school life so far. None of that was particularly useful in this new world he had been on for the past two days.

Steve noticed something; Ash hadn't moved yet. "Ash, what are you doing?" Steve asked.

"God Steve! I mean no offense when I say this, but I'm not comfortable with my sister being here." Ash wanted to protect his sister. He knew her temper and her attitude very well. If she lost control of herself here, then Steve might…

"There's no problem. Go check up on Loop and Leeroy's Workforces," Steve ordered Ash again.

This time Ash left. With him gone, there was only Steve, Azra, and the occasional loud snore that drifted out from the residence. The man sure did know how to sleep. Although, to be fair, he did have his mana and part of his energy sucked out of him just last night.

"What do you want from me?" Steve asked Azra.

"I-I want to learn magic from you!" Azra had stuttered a little. Maybe he had been too direct. Then again, it was probably better this way.

"Nope!" Steve answered.

She looked crushed. But she didn't give up with just that.

"W-Why? You're teaching Ash, right?" she managed. Her eyes looked a bit watery. Steve wished he were able to look away.

"I'm not. I told him I'll consider it after his Naming ceremony," Steve answered back. There was no harm in telling her about the deal he had with Ash.

A light suddenly flashed in her eyes at this pronouncement. But it faded away as she said, "My Naming ceremony isn't for another year…" She trailed off at the end.

"How's your talent?" Steve suddenly asked. He was curious. "Are you better than Ash?"

"W-well, um, I guess I'm the same as him," she answered, not having expected the question.

"Well, same deal then. I'll decide if I have need of you as a student, a few days after the ceremony," Steve said good-naturedly. If the girl had the same talent as Ash but even younger than him, then it seemed promising. Steve just wanted to keep his options open. There was one thing for sure; he wouldn't be going out into the world alone.

A sudden thought struck Steve. Where had Bonnie been this whole time? Why was she so silent now? She had been so talkative in the beginning, but hadn't said anything at all in almost fourteen hours.

Bonnie? I've noticed that you speak up less and less often now. What gives? Steve sent mentally.

"Can't say!" Bonnie retorted cheerfully. "Who knows?"

That was a weird response, but Steve understood. He was probably boring her with his constant training but he really had no choice—this was necessary. Steve couldn't spare any time now to entertain her, so he decided that he would make it up to Bonnie after he evolved.

Steve spent the next hour or so training up his energy levels, until another flashback overcame him.

Chapter 12

"See this place?" a voice said.

Steve blinked. He looked around and did not see 'this place', or anything for that matter. He had no idea where he was; everything was dark. He felt like he was sitting in a chair, but he couldn't see anything when he looked down. He felt something strapped to his face too. What was going on?

"Uhh…No?" Steve tried.

"Whoops. Sorry about that, I didn't even turn it on. Let's try this," the voice said.

Suddenly, there was light. It was dim, but slowly rose in intensity until he was able to make out the small lights scattered around the blackness of the screen he was looking at. There was a small circle around one of them.

"Ok, it's working, right?" the voice tried to confirm with him. It sounded unsure. Then it muttered, "VR technology…so bad."

"Yeah it works," Steve affirmed with a nod. "This is cool."

The memories came flooding back. He was talking with his father. What was his name again? Steve was unsure. The memories were still incomplete.

"…you can see, we're here." Steve came back to himself and heard his father talking. "We are in orbit of the solar system Xolnea, solar system X. The closest habitable planet that we could colonize is here, in solar system T." As he spoke, the star systems he was referring to were circled with blue lines.

Steve remembered now. As a young boy, his father explained many things to him about the universe. They were running out of resources on their planet; the humans hadn't exactly treated their world well. So, humanity had looked to colonize another planet.

"Steve? Are you listening?" His father apparently hadn't stopped talking while Steve was reminiscing. He hadn't been listening at all.

"Yes," Steve answered. He heard a soft smack which he recognized as a facepalm. That was a gesture from decades ago, when his father was still growing up. Steve knew all about that as he often heard his father talking with his old friends about their youth.

"Okay, doesn't matter. Pay attention, I'm going to share a family secret. It's very important, OK?" his father said. "Your grandfather's father discovered this. Remember grandpappy? My dad told me, and now I'm telling you."

"Okay." Steve found that his voice was very high-pitched. Maybe there was something wrong with him.

"When you go to the academy, you have to remember this," his father went on. "Never forget it, and don't share it, okay? Family secret, and all."

"Okay!" Steve was confused. What was so important that his father had to keep repeating himself?

"See this thing right here?" His father circled it with red. "And this thing right here, and this thing…"

This went on until there were several red circles around the dark space on the map.

"We don't know what these things are. Scientists right now call these things globs of anti-matter," Steve's father explained. "But my grandfather discovered something and mapped it throughout his lifetime, from when he was a boy to when he was an old man.

"These spots move around sometimes, Steve." His father paused. "I think that they're dangerous. He never explained to me exactly why or how these things move…but, you have to promise me to never go near these things when you're all grown up and space-exploring and stuff...okay?"

"Okay, Dad," Steve answered. He could care less about this memory. Not only was this memory useless to him in his current situation, he also noticed that his father wasn't even explaining what he was talking about very thoroughly. Though, based on this memory, his dad did seem like a nice guy.

"Swear on your family's honor," his dad pressed. He took Steve's hand and held it, apparently unwilling to let it go.

"I swear," Steve promised.

***

Steve came to with a single thought, *What a weird, random memory.*

Then the pain struck his mind. What had happened to his family? What was his own surname?

Damnit, I should have tried to say goodbye! Steve opined. *Or...maybe I did? In that flashback, when he was showing me those spots—why did they feel so familiar?*

Steve racked his mind for a while, then gave up. Those memories were still locked up, Just like two of his evolutions. And the names of people he cared for.

Gods damn. Somebody locked my memories with Ancient-class magic. Steve recalled what Bonnie had said before. *When I get to the*

Capital, surely I can find someone who will know about that. Even better, they may know a way back.

Steve sifted through his memories for a while longer, until he was interrupted by someone. Ash was back. Steve watched as Ash looked around for his sister but couldn't find her; she had left earlier to get some breakfast.

Apparently, it had taken a while to get everyone together, fed, and headed off to harvest the Elemental Bark again. Leadership had changed for the workforce, but they were making good progress, but still had a lot to do.

Steve had decided he would only use the lumber in the worst-case scenario; if even after using all the Crystals he still didn't have enough to evolve into one of the top few evolutions, then he would use the lumber.

Steve wondered about the evolution rankings as well; they seemed to be based only on what was powerful in relation to his current self. He was especially curious about his newly unlocked evolution.

Deity... Steve mused. *A whopping 150,000 energy cost, but it's currently only the second-strongest. I have good reason to believe that it always was. There's a 33% chance that it always was the second-strongest, right? No, that's not right...Oh well.*

Rather than getting too wrapped up in calculating probability,

Steve moved on. Being hunted by all 'Celestials' definitely didn't sound good. It was probably a major drawback.

Although the pros and cons of this evolution were a moot point, there was no way that he was turning into a Deity. He'd have to absorb all of Niti Village to gain that much energy, and that was assuming the cost didn't go up further as a result of the attempt. In Steve's mind, the best course of action was to train up his energy levels some more, then wait for another chance at unlocking a new evolution.

Bonnie should help me again, like she did with unlocking Deity, Steve thought dubiously. *Hopefully.*

***

After training the rest of the morning, they had lunch then set out, away from town. This time, there was a party of four, with Azra and Fom having joined them. The Elder had agreed and even encouraged it, surprisingly.

Fom was driving the wagon, which was now only half full of Crystals. Steve had used the other half up at a prodigious rate, in his nightly training. Nobody really minded, though. Too much wealth for a village could also be a bad thing, as illustrated by the attack last night. Plus, they were god Steve's property to begin with. Nobody questioned this 'fact' anymore, besides Steve himself.

Their destination was the lake Ash had mentioned before. Steve had wanted to go there yesterday, but there wasn't enough time. Then there was the attack which had almost made him forget about his plans to go today. Those raiders had been weak, but the Elder had warned that there would be stronger enemies arriving soon. That hadn't really changed Steve's plans, as he figured upgrading his energy was the best way to defend the village and himself. He did plan on helping them fight their rival clan, anyway.

The four of them rolled along in relative silence, besides the clopping of horse hooves and the rumble of the wagon wheels on the uneven path. Steve, because he was contemplating his memories and practicing his Blink. Azra remained silent because she didn't enjoy socializing. Ash, because he was too polite to start up a conversation. And Fom, because he wasn't sure what to make of his position within the group, other than being the driver.

Steve really wanted to learn something new now. There just hadn't been a good opportunity, yet. Honestly, the spells out there were too numerous to make an entirely informed decision. Bonnie basically gave him access to every spell in the world. That was great, except that the more he looked into it, the harder it became to decide what to strive for.

There was the obvious advantage of becoming more powerful

with each new spell, but what would happen if he learned too many? Steve assumed that each spell he learned would affect his evolution paths since he had already seen it happen. Maybe it would dilute the power of his future paths if he explored too many areas? He also didn't have the time or energy to master all the spells. In fact, Steve doubted that he could ever master more than five complex spells.

Some of these spells were so powerful, he doubted that he would be allowed to keep them after the evolution. There was a Black Hole Vortex Sphere spell, for instance, which was world-breaking, in his opinion. The description stated that it generated a permanent black hole that sucked in all matter and light nearby. Learning that spell sounded like a great way to accidentally end his life, and maybe take the planet with him.

All things considered, Steve decided against learning another spell at the moment. If the countdown reached two days and nothing new happened, he would learn a new spell. Probably.

This is so hard. I wish I had something to guide me! Steve mentally grumbled. He then pointedly directed his thoughts right at Bonnie. *Oh wait, I do!*

He waited a while, but there was only silence in his mind. Steve was so done with this. Bonnie was absolutely useless now. Even when he asked questions, half the time she didn't answer at all, or told him that she couldn't answer. And when she did answer, it was in that annoyingly cheery voice.

Steve metaphorically sighed. Training indefinitely wasn't good for his mind, which was most of his being now, as he didn't have a corporeal body anymore. It had already been an hour of traveling and training in silence. Doing so under the gaze of a group of others was unbearable, especially after remembering Xander and their friendship in that earlier flashback. It was time to fix this problem by starting up a conversation.

"Anyone know any good stories?" Steve asked, copying Xander's usual tone. "Any volunteers?"

At this point, Azra tried to speak up as she was anxious to prove her worth.

"I—" Azra began.

"No? How about you, Fom? Tell us about yourself," Steve said, enthusiastically cutting Azra off.

Fom looked amused. He looked young, maybe five years older than Ash. Though the age gap made him more mature and quicker-witted.

"Well...I grew up in a town called—" Fom started.

"Gods damn it, man, I said tell us about yourself, not tell us about your life story," Steve cut in again, very Xander-like. He was laughing inside, unbeknownst to the shocked, young humans. It felt good to have fun like this; the past two days had been far too stressful.

They were mortified. What had they done to deserve this? Azra looked upset, while Fom looked surprised. Ash was even more surprised, as he had known Steve a bit better than the rest.

"God Steve…are you feeling alright?" Ash managed to speak up after a minute of silence.

"I'm good, I'm good, man," Steve replied.

"Do you still want to hear about me?" Fom hesitantly spoke up again.

"Nah."

***

They reached the lake after a while. It was large, about two miles long and almost a thousand feet wide.

"As you can see, it's a good water source," Ash began telling Steve all he knew about the lake. "The reason we haven't developed farmland over here is only partly because of the distance. Starting a second village here wouldn't be hard with our resources.

"It's just that…the lake is infested with hostile fish. It's also an extremely deep mana well. The hostile fish breed within and become unstoppable. We tried to kill them before, but lost some of our

warriors and a mage. After that, we gave up, it just wasn't worth it."
Ash got straight to the point. "We don't know how deep the lake may be, nor do we know exactly how much mana is infused within it. Niti Village tried to tap into it once, but it backfired. Now the lake is usually avoided and is known as Deadly Fish Lake."

He glanced at Steve for a reaction, then immediately looked away. Too bright.

"Can you do anything about this, god Steve?" Ash asked directly. "Starting a second village here would bring prosperity to Niti. There was a reason I mentioned the lake to you yesterday. We would be grateful if you could clear the waters of mana-infested fish."

Steve felt that it would be interesting to check it out and explore the area. Instead of responding, Steve held a Blink spell in his mind as he slowly ventured out into the lake.

Steve hovered out above the lake, just a few feet from the shore. Although the water was mostly clear with just a slight blue tint, he couldn't see more than a few feet into it with his omnidirectional vision. This was surprising. It was almost like the water had a magical veil, about ten feet below the surface, interfering with his sight.

He tried getting closer. Steve still had the Blink spell prepared, in case of an attack from mana-infused fish. As he neared the surface, he could see a few feet further into the water, which seemed like a good sign, but that was about it.

Nothing happened for a few minutes, as the group stared at their god hovering above the dangerous waters. The two children were worried for him, while Fom watched impassively. He had never seen, nor even heard of the horrors of this lake.

Steve then shot a Shock spell into the water. Bubbles floated up to the surface where the electricity had penetrated for a second, but there was no other reaction. Having heard about the dangers of this mana lake from Ash, he was taking no chances and completely focused on being ready to escape. After a few moments though, Steve relaxed his hold on Blink.

The moment he did that, a large fish-man sprang out of the water, straight at him. Its jaws splayed wide enough to swallow Steve's entire light body. It had been waiting for him the whole time.

***

Steve immediately Blinked. The fish-man arced through the air and landed on the ground behind where he had been. It flopped a few times, then picked itself up and walked back into the lake.

The creature that had popped up out of the lake had bright-yellow eyes which had flashed a dim green when it looked at Steve, before returning to the water. Steve felt a pull coming from the fish-man when the eyes glowed, but he couldn't quite explain it. It seemed strong, having a sleek, powerful body. Judging solely by the aqua-green physique, it was stronger than most of the Niti Villagers.

Steve had felt he was being watched from the moment he floated out over the lake. It was just a sort of intuition that he developed. Perhaps it had something to do with his skill, Greater Mind? He really wasn't sure.

He had relaxed his concentration to test his theory. It seemed that the reason he hadn't been immediately attacked, was the strong magical energy he radiated when holding the Blink spell. The moment the fish-man sensed that it was gone, it had attacked.

"Deadly Fish Lake," Steve remarked as he regrouped with his escorts. "Lives up to its name alright. Sadly for them, I have just the thing for this."

His escorts were amazed. Even though he had Blinked in front of them many times already, they couldn't help but admire it. They were all magicians and as such, had sensed him release the magical energy he was holding. Even so, in an instant, he executed the spell and escaped the danger.

"What will you do?" Azra asked. She now saw that Steve was on an even higher level than she'd thought. Not only did he hold a high-level Spatial spell for so long, he had played the dangerous fish for a fool. This was the kind of high-level magical combat she hoped to learn some day.

"Well, you'll just have to watch!" Steve was enthusiastic; this was an ideal reason to learn a new spell. "By the way, can you guys do Earth magic?"

Steve figured that he couldn't cast his new magic and his Shock spell at the same time. It would take too much concentration and energy just to hold up the spell.

"Large Anti-Gravity spell," Steve read aloud from the list. "Allows one to exert anti-gravity on large-sized bodies." Steve had chosen to spend some of his energy to learn this. Bonnie obliged him this one request, even though she had seemed sulky the entire day. Steve didn't know what her issue was now, but he didn't want to spend too much time thinking about it. That kind of thing wasn't his strong suit, anyhow.

Steve was confident that this spell was going to work wonders. They had worked on the preparations for his plan for the rest of the afternoon. When the sun was just about to set, the young mages had recovered enough mana from their training session and were ready to go.

"Ready, everyone?" Steve asked. The group murmured their assent; they had been waiting on Steve. Ash was in the front with Azra behind him and Fom was standing behind Azra, acting as support.

They stood on the edge of the lake as Steve began to cast his new spell. The energy that was released from his body began forming green symbols above a part of the lake. It drew a box at the ends of those symbols, only a few hundred cubic feet in total volume. After the box was formed, it began to spread out to the furthest corners of the lake. Once the target zone was defined, they witnessed the odd sight as a few thousand gallons of light-blue water floated into the air every second.

Steve watched his energy slowly but steadily drain downwards. He had brought enough Crystals to fuel him, but he would need to consume a large deep-blue Crystal, for both water affinity and energy purposes. Maybe with increased affinity, the energy cost for lifting many millions of gallons of water would go down.

The spell was already in place now, and the water was streaming ever more quickly into the sky. Steve let his concentration on the spell go; the symbols above the water would maintain it now, so long as he provided the energy. Though Steve didn't know exactly how the symbols worked to do this, his knowledge of the spell allowed him to understand that they did.

The mages began chanting. Even though Fom was technically a one-star magician, he was right on the cusp of becoming a two-star magician by now. The only thing that was holding him back was his mage robes. The three two-star magicians worked together to launch a stone slab they had prepared beforehand, onto the top of the water Steve was levitating. It was thick, with holes through it that turned it into a massive sieve.

The pressure of the water being forced upward through the rock made the mages expend a lot more mana than they initially thought, to hold it in place. The plan to strain all the fish-men out of the lake water seemed to be working, but it was clear that it would take too long to completely clear the lake; this way was too inefficient.

Steve focused on the wagon full of Crystals. He began topping himself off with the small Crystals, until none remained. Then, he looked at the two large dark-blue Crystals available to him; it was time to consume the affinity Crystals. Steve had a plan, although he wasn't sure if it would work.

The Large Anti-Gravity spell was right next to Small and Medium Anti-Gravity spells in the listings. It said that the user could control a large body's gravity and invert it for as long as you were casting. Steve wasn't sure he could accomplish this, given the size of the lake, but he continued, lifting the body of water even higher. He realized that this was probably going to kill all the normal fish as well, but that was a problem for the village to deal with later.

As his energy drained, he tried to adjust the magic so that it would only suspend the water and not the creatures within it, but as Steve had suspected, that didn't work. He ordered the young mages to place the Crystal into his being. They half dragged it off the wagon, into his body. Magical assistance seemingly wasn't enough to offset the strength difference of kids and adults.

He felt the deep-blue color of the Water element enter his being. He found himself almost breathing the Crystal in, soaking the color into himself as he drained its energy. Even as he absorbed, he was also expending energy through his spell cast over the entire lake. It took an incredible amount, around a thousand energy units every fifteen seconds. At this rate, he could maintain it a couple more minutes at most, before all the Crystals and his stored energy were depleted.

Steve used his newly improved understanding of Water to probe the lake. He wanted nothing but the pure Water element. He intended to drop all the fish-men onto the lakebed, then drop the hovering lake onto them.

He searched with his magical sense and racked his brain, so to speak, but it wasn't working. He couldn't find a way to drop the fish-men out of the water. Then, he felt something in the lake; some of them had already swam their way out the bottom of the water. Unlucky day for them.

The young mages watched as their god lifted the entire body of water up. The lowest point of the water was ten feet above the ground by now and slowly rising. Amazingly, the water remained held in by the green symbols. They didn't know what kind of high-level spell this was, but watching it was amazing.

Steve felt his energy levels drop below two thousand and he didn't want to absorb more of the large crystals. It was just about time.

"Get back, everyone! I'm going to drop it soon!" Steve roared. The young mages had been so captivated that they hadn't moved away yet, even though that had been the plan.

At his shout, his companions realized the danger they were in and flicked the reins, causing the horses to run away as quickly as possible.

Steve finally found the right technique; he had obtained a feeling for Water affinity from the huge blue Crystal and separated that feeling from everything else. He forcefully ejected everything that wasn't water back onto the mud of the lakebed. They struck the ground with small splashes, as Steve hadn't been able to get all the water floating, just most of it. He felt his energy level dip below one thousand. Even though it was dangerous to hold on longer, he didn't want to kill the forgetful mages with what he knew was coming.

They needed a little more time.

Then, he noticed a large blue Crystal near the lowest point of the lake. It was huge, several times larger than the one he'd had in the wagon and the color was mesmerizing. The fish-men that had dropped down encircled it, as if they were trying to defend the humongous Crystal. Now that the water wasn't in the way any longer, Steve could feel the power emanating from the massive Crystal down below.

In this moment, there were hundreds of fish-men and other creatures milling about in the shallow water beneath the massive floating mass of water. A sea of white structures caught his attention. Interspersed between them were different kinds of fish-men. Some were on their knees, in a state of panic. Some looked significantly different than the others he'd noticed before. Were they fish-women? They most likely had absolutely no idea what was going on. Steve saw a lot of creatures that he couldn't identify, but it didn't matter to him. There was no time left; his energy reserves were nearly gone. It was too late to think about that now.

He dropped the millions of gallons of pure, mana-infused lake water onto the fish civilization.

***

"The spell we had over the lake has been defeated as if it weren't even there. It was supposed to block any visitors, but someone or something must have passed through it and somehow killed the Naga King. They might be looking for the Greater Water Elemental Crystal. If so, they are a serious threat," a voice reported. "What is our course of action, my master?"

"Don't worry about it. We can't spare the resources now. Nobody could collect the Crystal that easily. Even if something has killed the Naga King, there's no way they can go through all the Naga in the Lake that easily. I can only think of a few powers on this entire continent that could accomplish that in one night," an aged voice rasped out in reply. "We can check up on them in a few days, if there is no news from them. For now, we aren't worried about the Capital's outskirts. We need to turn our attention inward."

Chapter 13

The three mages shouted; they had been hundreds of feet away, but still got doused by the water. The horses were even worse off; they'd been drenched completely by the miniature tsunami.

As they ran away, Ash had turned his head back, just in time to see the water fall from up above. He imagined vile creatures perishing to the sheer force of the water. The Elder would be happy to know that god Steve had avenged the Niti warriors that had fallen here years ago. They had lost important villagers to the lake, which caused their village to decline in power. It was one of the key reasons why they were in such dire economic straits before god Steve arrived.

The mass of water had been so large, that it first seemed to fall in slow motion. It had sped up as it fell, until it shook the ground with the massive weight as it made contact. A huge wave had swept toward them not too long afterward. Even though they were far away from the impact, water fell from the sky on them. Luckily, it was still slightly warm outside. Otherwise, Ash figured he might get sick. Having a cold for the Naming ceremony would have been bad, as he needed to be in peak condition.

After that, everything was still. Ash turned toward Fom and Azra to see them staring back at the lake with wide eyes. They were all dealing with the aftereffects of the adrenaline and feeling of awe. They had all grown up listening to legends of things like today. Now, they were witnesses to the great feat that god Steve had accomplished today—

"You can come back now!" Steve called out. The waves moving across the surface of what remained of the lake had died down a while ago, and now he wondered where the kids were. He was sure that he held it long enough to let them get to a safe distance...but maybe his calculations were off.

"Anyone there?" Steve tried again, using a little energy to amplify his voice this time.

As he waited, he heard a faint shout from Azra. Perhaps they had injured themselves? As they came back into view, he saw his guess was half right. He could see a look that was somewhere between awe and trauma on all their faces.

Oh well, better that they understand what they're getting into now, rather than later, Steve thought.

Azra had a gash on one arm and a scrape on her other forearm. It didn't look that bad, honestly. Fom had a small gash on his head and looked like he'd had a bad fall. Ash was shaking as he drove the wagon, probably from excitement.

Fom's face looked odd, though. Steve searched his mind for any information about humans shedding skin. But no, that simply didn't happen, humans didn't shed skin. Then why was half of Fom's face like that?

After a bit, he learned what had happened. Fom had worn a face mask to hide his age, believing that nobody would hire a fourteen-year-old mage, regardless of their power level. Too young and inexperienced. But when Ash and Azra had looked at him a bit after their soaking, they saw a monster whose face seemed to be melting off because of the water. Azra had hit him and they both fell off the wagon, resulting in their injuries. Ash was just shocked.

Peeling the rest of the mask off, Fom looked young. He looked younger than Azra even, but insisted that he was fourteen. It seemed the kid was extremely embarrassed about his youthful appearance.

With the lake completely cleared of its namesake, they needed a new one for it. So, for now, they were calling it Steve's Lake. The kids had wanted to name it something else, but Steve directly rejected it. He didn't want to have to say 'Lake of the Fish Vanquisher God Steve.' It was inconvenient, if not outright cringeworthy. Steve had heard his dad use that term before.

"That's cringe though," Steve had said, but the kids didn't understand at all. Steve didn't fully understand, either, he'd just felt compelled to say it like his dad had. Upholding the family traditions, and all that.

The group prepared to head back to the village for dinner. While the kids were preparing the wagon and groomed the horses to calm them down, Steve stayed on top of the water and started draining energy from the lake. Then, he tried going into the water.

It was an interesting sensation. Steve felt the water all around him, even within him, but it didn't hurt his light body. He continued topping off his energy with the water around him. It was just like draining the energy from the Water Elemental Crystal, but the feeling was much greater.

This must be related to the Crystal I saw at the bottom, Steve thought. After another few moments of absorption he was feeling full, and his energy read:

Current Energy – 7,742

Max Energy – 7,820

He had more than doubled his capacity since this morning! Steve quickly checked for changes to his top evolutions list. Aside from energy value changes, there wasn't anything of note.

Perhaps the evolutions near the bottom of the list have changed more, Steve mused. *Maybe I'll check another time. It's interesting that Turtle hasn't passed Elf though, even with all the Water affinity I've gained...*

The group made their way back to Niti Village to share the good news.

***

"Here's what we know." Leffer was stating the facts. "The Mottor will be here sometime after noon tomorrow. We know that we are more than a match for the Mottor in will to fight, but potentially not in power. We don't know how many mages they have hired. The advantage still lies with us, given our information about when and where they'll attack. But this advantage won't be enough, if we are overwhelmed by their mages' power."

The villagers were all wearing their ceremonial caps, as this was a serious village meeting. They had started it in the afternoon and were just wrapping up. The Elder was delivering his ending speech. The Workforces had returned earlier that day, with more than half the Elemental Bark in the whole forest harvested. They were faster today, now having at least a little experience in felling trees.

"Fom, when he gets back, will tell us exactly where and when they'll strike. We'll set up a large mage ambush near that area beforehand," Amon spoke up. They had already decided this before the meeting and were just sharing it with the villagers now. Most of the time was spent answering questions from the villagers. They were all concerned about the attack, as they should be.

"We cannot ask for god Steve's help in this matter since our village wars do not concern him. However, if he feels threatened, like that time last night, I think we can expect him to act. If the enemy can be lured into assailing his position...then god Steve will wipe them all out. This is what we'll do to even the odds. However, if that plan fails, we will use the village treasure to combat the Mottor," Leffer addressed the issue of Steve's role in the upcoming battle.

"Joffrey will lead the ambush. Amon will lead the frontal charge afterward. You will be split into two squads, the ambush squad, and the frontal squad. Are there any questions?" Leffer asked.

A man with an insignia on his pointy hat spoke up; he was a wealthy merchantman in their village, one of the best at his trade. This was a man who would be useless in the upcoming battle; he'd never learned any combat art, but that was fine by the village. Not everyone had to learn to fight.

"Why risk so much in this battle? I say if we have a god in our village, then we need to take advantage of this opportunity. Seize this chance to offer him gifts for his...friendship!"

Bribery was one of the arts that must be mastered to become a successful merchant. Otherwise, the taxes in the larger towns and cities would bleed away all the profit. This was an accepted practice...if one wasn't caught.

"We cannot bribe a god. There's nothing we can offer save for the village treasure that he might want," Leffer answered. He was not going to stoop so low.

"I wasn't speaking of that kind of bribery." The merchant held firm. "It's more like, mutual interest, given that he has shown us what he requires..."

"We can't sink to the same level as the Mottor! We will not bribe the god by sacrificing our own people!" Amon suddenly spoke up angrily. He knew that the merchant had made a decent point. God Steve had expressed interest in their village people before.

"I've heard that he was willing to trade Elemental Bark and Crystals for manpower," the merchant continued, ignoring Amon's outburst. "I think he would be willing to help our village if we offer more of the same deal. This...god, is a benign one, but he doesn't work for free."

Leffer had to consider this seriously, Steve wasn't like the other gods in the legends. Those gods would rarely, if ever, deal with humans. This plan might actually work.

"We could offer up all of the prisoners and more livestock, as well as permanent command of the Squad of Scoundrels…" Leffer's heart ached at the last part. The Squad of Scoundrels contained his family, after all. His mind balked at the notion, but if it was for the good of the village…Leffer was at a crossroads.

"He might accept, and we would suffer no losses to manpower. Sacrifices to the gods have always been a tradition, too."

Joffrey signaled to the Elder, pulling his attention from the merchant to him. God Steve was back.

"We need to consider this matter carefully, we will have another meeting tomorrow morning, after the Naming. The meeting is adjourned," Leffer announced.

***

"We're heroes!" Azra was giddy with joy.

"Legends!" Ash called out.

"S…Saviors?" Fom tried. It wasn't a good try, but it was a try. The other two had taken the good ones.

"Destroyer god Steve, with the help of three young mages, vanquished the Deadly Fish Lake's inhabitants in one afternoon," Azra announced. She then imitated a bard and in her best falsetto sang, "We're like the heroes, in the legends of yore!"

"Legendary heroes!" Ash had dropped his facade of politeness, infected by Azra's enthusiasm. Now he was just like any other excited kid.

Though there was a glimmer in his eye, there was no response from Fom. The young mage had accepted that he couldn't keep pace with these two.

They were almost back to the village by now. Steve had checked the countdown timer before they left. It had read:

3 Days 4 Hours 30 Minutes 20 Seconds

He estimated that he would still have a good ten minutes after arriving at the village to prepare for a sudden feeling of whatever was to come. Steve was getting used to the cycle. It went, feeling – memory – feeling – memory – feeling, and so on.

When they arrived, they could see a lot of village men acting as guards now. There was a tense atmosphere; everyone knew that the Mottor would arrive soon. It was just a matter of exactly when.

Steve led the group of children to the Elder's residence. He noticed a lot of people putting away their weird pointy hats. Steve guessed that there must have been a gathering of some sort since that was the tradition. Weird pointy hats for Niti Village meetings.

Well, I guess there's no reason to delay in letting them know, Steve decided.

***

Lord Mottor glanced at the stars. He was expecting a notification from Tenk about now. Usually Tenk did all the talking, Fom was always more of the quiet type.

He had bought their contracts from a mercenary group called Rogues for Hire. It was a subsection of a much larger mercenary group in the Capital, but a mere village Lord couldn't afford hiring an entire mercenary company, so he'd settled for five rogue mages, to bolster his forces.

Lord Mottor was a decent three-star mage himself, but as all mages knew, there was safety in numbers. At least, until the five-star rank or above. After that, it was more a matter of quality over quantity.

Rogue mages were usually better than normal, Capital-trained ones. Until the five-star rank, or so Lord Mottor had heard when he had hired them. They were more accustomed to battle and used to using magic against anyone. The kids at the Capital who trained in magic were usually soft-hearted and weak. Rogues were much better for his purposes.

Any time now, Lord Mottor thought impatiently. *They must have finished their second raid by now, right?*

The Crystal blinked. "Was the raid successful?" Lord Mottor didn't waste any time. They had marched all day today and would need to march another half day tomorrow to get there. He needed to quickly confirm their status and set up a rendezvous.

"Yes. We lost two more men today, they were prepared," came Fom from the Crystal. "One fell to an ambush by regular militia, the ball of light took out the other. We think it may have been conjured by a four-star mage, it isn't that strong. The mage has kept himself hidden, though."

Four stars, huh? Not good, but not too bad. Lord Mottor could overwhelm that mage with his ace. As for the ball of light he conjured, it would be too easy. Usually conjured images didn't last too long in combat because of mana restrictions. There was usually only so much mana you could imbue into an object or summon.

"Hold off on any further action until I give the command. Now, tell me, where should we meet up?" Lord Mottor was fine talking to Fom. He was somewhat mysterious and Mottor found himself curious about his origins, as he was a decent mage for his price. This was the most they have ever spoken.

Tenk, on the other hand, was immensely greedy and would ask for bonuses in the form of Ekem village girls. The younger, the better. Lord Mottor didn't have an issue with this on principle;

however, it did lower morale substantially in the conquered village. Lower morale would eventually lead to lower productivity. Though, that was a matter to address another day.

"As you approach, you will see a lake near the village. Next to the lake is a rocky area where we can meet up if you're following the dirt path all the way," Fom replied in his usual gruff voice. "Once you see the village, you might want to duck off of the path and stick to concealment as much as possible. They have sentries out now."

"Fine. Tomorrow afternoon I'll contact you for the exact location, make sure you're prepared," Lord Mottor commanded. "Good work, we'll see you tomorrow."

"Father, is everything going according to plan?" It was his useless second son, Mottle. He was just checking in, for no good reason. It wasn't like he would be much help in the upcoming battle. Lord Mottor didn't have the time to—

"Father, when do we conquer Niti? Is the plan on schedule?" This time it was Mithe, his first son. Mithe was a better fighter and had a better attitude about these things.

"Tomorrow evening. The plan is on schedule. We'll use the light of the two moons to raze Niti Village," Lord Mottor declared.

"But that doesn't make sense, the moon…" Mottle went on to explain why one couldn't use the moon to start fires.

Absolutely useless, thought Lord Mottor as he ignored his rambling son. *At least I have one decent son.*

***

Leffer paced back and forth in his residence, with his pointy hat still on. This was exciting news. When god Steve's party arrived, they had told him that Deadly Fish Lake had been completely cleared out by Steve and the three young magicians.

This opened up so many new opportunities for the village. They could expand to a second village, harvest the mana-water to make potions, or mana-infused alcohol even. Both of which could be sold for exorbitant prices. New Nitian businesses would flourish, with the addition of this free territory. The possibilities of this new area were endless! Leffer couldn't contain his newfound excitement.

The problem they'd faced when trying to claim that lake before, was that there was so much mana in the surroundings. It was harmful, possibly even deadly for anything living to go into it. Only the best warriors and mages could even attempt clearing it out.

When they had set out on sturdy boats, they all almost died. It was only through sheer luck on Leffer's part that they managed to survive. He had lost two old friends that day, pulled down into the lake by the fish. He had been sure that there was a treasure in the lake, just waiting for him to claim it.

It was at this point he realized that everyone was staring at him. Who knew how long he had been slowly pacing, lost in his own thoughts? He had been rude to everyone, including god Steve.

"Ahem, this is incredibly good news!" Leffer cleared his throat and recovered his bearing. He went on, "I'm jubilant to hear that our young heroes, along with god Steve, have cleared out a dangerous part of the village surroundings. You've done an incredible service to the village. Ash, you need to go sleep. Tomorrow is your big day!"

Leffer doubted the young man would have an easy time falling asleep with all this excitement going around, but he had to. Not having enough energy for the Naming would be disastrous. One needed to be as rested as possible to proceed through the pain. The Naming ceremony would be the most agonizing thing that Ash would ever experience, or at least Leffer hoped so.

Ash bid the group farewell, saying he would go meditate. Leffer approved, as it would help him collect his emotions and prepare his mind for tomorrow.

Fom had spoken to Lord Mottor earlier, but for security reasons they needed to keep him in their sight, at all times. Azra, on the other hand, really had no reason to be there. She had taken a liking to standing beside Steve. Maybe the young girl still had delusions of grandeur. It was fine, for now at least. She would understand soon enough.

"God Steve, we have a request." Leffer had made up his mind. He would protect Ash and the village, even if it went against his values.

Even if it cost him his only son.

***

When Steve entered the residence, he suddenly felt euphoric. He checked the countdown as the feeling overcame him. It read:

3 Days 2 Hours 59 Minutes 55 Seconds

The feeling warmed his light body and flowed through his mind, sort of like an org…A what again? The memory block on his mind shifted, preventing him from remembering what he was about to think.

That didn't matter; he felt great, this was the best feeling he had experienced over the past two days. Steve saw that the group was talking as Leffer walked around. They were excited about something; Steve was excited about it, too.

After a whole minute, Steve started to come down. Bit by bit, his joy diminished. *What just happened?* Steve wondered happily. *This system is pretty good after all, heh.*

Then he noticed that the Elder was talking to him directly. "In short, we want to offer you full control of the Squad of Scoundrels and the prisoner squads," Leffer was saying. He had apparently been talking this whole time. Only now did Steve really focus on what he was getting at. "Permanently."

Steve felt that this offer was okay, but not as high as it should be. He saw that he was regarded as a god or higher being everywhere he went, because of his power, so it wouldn't be difficult to gather more people. Surely, he knew better than to lead with his best offer; he must be willing to go a little higher. So, Steve waited impassively for Leffer to sweeten the deal.

"We'll also give you a small portion of the village resources, in return for your help in this upcoming battle," Leffer added. He knew people weren't in high demand, at least not nearly so much as supplies were. If one had people but no supplies, then you were in worse condition than if you had no people at all.

The deal sounded good. A portion of Niti's resources, as well as his own force, to use as he saw fit after his evolution. The binding ritual, however, was a little sketchy. Steve didn't feel that he was actually a god because he could transform into a Deity. That meant that he wasn't a Deity now, right?

"Sure," Steve agreed. He couldn't think of a reason not to. The power level of the humans in the village wasn't great, save for their few older elites. Helping them out wasn't a big deal at all, in Steve's mind, especially since he still had a bit of time and energy to burn before evolving. Though, what he could accomplish would depend on the forces of the Mottor.

Bonnie, any thoughts about this ritual? Steve asked. There was no reply. This was actually a little unnerving, how Bonnie's commentary and even assistance was so erratic now. Over the last day, she had been especially quiet.

Something felt off, but Steve couldn't quite pin it down. He needed some advice, right about now. Also, as the 'big moment' was getting closer, he needed a direction to go in. His energy storage level should be fine in time, as he had been working to enhance it. The only issue was that Steve wanted the best evolution, since it would probably help him get home. He was a bit interested in Vampire, but Ash had said the other races would seek to kill him.

Steve wanted a powerful, mobile evolution. This was only so that he could go and find more information about his predicament. The only goal was to get back to his girlfriend, wherever she was.

"I'm going to go practice some more magic now," Steve told the three that were still gathered. "We can talk about details, later."

He then opened up his list again, after he left the residence. Steve planned to practice his Large Anti-Gravity spell. Perhaps if he grew more proficient in it, the list would change to his benefit. Right now, it looked like this.

1) ??? - ???

2) Deity – Cost: 125,000 Energy. End evolution is Undetermined. Evolution starts out extremely high-powered. Will be hunted by all Celestial beings.

3) Vampire – Cost: 5,000 Energy. End evolutions are the Legendary Vampire or Undetermined. Evolution starts out extremely low-powered. Will receive help from the current Vampire clan.

4) Dragon – Cost: 55,000 Energy. End evolution is the Dragon God. Evolution starts out medium-powered but gaining energy and consolidating it is difficult. Will receive help from the current Dragon race.

5) ??? - ???

6) Undead – Cost: 45,000 Energy. End evolution is the Undead Emperor. Evolution starts out low-powered, however amassing undead is easy. Gaining power is easy, however keeping it might prove difficult. Almost all other races will join forces against you if your nature is discovered.

7) Elf – Cost: 25,000 Energy. End evolution is the Greater Elven Magister. Evolution starts out low-powered. Gaining energy is medium difficulty while keeping energy is easy. Races will tend to trust you, making interacting with most of them easy.

The upper few evolutions had become cheaper in terms of energy cost. It wasn't bad news at all. Gaining an affinity for water hadn't really changed his evolution paths that much. Deity's cost had been lowered, though. Steve wasn't sure when it had happened, however.

I should have been watching, Steve thought. *If I kept track of when the cost of these evolutions changed, I would already have a better idea of what influences it.*

Steve wasn't sure whether the water affinity or gravity spell mattered more. So, he was now going to focus on training his gravity spell, while he observed changes to his list.

He went to a grass field with some gray rocks lying around. Steve focused on bringing those rocks up with his spell, but this time he focused on speed. A spell needed power, speed, and utility. If it was too slow, it would be useless in a lot of situations. It only took Steve ten seconds this time, but it was a far smaller body than the lake he had previously lifted. Energy cost was minimal as well.

After a few hours, Bonnie spoke to him again. Only, it wasn't the cheerful Bonnie that spoke. It was the forced voice that he had heard only two times before.

"Greater Mind consequence lifted," Bonnie deadpanned. "Due to two days of Greater Mind consequence, some information will be released."

Steve blacked out.

Chapter 14

"Steve! Wake up!" Bonnie shouted into his mind. "You really shouldn't have broken that rule!"

Steve's omnidirectional vision returned. He found that he was a lot more clear-headed than before. On top of that, he found that he didn't have any new information or memories unlocked.

Where is my information? Steve asked.

"I have your information," Bonnie replied, still sounding peeved. "Greater Mind blocked me out. I could resist it a little bit, but as your mind gained in power I couldn't keep up. I could barely speak at the end. Good thing it was lifted."

It sounded like Bonnie had wanted to tell him that for a while now.

"But we gained a lot from it, Steve!" Bonnie was enthusiastic as ever again. "I know how to unlock the two question-mark evolutions!"

Steve's interest was piqued. He had wanted to figure out that mystery for a while now. What would the top evolution be like?

"You have to--—" Bonnie tried. "Have to—uh. Hmm, it seems like I can't directly tell you! Let's just say the opportunity will come up very soon. I think?"

It didn't seem like much information, but it was immensely useful. Bonnie had been suppressed by the consequence of breaking a rule. It made sense for there to be upsides and downsides to it; on the one hand, he couldn't be controlled or influenced by enemies. On the other hand, he couldn't be influenced by his helper.

It was an interesting situation that Steve found himself in, at least he now knew that the opportunity would come soon.

It's fine, you've helped plenty already. Steve had become accustomed to life without Bonnie's assistance, but wanted to make use of his newly freed helper. *Thanks for the information. Also, can you watch what happens to the evolution list values when I practice my spells? Let me know if there are any noticeable changes.*

Steve kept on practicing the Gravity spell on different objects, trying to get a feel for it. He knew that this spell would be important in the upcoming fight. As of right now, if he focused extremely hard, he could cast the Gravity spell in around five seconds and maintain it while he fired Shocks, though not rapidly.

Steve wanted to get to the point where he could cast his upgraded Area Energy Drain spell while maintaining the Large Anti-Gravity spell. It was a necessity if he wanted a way to affect his opponents en masse once he got them in the air. If he just kept them there, they would find a way to strike back.

He had never been seriously hit before. The Blink spell was too effective a means of escape to allow for mistakes like that. Though, he still wasn't entirely sure what would happen if he did get hit by something.

Thinking of all these spells, Steve had a sudden question.

Will I get to keep these spells and abilities after my evolution? Steve asked Bonnie. He was sure that she was able to help, now that Greater Mind had been lifted.

"Yes and no. If the evolution you choose is unsuitable, or the spells are too powerful to transfer, then you can't. If it is suitable and the spell isn't too powerful, then you can." Bonnie was very direct in this.

Steve figured that would be the case, but it couldn't hurt to ask. If he evolved into a Rock Being, then he probably wouldn't be able to cast many spells. Steve imagined himself as a Rock Being. He felt a tingle in his mind and immediately stopped. One of the rules had said no evolving until the countdown was finished. Steve wasn't willing to risk breaking another rule so soon; the consequences might severely hurt him this time. For all he knew, they already had. It was impossible to say what he may have learned if Bonnie had been free to speak to him all this time.

He checked the countdown again, it read:

2 Days 19 Hours 10 Minutes 23 Seconds

This meant that he had a bit more than two hours until the next memory.

He focused on the two moons up above. On his planet, there had only been one moon. It was just known as the Moon. Steve still didn't know what these two moons were called. He would try to remember to ask Ash tomorrow.

The large Crystals he hadn't yet consumed were still sitting in the wagon they brought to the lake. The other wagon was still mostly full, though some of the Crystals had already been consumed. Steve wondered if he would need to pay another visit to the Lake before tomorrow's battle. The energy in the Lake was so dense, even though the humongous Water Crystal was located so far down in the depths of the water. It was a purer and stronger type of Water Elemental energy even compared to the largest Crystal inside his wagon.

Steve assumed that all the creatures and 'fish' that had lived in the water had been feeding off the Crystal for a long time. Right up until he smashed them with their own lake, that is. He doubted there would be any survivors of such an attack, but anything was possible.

I might have to go down into the structures to check for any surviving fish, Steve thought to himself. He hadn't considered this before. *If I don't make sure, then Niti Village won't be able to flourish under the threat of any hostile fish survivors.*

The vivid red sun interrupted his thought processes. The massive ball of fire in the sky appeared several times larger than his own sun back home. Steve remembered that temperature was related to the color that stars appeared but couldn't remember any of the details. This one was nothing like his own yellow sun back home.

As he thought, he kept on practicing his Gravity magic. It was getting tiresome, even for Steve, practicing magic for days on end. *Is there any other way?* Steve thought. How could he practice smarter, not harder?

Then, he felt yet another improvement. This time, noticeably larger. This was unusual; it was usually a slow, gradual improvement, rather than a sudden larger one.

"Turtle has moved up to the #6 spot and Slime has taken the #7 spot," Bonnie reported in, as promised. She had been diligently keeping track of and updating him about any changes to his evolution paths this entire time. Though, Steve had only wanted notifications for the more drastic changes. The sixth and seventh places on his list didn't really matter to him. "Energy costs have changed as well."

Nonetheless, it was good to know.

1) ??? – ???

2) Deity – Cost: 120,000 Energy. End evolution is Undetermined. Evolution starts out extremely high-powered. Will be hunted by all Celestial beings.

3) Vampire – Cost: 8,000 Energy. End evolutions are the Legendary Vampire or Undetermined. Evolution starts out extremely low-powered. Will receive help from the current Vampire clan.

4) Dragon – Cost: 50,000 Energy. End evolution is the Dragon God. Evolution starts out medium-powered but gaining energy and consolidating it is difficult. Will receive help from the current Dragon race.

5) ??? – ???

6) Turtle – Cost: 75,000 Energy. End evolutions are the World Turtle or Undetermined. Evolution starts out low-powered. Gaining power is easy, just eat! Monster-class being, however, other beings will help you.

7) Slime – Cost: 20,000 Energy. End evolution is Undetermined. Evolution starts out medium-powered. Gaining power is easy, just absorb! Monster-class being, other beings will want to hunt you.

"I see…So the Gravity spell improvement had somehow pushed Turtle and Slime past Elf and Undead, on the list," Steve gathered. Obviously, this meant that the paths of Turtle and Slime had a positive relation to gravity. That also meant that there had to be other factors more relevant to the top five evolutions, as they hadn't budged much. Also, Steve assumed Vampire going up in energy cost must mean that it was not very compatible with Gravity-type magic. *Well, nothing to do but continue training until morning,* Steve thought.

***

Ash was nervous. No, if he was honest with himself, he was scared. It was a restless anxiety, that caused frequent waves of nausea if he didn't keep his mind off it. The fear rolled around in his stomach, like a never-ending tidal wave of energy.

Today was the big day. The village Left's own son, the village's top young mage, was going to undergo his Naming ceremony. Expectations were sky high; everybody in Niti gossiped and speculated about the outcome.

The Naming ceremony was something performed for young mages only. The Elder would customarily perform it, though there were exceptions. Sometimes, a close family member who was a three-star or higher mage would perform it. This was the norm in the entire Empire, to unlock the potential of young mages when they became young adults.

Ash put on his pointy hat with the A insignia emblazoned on it, signifying that he was of the A family. Anyone who wore their hat on a regular basis would appear arrogant in the eyes of the other villagers but this was a serious ceremony, so he had to wear it.

Ash then thought about god Steve. Maybe he would be able to become his disciple or follower and then be able to learn magic from the god himself. He felt that it was all moving too fast. In his mind, it seemed like he had just started learning magic yesterday.

Ash then turned to walk out of his residence. They lived in a relatively nicer home in the more affluent part of the village. The surroundings weren't bad at all. There were some green trees, a clear pond, and a small garden nearby.

They would be conducting the ceremony in the village center, so Ash started heading there. The 'village center' was actually somewhat off-center, because of poor settlement planning in the past. It wasn't a big problem; it still served its purpose, though some of the villagers that lived on the farther side complained about the longer route.

The whole village was gathered there now, a few thousand

people, all standing around, chatting and occasionally glancing at the tall podium in the middle, where the ceremony would be conducted. It was still early, but nobody wanted to miss this occasion.

As Ash came into sight, everyone went silent, aside from the sound of a few babies crying and a few people whispering. Everyone made way for Ash to get through, as they recognized the soon-to-be man. He was famous in the village for his talent, not just because his father was the Left. People recognized his hard work and respected him as a result. That coupled with his talent, made it difficult to not like him.

Ash reached the base of the wooden stairs which led to the top of the podium. Leffer was already patiently waiting for him. The Left and Right were also there, standing off at the side. Nobody spoke as he neared the top; that would only wreck the boy's concentration at this point. Trying to break the tension with levity was futile, too. Anything said would only make it worse. If Ash fainted during the ceremony, it could be disastrous.

Most of the time, Naming ceremonies were painful. Most children openly wept, as they tried to endure it. The procedure was often agonizing, because the Elder had to reach deep within the child mage, to tug at and enhance their mana veins, since humans generally couldn't freely manipulate mana.

This was a weakness inherent in humans; they were typically born with small mana veins or none at all and would have to learn and practice working with mana for the rest of their relatively short lives. The only advantage was that once they'd learned to deal with magic, they could potentially channel more, and work together more easily than other races as well. Before that point, however, humans were generally weak.

This was also why two mages were generally better than one. Unless there was a huge disparity in skill, the two mages would have double the resources of a single mage. As humans had little innate magical skill, they learned where the mana veins were located and therefore had an easier time synergizing. Combining energies became extremely easy at the higher levels, if voluntary.

Humans couldn't change shape; their bodies were soft and weak, and they were practically useless until age fifteen or later. Other races were fundamentally better off in most regards. But, to make up for this power disparity, humans had developed ways of thinking and techniques more advanced than that of other civilizations. They banded together more readily than other races as well. The reason the Empire had survived for so long, in the midst of all the monster nations around them, was due to their sheer will to stay alive as well as their ability to stay together during times of hardship.

That's what Ash had always been told as a child, that humans needed to work together to survive. He knew the gist of what would happen. The Elder would first tug at his veins, so he would have an idea of what was to come and a moment to brace himself for it. If it wasn't blinding pain, then he was lucky.

Ash was confident that he would gain a special ability from the Naming today; his mana veins were different from birth. They were the most vibrant and powerful anyone in the village had ever seen, or even heard of. As a child, Ash had realized that he was a little different from the rest of his peers. He was treated better than the rest of his classmates at the small village school that all the children had attended twice a week.

It was considered a gift to be able to attend school. Ash was able to go and study whenever he wanted since he had the most latent potential. He was also given the best food and instruction, as well as the unique opportunity to learn magic straight from the village Elder himself. When Steve had appeared near their village, he was naturally given the opportunity to follow him around.

Ash remembered what the Elder had told him. "Make sure you do not waste this opportunity. We, as humans, are not able to make contact with the other races of the continent anymore. Take this chance to learn from god Steve and improve your own magic. I hope you'll be able to become a 7-star mage in your lifetime," Leffer had said gravely, the night Steve appeared. They were both very aware that their village was minuscule and insignificant when compared to the rest of the continent, much less the world. The talent that Ash possessed meant that the village had an opportunity to become a Town or, if lucky, a City within two generations.

Ash knew that Leffer hoped that he would be able to send Ash to the Capital to learn magic from the best in the Empire. Thus, he never grew cocky or conceited over his advantage in his small village. There were much grander plans in motion than being the best village mage and Ash had been terribly aware of that for as long as he could remember.

The Elder came up to him and placed his wrinkled hands over Ash's. Energy filled the air as the Naming began. By now, the whispering of the crowd had stopped and the kids had all been silenced. It was considered taboo to disrupt a Naming ceremony in any way. A split-second lapse of concentration could mean the difference between life and death since Ash was so powerful already. Any mistake would ripple through his powerful mana veins and be amplified several times over. Any misstep in the Naming would smash Niti's chances of becoming a Town.

Power accumulated in the air and the crowd held its breath,

then—

"Stop the ceremony!" Steve's loud voice rang out across the village center.

Chapter 15

A few minutes earlier...

"It's about time," Bonnie said, shaking Steve from his training. "Go over to the village center, it's not too far from here. You'll unlock an evolution if you perform the Naming."

How do I perform the Naming? Steve wondered to Bonnie. *Wait... What even is a Naming, really?*

He had started floating over, as he obviously wanted to unlock the evolution but so far, Bonnie hadn't made what he needed to do at all clear.

"It's easy! Just take some of his mana and replace it with your Energy! Fill him until he almost pops. You'll feel it, don't worry," Bonnie replied happily. That was reassuring. Then she added, "If you don't, it's only a human. No big deal!"

Steve was now hesitant; he had nothing against humans, as he knew he had been one in his memories. Bonnie's way of thinking lacked any respect for human life. Steve eventually decided to go along with the plan. Bonnie hadn't really led him astray before. Sure, she was being vague, but it was fine. Besides, without much other counsel, he couldn't help but be influenced by her advice.

As he approached, he saw the sea of villagers and realized they were already starting the ceremony. He had yelled, probably loudly.

Everyone startled and turned their attention to him. Steve wasn't sure what to say in this situation, so he just continued floating towards the podium. He hadn't ever had so many eyes on him before, and with his omnidirectional vision, he couldn't even look away as he floated above their heads. All the attention made him feel anxious—anyone would be, right? There were at least a few thousand Nitians focused on him right now. He had never been a good public speaker back at the academy; in fact he was more the quiet, laidback cadet stereotype.

"Let me Name Ash!" Steve addressed to the crowd, rather than directing it to the Elder.

Leffer looked extremely confused right about now, though Ash was even more so. Steve had made this dramatic entrance…just to name him? To be Named by a god, it was an unheard-of opportunity.

Leffer looked at Ash. "It's your awakening, young man," he said with expectation clear on his face. They were still touching hands, about to start the ceremony. Ash was still shocked and hesitated for a whole two seconds.

"I'll accept god Steve's offer, I believe in him," Ash responded. He had seen too many wonders not to believe. In fact, he was starting to believe that god Steve could do anything. "Please do not take it as a slight, Elder."

Steve was thrilled when he heard this, as it meant he would be able to unlock his next evolution. The villagers on the other hand, began to buzz with speculation about why this was happening and what it might mean.

The Cult of Steve immediately knelt and mumbled praise for this blessing from their god. Rumors of Steve's divine appearance, coupled with his magical prowess, fabulous wealth, and generosity, had been circulating the village almost since his arrival. For a few dozen of the villagers, their interest and reverence had coalesced into open worship, when he had singlehandedly defeated the invading mages.

Leffer nodded to Ash and took a step back, as Steve hovered onto the podium before the thousands of assembled villagers.

It was a magnificent view for Steve, with his omnidirectional vision. It was also a magnificent view for the villagers, who once again became reverently hushed in preparation for the Naming.

Okay, Bonnie, I want to be sure I understand. I take some of his mana and replace it with my Energy until the kid is full. Right? Steve couldn't afford to mess up here. Ash was beloved by the villagers, for both his attitude and aptitude. If he messed up, he'd probably be forced out of the village by a mob of thousands of angry villagers. He doubted he could fight that many people at once and he wouldn't even want to try. Plus, he liked Ash more and more, as time went on.

"Yes!" Bonnie replied.

Steve moved closer, until he would have nearly been nose-to-nose with Ash, at least if Steve had such a feature. Ash stood as still as he was able, hands trembling slightly, and eyes closed. He seemed prepared, so Steve began the ceremony.

Steve focused intently and located Ash's mana veins. They ran evenly throughout his entire body, besides the core. His core seemed like it was the source of all of Ash's magic, as it was the largest mana pool within the body. Steve began absorbing Ash's mana, siphoning slowly, since he didn't want to mess up the ceremony by rushing.

Ash tensed up and released a groan through his clenched teeth. He was growing visibly weaker as his mana waned away. When Steve had siphoned a bit over half of Ash's mana, he concluded that, though there wasn't a lot of mana within Ash, the quality was high. The mana's purity and the fact that it was spread through his body on a regular basis, must have made it easy for Ash to access and utilize it.

Is this why Ash is considered so talented in Niti? Steve wondered as he continued to drain the rest of Ash's mana. Ash fell heavily to his knees with a thud. He was sweating and looked a sickly pale. Ash thrust his arms out to prevent himself from completely falling over, as his breathing became heavy and erratic.

"Easy, Steve," Bonnie warned. "You need to make sure he still has some left when you break through and open his veins, otherwise the amount of energy he will need to take in will be more than he can absorb."

Steve noticed there was only a sliver of pure mana left in Ash's core; the rest which had been spread throughout his body was gone, almost as if it had never been there. Steve immediately stopped his absorption. Just out of a morbid curiosity, he glanced at his energy numbers. It read:

Current Energy – 5,600

Max Energy – 10,326

He had gained nearly three hundred energy from the slow

absorption of Ash's pure mana. Steve then focused on his own light energy storage and tried to inject it into Ash, a simple inversion of what he had been doing so far. It didn't work.

The light that he was trying to inject was blocked by Ash's firm mana veins. The boy's body seemed to reject Steve's pure light energy, completely stalling Steve's attempt to fuse energies. He tried for another few seconds, before he became genuinely worried about what was happening.

"Push harder, Steve!" Bonnie was right there with him and offered advice without being asked. "You have to force your way in, through his mana veins to unlock his true potential."

Steve focused all his attention onto Ash. The young man was now on his knees, folded over and cradling his stomach. Steve lowered himself so that he was nearly in contact with Ash once more and reinitiated the link. He increased the amount of energy he was transferring to Ash and forced it into his body with a new intensity. Steve was forcing so much energy into the air that it surrounded Ash and slowly began to seep in through his pores. It wasn't a direct link, with this intermediary step.

This was starting to work, but he needed more of the energy to make it into Ash's core—he had to make sure there was no other path it could take, besides into Ash. Steve expelled an even larger mass of energy, slowly forming a glowing circle of light around Ash. He then compacted it into a shell which enclosed the hunched-over mage, entirely. Then Steve condensed the energy within the shell and pressed it inward.

Ash screamed and slumped entirely to the floor; his limbs thrashed erratically but he didn't try to get away nor seem to resist. On the contrary, Steve felt him go rigid as he forced himself to remain still, as if preparing to receive the energy.

Steve pressed on; he added even more energy, then compacted it once more. After repeating this process many times, the energy around Ash was so pure, it glowed with a brilliant yellow light. Then the light enveloping Ash's midsection turned completely white. He braced himself, then pushed one final time. Steve felt Ash's mana veins shift and open, allowing his energy to stream in, through his pores and into a second magic core.

Steve checked on Ash; he was surprised to find he had passed out and was lying in the fetal position on the podium. The mana veins were now fusing together with Steve's own pure light energy. Steve made sure the last of the energy reached Ash's core, then finally stopped.

A stunned silence reigned in the village center.

Steve checked his energy reserves.

Current Energy – 4,600

Max Energy – 12,324

Congratulations, Bonnie cheered. *You have unlocked an evolution!*

1) Changeling – Cost: 250,000 Energy. End evolution is Undetermined. Evolution starts out based on Energy, attitude, and Elemental aptitudes.

2) Deity – Cost: 120,000 Energy. End evolution is Undetermined. Evolution starts out extremely high-powered. Will be hunted by all Celestial beings.

3) Vampire – Cost: 8,000 Energy. End evolutions are the Legendary Vampire or Undetermined. Evolution starts out extremely low-powered. Will receive help from the current Vampire clan.

4) Dragon – Cost: 50,000 Energy. End evolution is the Dragon God. Evolution starts out medium-powered but gaining energy and consolidating it is difficult. Will receive help from the current Dragon race.

5) ??? – ???

6) Turtle – Cost: 75,000 Energy. End evolutions are the World Turtle or Undetermined. Evolution starts out low-powered. Gaining power is easy, just eat! Monster-class being, however, other beings will help you.

7) Slime – Cost: 20,000 Energy. End evolution is Undetermined.

Evolution starts out medium-powered. Gaining power is easy, just absorb! Monster-class being, other beings will want to hunt you.

***

Mottle mumbled about as he walked, his eyes downcast. He knew his father didn't care about him, or what he did. His father made it clear to him that he was useless, even if he didn't outright say it to his face.

Honestly, Mottle found that this treatment was even worse. The constant subtext of 'You're worthless' was there whenever his father praised his brother. Being the second child was the worst.

I wish I had another father, Mottle thought, then frowned. *That didn't come out right...* Mottle immediately recanted his thought. *Different father I mean, the one I already have is bad enough, I don't need two.*

When Mottle finally broke away from his thoughts, he found that his aimless, sullen wandering had left him in an entirely unfamiliar place. They had arrived near Niti last night and were camped out in the forest as they were exhausted by the long march.

It was now early morning and most of the village troops were still sleeping. They had brought a thousand warriors. Coupled with their mages and hired rogues, they were a formidable force. At least, at the village level. Mottle knew that these forces couldn't be compared to the town level at all.

Mottle looked around at the plants, trees, and rocks that he didn't recognize. He was definitely lost. *Well, fuck,* he thought dejectedly. *Oh well, it's not like Father would miss me, anyway.*

Mottle walked in circles for a while, trying to find the way back, but he hadn't paid any attention to how he got here. After half an hour, he was still completely lost. He walked a bit more, until he arrived at the top of a small cliff. By now, he was tired. He had never been the outside type of child growing up. While all the other village children had played in the sun and would come home bruised, he stayed at home and read books. They grew strong and tanned, out in the world, while he gained abstract knowledge of it from his books. Because of this tendency, nobody had wanted to play with him, even though he was the son of the village Elder.

Some were forced to by their parents, because of his status, but Mottle picked up on this early on. It was depressing to know that the only reason people talked to him, was because of someone else, not himself. Books soon became the only good thing in his life, but all that reading had never gotten him anywhere. The knowledge that he gained was never put to use, since he didn't have connections.

Mottle had learned over the last few years that in order to succeed in this world, one must have connections, but it was too late for him to form them with the people of his village. He had made himself a pariah by never getting to know anyone very well. To make it worse, he was now known as a 'useless' second son of the formidable village Elder. Now that his father had become a Lord, the feeling had grown even worse. He was a young adult now, with nothing to do or live for.

Mottle considered the cliff. Maybe he should just accept that life wasn't worth the trouble. He sighed, something he'd been doing a lot recently.

Better at least be sure it's high enough first. It'd be painful and embarrassing to screw up even this. Mottle cringed at the thought as he walked over to the small cliff.

Those are... His eyes widened at the sight of hundreds of swarming insects. *Why is there an army of ants so close to Niti?*

***

The whole crowd remained frozen and silent for an entire minute at such a display, then at a signal from the Elder, they began to disperse. They had to prepare for the upcoming fight.

Leffer and his Left and Right all bid Steve farewell and headed off to direct the preparations. Ash wasn't going to wake up for a few hours, anyways. His body was undergoing a change now, and he would need time to understand what gift had manifested from the power that god Steve had given him.

Steve wasn't sure what to do after this. Changeling was his number one option right now, but it was astronomically expensive. He would have to hope that the cost came down with further practice, or it was going to be impossible. Though the currently high cost might be for the best. He couldn't evolve until the five-day countdown was over without breaking another rule, and he wasn't willing to do that, even though not all the consequences had been bad. At least this way, he wouldn't be too tempted to evolve early.

"Changeling depends on your Energy mostly, then aptitude." Bonnie was volunteering information, once again. "They are a unique race that is extremely rare. This option is powerful, but, like it says on the list, it depends on your own power. You'll get more information about the races later. This is the trade-off you made when you broke the rule."

Steve understood this. He was going to have to wait. The countdown timer read:

2 Days 17 Hours 40 Minutes 35 Seconds

The ceremony had taken a good amount of time. This meant that the next memory would come in 40 minutes.

Azra had come up to him while he was checking in with Bonnie.

"What will you do today, god Steve?" Azra asked hurriedly. It was obvious enough to Steve that she was trying to get her mind off the upcoming battle with the Mottor.

Steve took a moment to consider the question. Originally, he planned to go to the Lake and train his energy. However, he wasn't sure what kind of aptitude or energy level was best for his evolution. It seemed like the Lake was a huge source of available Water elemental energy, due to the large Crystal inside of it. At least several times as much as all the crystals he owned combined. Even though he'd been nowhere near it, the sense of energy he'd gotten from it was immense.

"I'll continue training in magic," Steve decided. For the upcoming fight, he would need to be able to simultaneously cast his Gravity and Area Drain spells. He was confident that this tactic would destroy any non-mage enemy in this world, as he found this world's technology was lacking in comparison to his old world. At least from what he'd seen in Niti—it could be better in the capital.

It looked like everyone here relied on magic too much, making them unable to advance technologically. Maybe after his evolution, he would be able to do something about the sad state of this world's technology; he did remember a few tricks from his academy memories. There was nothing he could do about it at the moment though, as all the technology he remembered required hands, so he didn't think about it too much.

Azra had gone off to do something else, so Steve headed back to his guest house alone. When he reached it, he began practicing again.

Steve had almost reached the point where he could hold both the Gravity and Area Drain spells indefinitely. He wasn't quite there yet. It had been a large mental strain when he had started using both the spells at the same time earlier; even now it became too difficult after about thirty seconds.

When his Gravity spell became easier to cast earlier in the day, he'd felt a breakthrough in his mind, and whatever that change was, it had been reflected on the evolution list. Steve was determined to make a similar breakthrough happen again, to help Niti Village combat this threat. The fact that the battle may gain him a lot of energy…that was just a bonus.

I wonder how the others are doing. Steve found his mind wandering once more. He was still training, trying to improve his chances of achieving a decent evolution within the next few dozen hours. *Bonnie told me I wasn't the only one.*

From what she'd said, about him being the first one to break a rule, he could infer that there had to be more entities just like him.

Practicing magic took focus, but not so much that Steve couldn't think about other things at the same time. Thus, he found himself going through his very limited memories and speculating about what the greater implications of every detail might be. It wasn't very mentally stimulating, being limited to this small village and its outskirts. He occasionally saw Niti villagers busily preparing for the upcoming battle, but generally, there was not much to keep him from becoming wrapped up in his own thoughts.

After a while, the countdown hit:

2 Days 17 Hours 0 Minutes 0 Seconds

Chapter 16

Steve opened his eyes, but there was nothing to see. He blinked a few times, but his eyes couldn't adjust; there was no light whatsoever. This was different from the previous flashback with his father; it wasn't that there was something in front of his eyes, there was just pure darkness.

Steve felt a gnawing sensation begin to build at the back of his mind. Then, it crashed into him—a massive wave of fear, nausea, and anxiety. He despaired.

He tried to move, to get away from this sensation but found that he couldn't. Something kept him immobilized; he couldn't move a muscle. It seemed that whatever was restraining his movement was also blocking his memory from coming back.

Since deep down he knew that this wasn't real and thus couldn't hurt him, he felt a little bit better and began to adjust after a while. Steve was glad this wasn't the first thing he'd experienced; he knew that if he didn't have his other memories of the new world, and understanding of what he was experiencing now, he'd be completely panicked.

The feeling didn't get any better after that though. The irrational fear that he would be trapped here forever, made him weak and desperate.

The dark and inability to move was awful; it was almost like being buried alive, except he could still breathe. Steve didn't know what to do, so he just waited for it to be over.

***

Steve did nothing after coming to. He tried to process what had just happened for long minutes.

He didn't know what that was or where the experience came from, and he just couldn't move without trying to figure it out. It had been a terrifying flashback—that was, if it really was a memory from his past life. Whatever it had been, it rattled him to the core.

It had seemed as real as his other flashbacks; he was in a human's body. Most humans relied on sight; it would be fair to say it was their main sense. Being trapped in absolute darkness as a human had been traumatic enough, but Steve wasn't used to being human. The flashbacks and memories gave him insight to what a human's vision was like, but it wasn't a lifetime's experience—it wasn't even a fraction of the few days that he had already spent as a ball of light. Steve felt out of place whenever he was forced into these flashbacks. Having an omnidirectional view of his surroundings, as he did now, was a far greater ability. So being robbed of vision was even more terrifying.

Okay, then, Steve thought. He was recovering, albeit slowly. *I think I'm alright.*

There was no way he could focus on training his spells now. It was time to take a quick walk, or rather, a quick float.

Steve decided to go find Azra. Quite honestly, he didn't know the way to the Lake by himself yet. He'd been there a few times now but had always been focused on practicing magic, as he was driven there by someone else. Ash was likely still out of commission, for who knew how long. Steve had been a little concerned but the villagers had acted like it was normal. So, Steve wasn't too worried about the young man.

He floated back through the village; there were a few of the villagers still milling around in the center. The majority were busy preparing for the upcoming battle with the Mottor. The two Workforces Steve had created were being used to carry supplies around and for other general preparation. Steve had temporarily put them back under the Elder's command so they could participate in the battle as well.

All the prisoners in the village were going to be given a chance to prove their worth to the village. This meant that if they did well, they would be pardoned for their crimes. Facing such a massive threat, the Elder had decided to use all available resources. After all, they would be fighting the forces of two villages.

In the past, the Niti clan had always been superior to the Mottor clan. Ever since the two villages were founded by the Empire, they had always been in competition, under the command of two high-ranking military leaders.

Niti Village and Mottor Village were initially created as rewards for service to the Empire way back then. The founders had been friends and the villages had enjoyed good relations initially. However, after so long, friendship turned into a rivalry, and now the rivalry had escalated into a war.

It's funny how history works, sometimes, Steve thought. Ash had described it as a long-lasting and totally meaningless feud, as nobody even remembered how it had started now.

There were two oddly dressed men watching over Ash, who still lay on the platform. Steve approached them for directions to Azra's place. They pointed then bowed to him as Steve went on his way.

As he neared the residence, he picked up on sounds coming from inside. It sounded like shouting. A few seconds later, he could discern what was being said.

"No! I will participate," Azra was yelling. "This fight includes all of Niti, which means me too!"

"You will not. We don't need you and you'll be a hindrance," Amon said flatly. "Just watch over your brother, he's still consolidating his future power."

"But I want to be near the frontline, casting or doing something useful," Azra replied petulantly. Amon seemed to think she was weak. Hearing them argue now, Steve wondered if it had always been this way. "I'm practically a three-star mage, only short a couple of spells. Ash isn't that much better. I bet if he was conscious right now, you'd let him go fight!"

"I wouldn't—" Amon started, but cut off as Steve floated in. It wasn't good to bicker and waste time in front of a god. "We'll continue this later."

"I hope I'm not interrupting anything. Azra, come with me." Steve didn't have time for whatever this was; he had something on his mind. Steve wanted to go to the Lake. Merely absorbing energy didn't take that much thought.

***

They walked along the path they had taken before. Steve recognized a few landmarks as they went, but it was still hazy. If he'd been forced to go by himself, there would be no chance of getting there before tomorrow morning. His memories now, just like when he was human, weren't perfect. In fact, he thought it was like his mind was still in human mode, just stuffed into another body. A light body. Memories were truly a tricky thing.

"My father thinks I'm useless just because I'm a girl," Azra started. She spoke freely, now used to Steve's presence. They had been walking in silence for a while and she just couldn't stand it any longer. "Like, I'm already almost a three-star mage. That's so much better than what he was when he was just fourteen. Just because girls don't have Naming ceremonies, that doesn't mean they can't be mages. I even hear stories from the local merchants about girls in the Capital doing something different for their powers.

"...you know? Like, it's hard to get my father to be serious about me doing magic. Apparently, it takes a lot of money to make a girl into a mage, rather than a boy. There's something specific about the ceremonies for girls that just...requires a lot of money. Or something, I don't know. Vim told me that. He's the village merchant, so he travels a lot and stuff. He's a cool guy. He wanted to bribe you, you know? Vim was talking about how the Elder should just, make a deal with you. I don't know…"

Steve listened in silence. He really couldn't relate; his own father had been kind to him, at least in the memory he'd relived of him. There was no way he could understand another person's experiences except by listening.

"There's no way I won't be able to contribute to this battle," Azra told him. She then looked below Steve. "You believe me, right?"

Something had changed over these past two days. She was no longer frightened of what he could do or what he was. Children adapt easily, after all. Steve sensed that Azra now considered him to be her ally, in a way. He brought her on adventures and showed her marvelous sights. That, for the young country girl, had apparently been enough.

"Yes," Steve said. He just told the truth. It was also the first time he spoke in ten minutes. Apparently, by village standards, a three-star mage was considered more than decent. This was because out of the thousands of people in a village, only a few hundred were considered to have any magical talent.

Being able to do magic and being talented at magic was not the same thing. Almost anyone could do an extremely basic spell. But few could do it quickly and efficiently at a young age; that was the difference. There were only a handful of children in Niti that had aptitude like Azra and Ash.

"But, instead of being on the frontlines, I want you to assist me," Steve said. He wanted to use her abilities for the upcoming battle.

Azra nodded enthusiastically. This was what she wanted. Would there be a better view of the battle from Steve's side? This was exciting! And besides, even her father wouldn't dare contradict Steve now that he had asked for her assistance. She understood the reason that the villagers didn't speak to Steve. Most of them, having never met a god before, stuck to tradition. Most of them, not including Leeroy, Jenkins, or their crew wouldn't risk giving even the slightest offense. They'd chosen to ignore the law; they'd incurred his wrath and were now paying the price for it.

One doesn't speak to a god unless it speaks to you. One doesn't deal with a god unless it deals with you. And so on. These age-old rules were established alongside the Empire, when it first came into being. Along with the charter for every village, town, and city came instructions for dealing with other beings. If a god or similar being came to a village, they were to be treated with the highest respect. Any village found to be in violation of these orders would be immediately cut off from the Empire's support.

The two continued their journey in silence. After about an hour, they had almost arrived, when they saw a curious sight. Azra was stunned, while Steve was curious.

It looked like the centipede he had absorbed when he first came into the world. It was a brown-colored bug, about a foot long. Only here, it had a couple of its brothers in tow. A lot of brothers, and sisters, it seemed. Steve wasn't sure how these things reproduced. Did female centipedes even exist? Why was he even thinking about that in the first place?

"We have to warn the village!" Azra suddenly understood the situation clearly. "The centipede army...This close to the lake. We can't venture out of the village's inner walls!"

A chill ran through her as her skin prickled with goosebumps. If these centipedes were here for what she imagined, Niti was in a precarious spot.

"We weren't heroes..." Azra turned to Steve with tears in her eyes. "We have to go back, now!"

***

A thousand people, all carrying weapons of war, were split up into fifty-man squads, each with a capable mage leading them. The squads were preparing to attack, just waiting for the signal from their Lord.

The Lord, on the other hand, had been waiting a good fifteen minutes for his rogue magician group. They were supposed to take the remnant of their original squad, along with some more of his men and sneak around the village to flank Niti.

The group had long since sat down in wait. They had brought half the force over, a total of ten squads, to escort the Lord over to the meeting point. The other half were camped nearby, overseen by the mages of the Mottor force.

Tenk and Fom never showed up. This told the Lord that they were compromised. That was disappointing, but not a real problem for him.

Lord Mottor was just about to give the signal to move on, when he suddenly sensed the presence of magic. It felt odd and was powerful enough that he wondered why he hadn't sensed it before, when something came hurtling out of the brushes, swift as an arrow. He instantly popped one of the seals on his arm and Blinked to safety.

"Enemy ambush!" There were shouts all around. The one that had come at him wasn't the only one. Apparently, they had been targeting all the mages.

There was no time to think. "Retreat back to the camp, men!" Lord Mottor shouted. They were falling all around. As he watched, five more humongous logs were magically flung through the air, though they couldn't see any attackers. The Nitians were literally crushing his men with brute force.

Originally, they had been seated close together, to avoid being too visible. As the first logs came through, the men had tried to quickly evade. Some tripped over each other, knocking still others to the ground in the path of the logs. Then they were flattened, like human pastry dough before a multi-ton rolling pin.

The sound was the worst part. Bones snapped and ligaments popped loudly under the massive force of the logs. In seconds, they had already lost twenty percent of the force and the rest of the men broke and ran in every direction. It was impossible to issue further orders over the sound of hundreds of men shouting or screaming in agony. There was mass panic in the forests of Niti. Nobody had ever trained for this kind of scenario.

By now, Lord Mottor had used two Seals. The Blink when he was surprise attacked, and a defensive one when he couldn't dodge another log.

"They're using formations to mask their mana trail; I can't track it!" one mage screamed out, amplifying his voice to be heard over the chaos. He was one of the few that wasn't completely useless. A three-star earth mage, from the look of his robes.

Lord Mottor was a five-star mage himself or at least he had the robes for it, albeit a little bit out of date. The true advantage he had over the other mages here were his Seals. Seals were extremely rare, and very expensive. For those reasons they were typically only used by the rich. Having a Seal in your body meant that you could cast a high-tier spell instantly, making them incredibly useful in high-pressure situations. Though the cost of having such a Seal applied was tremendous. Lord Mottor, being a Lord of two villages, only had three such Seals. They were well worth the cost, having saved his life twice in such a short time.

Unfortunately, they couldn't be used reused. Seals broke and disappeared after being triggered

The mages that he had hired did not have any Seals on them. It was possible that one or two of them had Lesser Seals, but that was about it. Any Seal would cost a ridiculous amount, as only seven-star mages or the equivalent could bestow them, or even understand how to bestow them. Finding these mages was difficult and getting them to give you a Seal was even more so.

They were all out of the rendezvous area now. They had been surrounded by trees in there, making it hard to figure out where their attackers were. Most of the casualties were normal troops, but a good number of the mages had fallen as well.

Lord Mottor glanced around at his losses furiously. The losses of these rogue magicians meant that the organization he had hired them from would never do business with him again. Especially for this kind of reason.

The remaining men who had scattered in all directions were only now coming back to him. As he took a rough headcount, it seemed he had lost eight rogue magicians, one of his own mages, and about two hundred men. His face darkened, and his eyes gleamed with malice as he contacted Remley's trio.

"We begin the attack, now!"

***

Amon clenched his fist in victory. They had taken out ten mages and forced Molke to use two of his Seals, just to escape with his life. Molke was Lord Mottor's name before he had taken the position of Lord. Nobody with any respect for the Lord would ever call him Molke. After losing so many mages and two hundred soldiers, the enemy would be more cautious in dealing with them now, but that was fine. They had struck a devastating opening blow and scored a clean victory for themselves.

They had a god on their side if worst came to worst. Amon was skeptical of asking for a god's assistance, but at this rate, they wouldn't need help at all.

"Great job, everyone! We completely pushed that cowardly Molke back," Amon triumphantly cheered. He had ten mages on his side of the ambush location; on the other side was Joffrey, with another ten mages. They had worked around the clock to set the formation circles which would mask their magical presence, in preparation for this. Even Fom had helped. The man was probably still angry that Molke had thrown him to the enemy as bait and was firmly on their side now.

"Clear out, prepare for the next ambush," Amon commanded. The mages followed Amon back to the village. They weren't that far off—after a good ten minutes walking, they would be there.

Niti only had four mage squads, meaning they had used almost half their force for this ambush. It had been worth it though. Amon had to admit they'd done an excellent job, even better than he'd dared hope.

As they approached Niti, they heard screams and shouts from the village. As soon as Amon realized what he was hearing, he set off in a sprint, casting a wind spell to increase his speed as he ran.

As he neared the inner walls of the village, he could hear deep, rumbling growls coming from the village center. *Dire wolves*, Amon thought, as he pushed himself to run as fast as humanly possible.

If anything happened to his family, he would tear the Mottor clan apart.

***

Azra and Steve moved as quickly as possible back to the village. Steve expended energy to push his light body forward faster, to keep up with Azra and her wind magic assistance. He didn't care if it was wasteful, it was necessary.

Azra had explained as they ran from the encroaching army, "The centipede army is usually inactive, they've never approached the village before. But the fish used to have control of the lake, now that they're gone, everything around us for miles around will come for the lake! The mana's leaking out freely." She was crying at that point, though just a few tears, so far.

"If the mana leakage isn't solved soon, we'll be overrun by monsters!" Azra sobbed. To her, there was no solution to this problem. "I…We…doomed Niti!"

Apparently, Steve had been too rash in his decision to clear the lake. At least she didn't seem to blame him for it. Even though he had been the one to do most of it, in the end, the three that were with him had all agreed.

"Don't worry, we'll find a way to get that Crystal!" Steve reassured her, on the assumption that the Crystal was the problem. He had seen the Crystal on the lakebed when he had been levitating the water. The main issue was, he wasn't sure he had the ability to absorb it all. He also didn't even know if he could go that deep down into the Lake. How would his body react to the water pressure?

It seemed likely that he would need to greatly expand his maximum energy in order to do it. His current max was only about twenty thousand. The Crystal down there seemed like it would contain a lot more than that.

"We might only be able to hold out a few days under such an onslaught." They were moving at this point. Azra was still a bit red-eyed, but she didn't want to embarrass herself in front of the god. She had stopped panicking. "Can you get it in that time?"

"Of course, I can," Steve reassured her once more. He had no idea whether he could or not but telling the truth in this moment wasn't going to help.

***

The dire wolves they had left near Niti had still been waiting for them when they came back. Remley and his two brothers had worked together for weeks to control them and even then, they could only influence the pack leader. They convinced it to wait for them near Niti, not moving unless they had to hunt.

At the command from their Lord, they began leading them towards the outskirts of Niti. All they had to do was tell the dire wolf pack that there was fresh food in the village. Extremely fresh food.

The weeks the trio had spent here, living out in the forests, were finally about to bear fruit. The hard work they had put in living off the land and learning about the surroundings, foraging to supplement their rations, was about to pay off. They knew the perfect route to sneak the dire wolves in.

They were all two-star mages. Low-class for sure, in the world of mages. But there was one thing they were exceptionally good at: teamwork.

"I'll do it," Ronnie said. They were with the dire wolves. The group had come with them into the tall grass that surrounded the village's front entrance. With the dire wolves hunched low, they wouldn't be seen. Ronnie, who was usually sarcastic, was completely serious now.

"Come." He was coaxing the dire wolves along. It would only take a few minutes for them to get into position. Then, they would sneak as far into the village as they could and set the dire wolves loose. It would be the perfect distraction for Lord Mottor's men to overrun the village from the opposite side. This would be it; Niti Village and all their resources would be theirs.

They crept along a bit longer; the dire wolves had already reached the village entrance. Reagan was preparing a spell under his breath, his hands glowing. Remley was holding up the rear.

Then, a young man who appeared to be headed elsewhere blundered into them. He appeared to be around age 16 or so, and though spooked, he didn't hesitate.

"Enemies at the gate!" he called out loudly, as he ran back the way he'd come, alerting all his nearby clansmen. The trio were taken by surprise by the suddenness of it all and failed to react in time.

"Guess we've been found out," Remley called from the back. "Let's get this thing started."

Chapter 17

"Help! Send help!" Loop ran madly back to the inner village walls. The 'outer wall' was more of a flimsy fence. But the innermost part of the village was the stronghold where they could hold out in the event of an attack or siege. All the villagers were gathered there now since the battle had begun.

"What is it, son?" Leeroy asked.

"Enemies by the entrance!" Loop gasped. "Three mages with dire wolves!"

Ordinarily, this wouldn't be enough to be a serious threat. But the problem now was that their Left and Right were out of the village, along with half the mages, conducting an ambush. Even god Steve was gone. This left them in a bit of a pinch, with more than half of their elite forces gone.

"Pass on the message!" Leeroy roared. "Let the Elder know!"

The designated messenger immediately set off at a run towards the village center where the Elder would be.

***

Leffer had been feeling optimistic, maybe even in a good mood, considering the circumstances, until the shout interrupted his meeting. He had been planning their next move with the advisors that hadn't gone out with the Left and Right. Amon had told him via communication crystal that the ambush was successful. Now, just five minutes later, he heard someone shout something about a surprise attack.

The messenger stumbled in, getting tangled in the curtain over the doorway and shouted again, "Enemy attack! Three mages and dire wolves!" It was clear he had run all the way; he was breathing heavily from the sprint. "They're already…Inside the walls."

"Gods damn it! The dire wolf pack." Leffer was furious, though mostly at himself. He should have seen the correlation. Now it was too late to prepare for dire wolves. "The Mottor…never mind, assemble the troops! We need to repel this threat at our inner walls."

Leffer was in full control of the situation. He stormed out to the village center and saw the sea of people—mostly women and younger children—waiting for him. They had gathered here within the last hour, to stay safe during the attack. The troops were already prepared, but they weren't gathered in one place yet.

His commanders, Amon and Joffrey, were gone. It would be up to him to salvage the situation. Sounds of fighting had already broken out near the entrance to the inner village.

Leffer cast a Flight spell. It took a minute, but this would allow him to fly to the action immediately. In the whole village, only he and Joffrey knew how to cast this spell. The previous Left had also known how, but he had died some thirty years back.

Leffer swallowed. Casting this spell always brought up old memories. The three of them had learned it together, while they were young and journeying in the Capital. Now, after all those years, he and Joffrey were the only ones left from the initial group. Before he left, he gave out a few commands.

Leffer lifted into the air and quickly traveled toward the sound of the battle and assessed the situation. There were fifty dire wolves and three mages were directing them from the back. The few hundred villagers Leffer had positioned near that side of the wall were currently managing to hold them back. The villagers fought the wolves three to one, since they outnumbered them by a large amount. But, with every cast of those mages, the defenders were falling.

The other villagers were pulling the wounded back out of the fray as well as they could, but the losses were mounting nonetheless.

In just the few seconds he'd been observing, Leffer understood where he was needed. He was about a hundred feet up in the air; nobody had noticed him yet, they were all too focused on the fight. So he began preparing his spells.

Mages typically took a lot of time to cast spells. That was why they weren't great in one-on-one combat. Fighting in an enclosed space, mages were at an extreme disadvantage. Especially if the mage couldn't start their cast before the opponent knew they were there.

Knowing that, Leffer was in a perfect position to end the fight. He didn't have to eradicate all the wolves or mages—not at all. All he needed to do was disrupt the battle and destroy the enemy morale. He began to cast his most powerful spell.

***

"What the fuck?" Ronnie suddenly said.

At his prompting, the other two noticed it as well. The three of them slowly turned their attention upward. There a man, floating in the sky. Next to him was a towering tornado. It looked to be about thirty feet tall and growing rapidly.

It was already too late to run away. The tornado would obviously be targeted straight at them, because they were the ones directing the dire wolves.

"Combine, now!" Remley ordered. Nobody questioned it; the three of them knew what to do. They had practiced this spell together many times before.

The three of them huddled up and put their arms in. Remley started the chant. Ronnie joined in soon afterward, with Reagan following their motions. A wind vortex began swirling in Remley's portion of the circle, then expanded to form a circle within the space defined by their arms. Ronnie added fire to create a smaller circle within the first. Reagan then summoned earth to fill the core of the circle, completing it.

The three of them kept on adding their elements into their self-made spell. They compressed the Fusion spell when it threatened to grow too large for their arms. It took a lot more mana to compress the spell and they felt it. The brothers were close and compatible enough to share mana—by splitting the cost three ways, they were able to succeed.

The compressed Fusion spell had been charged for a full minute now. While they were doing that, the tornado above hadn't stopped growing. It was at least fifty feet tall now and gathering power by the second. The man controlling it had long since moved far away, lest he be sucked in by it.

The multi-colored Fusion spell was fired into the center of the tornado that was about to come down on the men and dire wolves, in hopes of dispersing it. By now, the Niti villagers had fallen back a bit, seeing what was about to happen. The dire wolves were confused, losing direction when the mages directing them were distracted by their spell.

When the fusion reached the center of the other spell, it imploded. With a flash of light and burst of mana, a ripple of spell residue washed over everyone in a one hundred-yard radius. The ones nearest to the center were decimated, namely the confused dire wolves. The ones farther from the center that survived, weren't in good shape either.

As for the rogue mages, they were a bit better off. The moment they had sent the spell up they had run towards the village exit. Even then, the blast caught them. Reagan went down with a stray rock to his head. Remley threw himself atop Ronnie, in an attempt to shield him. It worked, though Remley's body was ravaged by the force.

As for the villagers, some of them hadn't made it far enough away in that short amount of time and also went down.

The blast spread across the sky and the land, as if signaling the start of the real battle.

***

Lord Mottor used his communication crystal to order his Left, who had been left in charge of the other camp, to attack. The mages in control of the squads cast wind spells to make them move faster, then he led the remnant of his own force to do the same. They would attack the village from the rear while the hired rogue magician trio sieged the main entrance with the help of their dire wolves. Lord Mottor assumed that the villagers would have trouble dealing with the dire wolves, unless the Elder directly intervened and expended most of his mana to stop them.

The two groups met up and assembled into a single force, near the rear entrance. They then stormed into the village, buff spells at the ready in the minds and hands of the mages. At a moment's notice, each mage could enhance their entire group of fifty.

They proceeded cautiously, looking around and sending out a recon squad. There was apparently nobody here in the outer village area.

They must all be inside the inner walls, thought Lord Mottor. His mind was racing, analyzing every piece of information he had. He then gave the command to rush ahead, deciding that they would have to reach the inner walls while the dire wolves were still fighting. *The Elder must have withdrawn their rear troops to focus on the front, against the wolves.*

It was then that all the mages sensed the mana pulse from near the front entrance of the inner walls.

"Go, now!" Lord Mottor roared the command as they neared the inner walls. He didn't care whether the trio of rogues survived or not, but he wouldn't waste this opportunity. Judging by the size of that mana burst, whatever it was had just put an end to the distraction of the dire wolves.

The villagers had barricaded the rear entrance, but they easily broke down the structure and burst in. The opening was just wide enough for the ten-man vanguard of the squad to pass through, shoulder-to-shoulder, with the rest following close behind and the mage providing support from the rear.

They were instantly set upon as they cleared the breach, by Nitian men who had been hiding behind the walls. Having had plenty of time to prepare, they'd made sure they had the terrain and cover advantage when attacking.

The vanguard was almost instantly locked down by the attacks of the Nitian militia. Though, as soon as that happened, the buff spells the rogue mages were holding were unleashed. A few great gusts of wind helped his squads press forward. The wind spells buffeted the defenders, making it harder for them to move, let alone fight.

After the first three squads, Lord Mottor came through on

horseback. He took in the situation instantly. There were rather few Nitian village fighters, desperately trying to hold the breach without sufficient support. He didn't see Joffrey or Amon, the Right and Left of the village, though there were a few other magicians. At a single glance, he estimated ten mages and a hundred odd warriors at most.

This meant that the diversion had worked as planned. The Nitians were unprepared for a simultaneous assault from the rear. The battle was going well; the mages ran away when it became clear that the fight here was hopeless. The Niti clansmen tried to hold but without proper command and organization, they had no chance. Lord Mottor's forces quickly disposed of the hundred odd men. When it was done, he observed the blood-splattered ground around himself, it was a mix of Nitian and Mottor blood, with the greater portion of it being Nitian.

At the end of the brief skirmish, some of the remaining defenders had run away. *Probably retreating to regroup with the main force,* thought Lord Mottor.

When the last squad was within the inner walls, Lord Mottor thundered, "After them!" then led the charge himself. Lord Mottor currently had a total of sixteen squads, though most were somewhat short of the fifty men they should have by now. He led them through the inner village as the few people they encountered fled, heading toward the village center, conveniently leading the way for the Mottor clan.

Lord Mottor's Left was riding beside him now, on his black horse, but he had left his Right at home to watch over things while he was gone. They didn't need him—not with the magical and manpower advantages he knew they had. Lord Mottor turned to his Left for analysis of the situation.

"We can assume that either Joffrey, Amon, or Leffer have expended their entire mana pools. They are the top powers in Niti Village," Lord Mottor stated. His Left was both a good mage and warrior, something quite rare in humans. He had done extensive research on the Nitian forces for Lord Mottor before the battle. "We'll hold the advantage from now on, assuming nothing unexpected happens."

When the Left nodded his agreement, Lord Mottor turned to his men.

"We take Niti tonight!" Lord Mottor roused his men into a battle frenzy. "Kill the warriors, take the women and children! Kill all who resist. Tonight, Mottor Village prevails again!"

After he took those Crystals, he would have enough wealth and power to completely dominate his two villages as well as upgrade them to Town status. It would cost half the Crystals, but it would be worth it. Officially becoming a Town paved the way for more development and power for the Mottor clan later on.

Everything hinged on being able to subdue all of the Nitians. If he couldn't win this battle, it would be the end for him. They would surely report this incident to the Empire and they wouldn't let him go with a warning; he would be publicly hanged. Even if he summoned his Right and another attack force, too much time would have passed. If Leffer and the other village mages had enough time, they would be able to teleport to the Capital and request assistance. He needed to take Niti Village tonight and it was already late afternoon, headed towards evening.

It was all or nothing now: either he would bring the Mottor clan glory, or he would be the one to preside over its destruction. His clansmen knew the risks as well and trusted in his ability, since he had done this once before.

It was time to make his ancestors proud.

***

One second earlier, and... Leffer hesitated to contemplate how near death he'd just been. The mana blast from the implosion moments earlier had reached him and disrupted his flight, making him crash-land in a bush. He was wounded, though mostly from the fall. He was grateful and a little surprised he wasn't dead. *I wonder if*

Amon or Joffrey are back.

He wouldn't be able to do battle in his current state; he had used up most of his mana pool and would need to spend at least a couple of minutes meditating to recover enough to cast anything. He quickly assessed his injuries—only cuts and bruises, nothing too severe. He would be fine.

Leffer sat down and meditated. After a few minutes, he had recovered enough to have his mana regenerate while he was on the move. It was stable, no longer in the chaotic post-casting state that it had been in. That spell always took a lot out of him.

Leffer moved quickly towards the village center, in spite of the pain it caused him. Not moving wasn't an option. He just hoped that his forces were somehow holding off the Mottor.

The dire wolves were meant as a diversion for sure, Leffer decided. *Considering that they attacked immediately after our ambush, and it wasn't timed perfectly to coincide with another attack, Molke probably lost his temper and set it off prematurely...that guy was always a hothead.*

They knew each other from the bi-annual meeting of the villages that usually took place in the Capital. Attendance of these events was mandatory; if a village did not send a high-ranking village representative even once, that village would be cut off. There was some flexibility to the rules of course, as travel was often dangerous, so being late was acceptable. As a result, most village representatives arrived as late as possible—none wanted to be the first ones there.

By village tradition, the first ones there would have to reveal what was happening in their village under truth magic. No village really trusted any other, since power struggles were frequent. There were at least several power-hungry clans like the Mottor who sought to control two or more villages. The Mottor were currently in control of both Mottor Village and Ekem Village. Leffer wasn't sure what had happened to Ekem Village exactly, as the Mottor takeover had occurred since the last Village Conference. The next one would be soon, as it had been almost two years now.

Assuming they survived this assault from the Mottor, Leffer would need to start planning for the next one soon. In the best-case scenario, they would win this battle and only have to attend one more Village Conference, as they would then become a Town.

As Leffer reached the village center, he could hear the sounds of battle.

We had around a hundred warriors stationed at the back entrance. I hope they're alright, Leffer thought. He was saddened that there was little chance of that. Every loss weighed heavily on him as he knew most of the villagers personally and every loss was catastrophic to their families, who were huddled in the shelters near the village center. If they failed to hold this last line, everyone would be at the mercy of the Mottor. Leffer would never let that come to pass, at least not while he was still alive.

As he drew closer, the sounds of the battle, shouts, and agonized cries became clearer. He immediately spotted Joffrey in the air, rapidly firing icicles he had probably readied beforehand. It was a dangerous tactic, but Joffrey was probably forced to try picking off the enemy mages. Suddenly, a lightning bolt shot out from the crowd of enemies and struck Joffrey. Leffer watched helplessly as his oldest friend fell out of the sky, smoking.

Leffer looked over at the area where the lightning had come from, where he assumed the higher-ranked enemy mages must be. There was a sea of people fighting on the somewhat flat ground, in between the inner village buildings. It was chaotic in the tight quarters. Though the Niti clansmen did hold the advantage in this kind of battle since they knew the territory, this advantage wasn't enough to offset the sheer numbers advantage that the Mottor held.

In total, if they were counting everyone useful in battle, Niti had less than five hundred combatants. The Mottor easily had double that, if they'd brought them all; that meant that they were probably still outnumbered two-to-one, even with the success of the ambush.

We're going to lose this war to simple attrition, Leffer quickly analyzed the situation. He was a little confused about one thing, though. *Where are Amon and god Steve?*

At this point, he had reached the fringes of the fight. He was on relatively higher ground and could see most of it unfolding before him. The Nitians were now losing badly. Joffrey seemed to be out of the fight and Amon was nowhere to be found. At a glance, he guessed they were down to about three hundred fighters in total, while the Mottor on the field were still too numerous and probably still had troops in reserve, waiting their chance to join in the action.

Leffer saw the village's best baker fall to the ground, a sword planted in his chest. He writhed in agony and clutched at the blade for a moment before he went still. Leffer was glad to be at a distance as people he knew fell all around; he didn't want to see the light leave their eyes.

Just then, Amon burst from one of the village buildings, with the Squad of Scoundrels in tow. He released the large area fire spell he had prepared beforehand, bathing the center of the enemy force in flames. The battle, which had already been chaotic, became a riot of death as Mottor soldiers burned and scattered in every direction.

The Left then shouted extremely loudly, "For Niti!" Then he led the charge of all the warriors and prisoners under his command. They had set themselves up in the perfect position to flank the enemy, by going through one of the carpenter residences.

It was at this moment a familiar ball of light came into Leffer's view. From his elevated position, he was likely the only one who could see Steve on top of Joffrey's house as he floated to the edge of the roof and hovered there.

They were going to be saved by a god.

***

Steve was on top of a building and channeling his magic into the crowd. He had arrived a couple minutes earlier with Azra. Thankfully, they hadn't been noticed by the enemy forces, having come in behind them, from the Lake area. His gravity magic made symbols appear in the air as he simultaneously readied his Area Drain. It was a slow process, but with nobody attacking him, he was able to take his time.

Steve floated to the edge of the building and cast his Large Anti-Gravity spell. The large group of Mottor he had targeted was suddenly lifted into the air. It was a full squad, along with the mage commander. They shouted and struggled, but being midair, there was nothing they could do. Steve quickly followed up with Area Energy Drain. As their energy was drained away, their struggling slowed and finally stopped. The mage that was leading them tried to cast, but was too slow—between the battle and the drain, his mana was already gone.

Steve's energy bar was fluctuating wildly as the energy he was absorbing warred with the cost of maintaining two spells. He couldn't spare the focus to really monitor how it was going now; he needed to make sure no elemental spells hit him while he was channeling.

Steve had worked on his Area Energy Drain while he was practicing his spells. He noticed that after a while of practicing, the effect would be stronger. It was just like with his Shock spell. The first time he had cast it, it was weak and barely scratched a tree. Now, the shock spell could easily annihilate half a person's body, if he wanted it to. It seemed like, as with most things, practice made perfect with magic as well.

He let the squad fall back to the ground. Steve hadn't finished them off, but had come close. They weren't going to be fighting anyone, at least for a while. Energy, like mana, took quite a while for humans to replenish.

Steve repeated this process for another group of Mottor. By now, the battle had shifted to a somewhat even state. The Mottor were flanked by the Left's ambush and also had to worry about their men randomly floating up and then winding up exhausted and devoid of energy. It was a strange magic, one they had never seen before.

Steve then noticed a group of Mottor going into the building below him—he'd been spotted. Azra had blocked off the roof hatch with a slab of conjured stone, but it wasn't going to last very long. At most, it would buy them a few more seconds. Steve finished with the group of men he'd been draining and turned his focus towards the roof hatch. The sound of pounding feet and movement came from the building below them already. He started charging up his Large Anti-Gravity spell, focusing on the hatch.

Azra was hiding nearby, where she would be safe, but able to watch. Steve had told her to stay out of the fight unless he gave the command.

The stone barrier was thrust aside and a man quickly scrambled up, followed by more. Before the first two could gain their footing, Steve blasted the upper half of their bodies off with his Shock spell. They didn't even have time to cry out.

Unfortunately, there was no way Steve could completely ignore cast times, cooldowns, and his own ability. If he pushed himself too far, the energy costs would multiply out of control until he was depleted, or he would lose control of the spell. He had used up a lot of energy coming from the Lake that fast, so he couldn't afford to keep dealing with these men one at a time. If too many came up, he would be left with no choice but to leave Azra and Blink. He wasn't sure how many there were in total.

He let the third and fourth man come up and gain their footing. Then, with his cast times and cooldowns reset he fired Shocks at each of them. Only, this time they were prepared.

One of the men was a mage and had cast a barrier beforehand; it absorbed the two spells but fizzled out immediately afterward. Unfortunately, that was enough to allow more men to climb up onto the roof.

Steve activated his Large Anti-Gravity spell and all the men before him floated upwards. He fired another Shock at the mage, but he escaped somehow. The man reappeared near Steve and was already gesturing, undoubtedly casting a spell.

"Azra! At the mage, now!" Steve commanded instantly. As he said that, he shot more Shock spells at the men floating in the air. They went down screaming as lightning seared random parts of their bodies. Aiming for their heads would take more concentration than he could spare now.

Azra had prepared her spell beforehand; now the two-foot-long flame spear tore through the air, towards the man who had just Blinked. It hit him in the back and he screamed, grasping at the wound as he fell.

By now, there weren't any more men coming through the hatch. Aside from the pained moans of the men on the ground and the sounds of battle outside, it was quiet on the roof.

Steve finished off the wounded men, then turned his attention back to the battle below. As he took it all in, he noticed that the battle was quieting down. The Mottor were surrendering, but so many Nitians had died that it was something of a pyrrhic victory.

After the last of the enemy had laid down their weapons, a cheer went up from the remaining Niti clansmen. Their god had come through for them.

The aftermath of the fight might have gone smoothly, if not for a few things that happened all at once. Steve was watching the Mottor being taken into custody from the rooftop, when a young man ran out from behind a nearby building. From the direction he was coming, Steve guessed he was a lookout. As he got within earshot of the main forces, he shouted, "Ant army invading from the rear entrance! They're already inside the village!"

Everyone turned their attention towards the unexpected, loud cry. That was when one of the surrendering Mottor lashed out at his captor with a surprise attack, stabbing him through the chest with a hidden dagger.

It was unclear from this distance if the attack was fatal, but apparently some of the Mottor forces weren't interested in surrendering. Following the first man's lead, many of the Mottor erupted into renewed violence, taking the Niti off guard with their sudden rebellion.

Steve acted immediately; he Blinked rapidly from roof to roof and once in range he shot a Shock spell at the first perpetrator, killing him instantly but it was already too late. The battle was in full swing again. This time there were no clear lines, the opposing forces having mixed during the brief ceasefire and attempt to secure the prisoners. The fighting was more chaotic than ever.

Before either side sustained many casualties, thunder shook the sky. Clouds gathered overhead, concentrated above the Niti Village center. Everyone paused for a moment, expecting a devastating spell. A random soldier took this opportunity to strike his opponent down, and the fighting once more resumed. Even accounting for all their losses, the Mottor still outnumbered the Niti by a wide margin.

It was at this point that Steve noticed something in his peripheral vision. Buildings in the inner village were taller than those in the rest of the village and that meant from his vantage point he could see almost the entire village. It looked like there was a line of brown coming into the village from the back entrance. The brown creatures looked somewhat familiar. As they drew nearer, Steve saw that they were kind of like a centipede, but smaller and with far fewer legs. Still, Steve guessed they were around nine inches wide and a foot long, easily. They were marching towards the fighting at the village center, in two neat columns.

Then, a massive lightning bolt struck down from the clouds that had just darkened the sky above, striking something in the town center.

Chapter 18

Ash was feeling quite good, great even. When the pressure of the invading energy had become too much, his mind had been transported to another place. Or maybe more like a subsection of his mind, where he felt no pain or worry at all. He had heard about Naming ceremonies where the child passed out from the pain; those were generally regarded as failures, and the child was left with no hope of becoming a strong mage in the future. Ash idly wondered if he was going to become one of them. Oh well, even if so, it didn't matter to him.

Ash was completely at peace as he stood in a stark, seemingly endless, white room. When he unfocused his vision, taking in everything at once, he could make out no walls or other boundaries.

It was odd, Ash had never even heard of a place like this, and being here felt eerie. After a while of trying to take in his surroundings, he finally noticed how strange his vision was. Since when did he have omnidirectional vision? What was this place?

Ash then felt a warm feeling coursing through his body and filling him with energy. A symbol appeared before him, but Ash didn't recognize it. After the symbol appeared, his body warmed even more, building to an intense but pleasant heat. It was like a rush of power…No, that's definitely what it was and the feeling was incredible, filling him to his core.

The feeling built higher and higher, until Ash's vision went black for a moment, his mind overloaded by the pleasurable rush. When his sight returned, Ash found he was lying on something hard; it was uncomfortable.

He was disoriented, to say the least. It was sort of like the morning after overindulging in spirits during a village celebration. Ash didn't know where he was, or who he was for a few moments. His thoughts were hazy, but everything slowly came back to him.

He was lying on the podium at the village center, his ceremonial hat lying where it had fallen, before him. There were a few wisps of smoke curling up from the podium, but what really caught his attention was the two men standing a way back from him, with astonished expressions on their faces.

It was now that Ash's mind fully cleared, and the feeling was stronger than ever before. He felt a god's mana coursing through him like a river. It had completely overtaken his own mana veins and replaced them with something different, something more powerful.

Ash cast a spell to try it out—halfway through the chant, the spell rushed out of him with a bang. It was more powerful than he had expected. Ash decided to quickly try again.

He wanted to use the lightning spell he had started studying right after he had seen god Steve cast it. Until now, even with the aid of one of the village's old tomes which explained the use of the spell, he wasn't able to do it correctly. It was too complex; it demanded too much of him. But now that he had been granted a god's power...

He tried it, how could he resist? The river of power coursing through his veins was intoxicating, making him feel invincible. He was the first apostle of the mighty god Steve.

Ash finished the chant and a lightning bolt shot from his outstretched hand. It struck the ground and left a crater the size of a man's head. The feeling of power only waned slightly as Ash then turned and stretched out his body.

The two men were still staring, unmoving in their astonishment. Only when he had been looking at them for a moment did they move towards him. One of them withdrew something from his pocket and held it up before Ash—it was a small mirror. For some reason, the mirror didn't show his reflection. Ash saw someone else, a man with bright-yellow hair.

What kind of trick mirror is this? Ash thought. Then it hit him. *My hair turned yellow!*

"You're needed at the front lines, Ash!" the other man told him. "The battle isn't going well."

They pointed him in the direction and wished him good luck. Ash now recognized the man with the vanity mirror. He was the most successful merchant in the village, which explained why he wasn't participating in the battle; the man didn't know how to fight.

Ash nodded and set off towards the fight; he could hear it clearly now. Ash increased his pace to a run and found that his body could now withstand this pace without any apparent effort. Everything seemed so easy as a result of the transformation he'd just undergone.

As he neared the battle, he saw his own Niti clansmen were fighting but still being pushed back. Then Ash noticed the bodies; there were so many dead bodies on the street! People that had just this morning walked these very streets, who had attended his Naming. His village was being torn apart, right before his eyes. A teacher, blacksmith, lumberjack, so many of his acquaintances now lay dead on the ground!

Ash felt anger surge within in, but he held it back. Now wasn't the time, not yet. He knew that if he threw himself into battle randomly and started flinging spells, it would only help a little. At most, he would disrupt the enemy's rhythm but the thing was, in this fight there were just too many enemies. A single mage could only do so much, even if he was powered up. He needed to wait for the right opportunity, so he could make the most of his limited power. After all, he wasn't a god.

Even as he had that thought, he saw god Steve unleashing spells into the crowd of enemies from the top of a building, trying to alleviate the pressure on the Nitians. A group of Mottor clansmen were lifted into the air, shouting and struggling. They came back down drained of energy, neutralized for now.

God Steve then used Blink and appeared just before Ash, startling him. "I need you to use your Earth magic to secure the inner village walls. There's an army of ants headed our way, we can't allow them in."

It had seemed somewhat like the Nitian forces were making a fighting retreat to the village center; this certainly explained why. If an army of ants made it into the inner village through the breaches the Mottor formed, Ash didn't need to be a general to know that could spell the end of the village.

With a nod, Ash set off. He was determined to make the most of his newfound power, so he'd have to trust god Steve to take of the Mottor. He avoided the fighting as he charged back towards the village's inner walls.

Arriving at the smashed barricade, Ash could see the incoming army of ants. It seemed to stretch to the horizon like a massive spear, aimed at the heart of their village.

***

Eventually the chaos died down, giving Steve a chance to look around. Both sides had been devastated. In Niti Village's case, they only had about a hundred and fifty warriors left; their enemy had even fewer. There were still scattered pockets of fighting after the initial surrender, but soon every one of the Mottor who was left alive could see they'd lost. One by one they dropped their weapons and lay on the ground, wherever they could find a space between the dead bodies and streams of blood. There was no other option given to them but to be killed on the spot.

Everyone was exhausted, even Steve. Firing all those spells in such a short period of time not only depleted his energy but had also mentally worn him out. Even in his flashbacks, he hadn't been a warrior, just a cadet in the academy. Nothing had prepared him for this level of carnage.

Joffrey was still nowhere to be found. Amon was leading the survivors, healers, and nurses to help treat the wounded who were all over the ground, moaning piteously or begging for aid.

After a while, Ash came back to Steve, who was floating somewhat in the center of the survivors, keeping the peace. Azra had gone to help her father.

"God Steve, I've sealed up the holes in the inner wall. I don't believe the ant army will be able to get in," Ash said confidently. Then he faltered as he thought of something. "Though, what about the other entrance?"

"Don't worry about it, I told Leffer to secure that area," Steve replied.

They had done it. Niti Village was safe from both the Mottor and the ants, for now. As the rest of the Mottor clansmen were securely bound, a victory cheer rose up.

This time it was quieter; there were far fewer men left alive to participate and they were hesitant to cheer at all, since the first time had gone so poorly. But they did it anyway, for morale's sake, Steve guessed. He had learned in the academy that troops needed to keep their morale up in times of war. It was the only thing that would keep them going when the battle got tough.

They began to clear away the carnage. When word of the victory reached the noncombatants, people streamed out to help. The wounded were treated, with Nitians taking priority, while the dead were moved out of the way. Nobody was eager to treat the wounded Mottor after what they had done.

Leffer came back, looking a lot older than before. The Elder had overexerted himself in the battle and aged visibly. He approached Steve and spoke up, "We can only offer our thanks for your assistance in this battle. Niti Village owes you a lot, I'm going to call for an emergency meeting as soon as we get everything cleaned up here. Please wait here, if you want to participate."

Steve was mentally drained, but he agreed. He wanted to know what would happen, now that the Mottor's main force had been taken care of. The ant army that was roaming around outside…that would be a problem for another time.

***

Mottle had seen it all happen from his vantage point. By the time he caught up with the troops, they had moved in and were attacking Niti Village. He didn't know what to do at this point, so he trailed along behind the rearmost soldiers. He knew that there was an ant army coming this way and they would be arriving soon; he just didn't know how to tell his father.

His father was probably glad that he had gotten lost, assuming he even noticed. Usually, an Elder's son would be capable enough to join in on the battle. He knew that Mithe was out there, leading a squad of Mottor warriors. But they had gone on without him.

Mottle didn't know how to feel about this. On the one hand, it was good that he wasn't participating in the fight. On the other, it was customary to at least discuss the matter with him. Instead, he had been cut off without any warning, just because they assumed he was useless.

He considered not telling anyone about the ant army, letting them all die together. It would serve them right for making him the outcast, the black sheep of the family. *No, I can't. That's wrong,* Mottle thought. The battle was already well underway at this point. His clan was winning, pushing the Niti villagers back. Of course they would win, they had hundreds more men. On just that basis, they would win almost every single time.

The tide began to turn a little when a man flew out from the Niti crowd into the air and started sniping away at their mage commanders. Flight was a higher-class magic; Mottle knew this because he had studied it before.

He saw his brother, Mithe, cast a lightning spell at this man not long afterwards. The older man fell from the sky, leaving a curl of smoke in his wake. Mithe had won glory for the clan, while he,

Mottle, hadstayedback and done nothing.

A part of him felt shame, while another felt anger. Mithe had always been the best;nobody needed a second son like him. Mottle suddenly wanted to die again.

It was at this point a large group of their soldiers were lifted into the air. From Mottle's vantage point on the second floor of one of the residences, it had seemed totally random, but then he saw it. There was a ball of light on a rooftop, the one that everyone hadassumed was harmless.

It certainly didn't look harmless now, as it brought a whole squad of men down. It put them back on theground, but they twitched and seemed unable to get back up.What had it done to them?

Mottle then saw his father rush along with his private guard, into the building that the light was hovering above. From here, he wouldn't be able to see what was going to happen. He would need to get on the roof to see it.

As Mottle rushed upwards, he realized that he was slow. Extremely slow. Even climbing a few sets of stairs and the ladder to the roof had him breathing heavily. Mottle wasn't overweight, just very out of shape, never having worked on his body.

Fuck. If I miss this… Mottle thought as he pushed himself harder. *Come on. Come on…*

Mottle finally reached the top of the roof, just as his father's bodyguards were coming onto the rooftop. Then, two of them were electrocuted as soon as they came up.

Weird, how is it using magic without any chant? Mottle thought. He had studied magic previously but seeing it in action like this made him reconsider. Mottle wasn't bothered by the deaths of those bodyguards, they were rude to him anyways. What he was really interested in was his father's magic.

His father came up, along with another bodyguard. They seemed to think they were safe, because the ball of light didn't immediately electrocute them.

Cooldown time. Mottle knew about this. Magic would control the world if one could cast spells indefinitely until they ran out of mana…That would be too powerful. Nothing could stand against that, save the beings from the legends. *This is where it ends.*

The ball of light levitated his dad and the bodyguard into the air. His dad then Blinked out to the other side of the roof, where he prepared a spell to attack the ball of light from behind. It would probably work, since the ball of light didn't seem to have any defenses.

Too bad he had to use a Seal to do it, Mottle analyzed the situation. *If he was better, he could've done it without. Oh well, he still has like two more.*

Even Mottle knew about the Seals. They were the envy of every mage in the village—both villages, even. They were so hard to get, but once you had them, you basically had a couple of extra lives. He was expecting his father to end it right there.

But, instead, a girl popped up from a nearby hiding place and hit his father with a flame spear to the back. His father went down as the ball of light finished off the other bodyguard.

Mottle couldn't move for a second. He was stunned. What had just happened?

Uh… Mottle at first failed to produce a coherent thought. Then too many thoughts crashed down on him all at once. *This isn't happening. How was Father defeated? Are we going to lose? What will happen to me? This can't be real; it must be a bad dream.*

This was unacceptable.

***

Droplets of blood flew from Loop's clothing as he swung his sword to attack his next enemy. He was strong, far stronger than these fools that had tried to attack Niti. At least, that was how he felt standing next to his father in battle. They were an invincible duo.

They had flanked the enemy force under the command of the Left. He'd already been considered a man for over a year now at age sixteen, so there wasn't anyone who would oppose his decision to fight alongside his father. He had been considering whether to participate before, as he wandered the streets of Niti, but as soon as he saw the dire wolves he knew he had to do something.

He had been there when his grandfather destroyed the dire wolf force and sent them packing. Now, he would be here when god Steve destroyed the Mottor force.

The feeling of battle was exhilarating, to say the least. Loop had trained his swordsmanship before, but it hadn't prepared him for the sensations of a life-and-death fight. He lunged, blocked, and parried, all the while knowing that one mistake could put him down for good.

He and his father were fighting side by side with the Workforces that they had overseen earlier. Now that they were in the thick of combat, he wasn't in command of the prisoners anymore. They were free to fight however they thought best but it had been made clear that traitorous acts would result in their summary execution. A lot of them had interesting fighting styles, Loop noted.

After fighting for what felt like forever but was probably only a few handfuls of minutes, the enemy force surrendered with their hands and weapons up in the air. Loop shouted in victory, along with the other Niti clansmen. They had succeeded in defending their village! He then accompanied his father to collect the enemy soldiers and place them accordingly.

He surveyed the prisoners-of-war, noting in passing that most of them were just like him: tan-skinned and strong. Even though their leaders had called for surrender, many of the men were slow to lay down their weapons. Loop could understand their mindset; they were still unwilling to give up, seeing that they held the manpower advantage. When the last of the soldiers finally disarmed, Loop and his father, as well as the rest of the Niti clansmen, began to round them up and lead them away.

Suddenly, someone shouted something about an ant army and his father cried out as he was stabbed through the chest by a Mottor. The perpetrator of this dishonorable act was almost immediately struck down by divine lightning, but the damage had been done.

Loop was stunned. His father... Then his vision went red. As everything around him erupted into chaos again, he felt his pulse beat faster and faster—it sounded like frantic war drums. He lifted his sword above his head, and began the slaughter.

Chapter 19

"Usually, an army of ants wouldn't attack the village itself. However, walling up was a good idea. This way, they would have to burn a lot of their stamina to charge up the walls, that is assuming they even can, since they're so large. Damn mana-infused creatures, they must be here for something else." Leffer had been talking for a few minutes now, trying to address everything that had happened earlier in the day. The emergency village meeting consisted of Leffer, Amon, Loop, Ash, Azra, and Steve, as well as a few other important village personnel.

"We did find an army of centipedes near the Lake," Azra offered. "It might have to do with the King of the Lake being dead. God Steve killed it the other day, and the freshwater mana spring would be very appealing to any creature."

"That might be the reason." Leffer nodded, agreeing with Azra. She had a good point. "Actually, it is the most likely reason. Nothing else I can think of explains why the ant army would be here, of all places. It seems that just like us, they want the Mana Lake.

"Eventually, that Lake might attract even larger creatures. We might have to be prepared for a lot more danger. Bug armies generally won't attack us, but other beings might." Leffer was in a bit of a predicament. They were essentially trapped inside the village now, for fear that they might be eradicated by beings drawn to the Mana Lake. He then turned to Steve. "What should we do, god Steve?"

"There's a Crystal at the bottom of the Mana Lake. I think it's supplying the Lake and the surroundings with mana. If I could get into the Lake, I could drain the Crystal to solve the problem. It's leaking out too much energy right now," Steve offered. He needed all the energy he could get, if he was going to have any chance of evolving to Changeling. He would just have to hope the affinity he absorbed from it wouldn't make him less compatible with the evolution.

Steve checked the countdown once more. It read:

2 Days 12 Hours 35 Minutes 30 Seconds

He still had almost half the time left to decide, anyway. For now,

Vampire or Changeling looked like good options to him. After draining a lot of the Mottor, his Vampire evolution had become even better in terms of energy cost.

Excess energy would buff up the evolution even more, Bonnie had told him. This meant that every bit of excess energy would change the outcome of the evolution. Whether that was initially or later, Steve wasn't sure, but there had to be something he was missing. He was certain that right now he didn't have the full picture of the situation.

Steve considered what had happened the last few days. He needed some time to review, and this was it. The last memory had given him some more insights.

First, he had woken up with absolutely no feelings or memories. This happened at countdown T minus five days. Every $n+1$ hours he would gain a feeling or a memory, alternating between the two. Then there were the pesky rules that had consequences attached to them. The 'Greater Mind' passive had blocked out Bonnie—somehow, she apparentlycounted as a tool of mind control.

The villagers were still discussing the repercussions of this attack. They were also discussing his abilities, but even so, Steve was only half paying attention as he reconsidered his position in the world.

Bonnie, was there anything you might've said during the time where you were blocked but couldn't? Steve asked. He hadn't considered this before, mostly because he hadn't had enough time to think. He was either training in his spells or rushing around, ever since Bonnie came back. They hadn't been able to truly sit down and talk, so this meeting was a good opportunity for that.

"As part of the consequence, I can't tell you!" Bonnie happily replied. Why was she so joyful all the time?

What were these consequences? What were the rules for? Who had created and enforced them? And why was Bonnie considered a form of mind control?

Countless questions flew through Steve's mind. Someone or something had placed him here with these specific guidelines for a reason, right? It couldn't have been random. Bonnie's existence was proof that the situation he found himself in and the rules he was subject to, had been created by some entity, for some purpose.

Unless he was insane…but no, Steve didn't want to go down the rabbit hole of questioning his own sanity. He discarded the terrible thought and continued.

So, my actions change the list. Steve went over what he knew again. The spells I learn affect the list. This means that in order to achieve the best evolution possible, I'll need to figure out what was originally the most powerful path I could have taken. Was the list at the start truly the most powerful? If so, then it must be either Changeling, Deity, or the still-locked evolution.

Steve regretted killing that chicken. What was he thinking? If only he hadn't, then Bonnie might have been able to point him in the right direction, or something.

The problem is, I wasn't thinking…I was a blank slate, filled with endless, baseless confidence, Steve remembered. That means the others are likely in a similar state as me. There's no reason that I should be the exception, unless there's something I'm missing.

The more he thought about it, the more he felt like he was going crazy. None of this made sense. He shouldn't be on this world, according to his memories he…Unless the memories he had experienced weren't memories at all. Steve considered the possibility that the experiences that he was being fed weren't real. What if they weren't events that had happened in his previous life, but bits and pieces of a puzzle?

Up until the last 'memory,' he had just been cruising along. He hadn't taken everything into consideration, but now he was hesitant. What did these visions mean? Steve was sure that they weren't random; the visions showed specific bits and pieces of his life, or at least a life. But why those scenes specifically?

There had been the chess game with Xander. Then there came

the night scene with his 'girlfriend.' Steve paused at that. He still wanted to know who she was, even now. The feeling hadn't gone away. But he forced himself to think beyond what he wanted. After that came the prank in the classroom. Then came the scene with his 'father,' showing him the stars. Last had been the despair scene where he was trapped in perpetual fear and darkness.

The only name he had from his 'memories' was Xander. So, that must be the clue that bound the elements of this puzzle together—that was, assuming this really was a puzzle. If he could just meet and confer with Xander, assuming hewas also in this world, then he would have a lot more information to work with.

Steve was sure that there were others in this world. So far, Bonnie hadn't lied to him—everything she said turned out to be true. She had told him of creatures, explained how to view the evolution listings and what affected the list, helped him learn how to absorb energy, and guided him through Ash's Naming ceremony. That meant what Bonnie said could be trusted.

He turned his attention back to the meeting. They were debating what to do with the Elemental Bark and their portion of the Crystals. Then, they began discussing what would happen to Ekem Village and Mottor Village. Steve tuned them out again; none of this had anything to do with him.

If Xanderwas in this world with him, he could assume that his visions were really his memories. If he could confirm the nature of his experiences by speaking with his good friend, then that would be a huge weight off his mind. Instead of finding his girlfriend, Steve needed to focus on finding Xanderfirst. It was good to sort out his priorities, even though he didn't like the conclusion he came to.

Of course, this was all based on the huge assumption that they were all brought here together. Steve had a hunch that they were, though. If not, then what purpose did these visions serve? There was too much he didn't know. He hated not knowing if he could even trust his own 'memories.'

Steve checked his countdown again. The meeting was going longer than expected. It read:

2 Days 12 Hours 3 Minute 2 Seconds

Dwelling on this too much would be bad for his state of mind, so he listened as the village Elder wrapped things up.

"So, we will need to send out squads to make sure the area is safe. We don't think that the insect armies will directly attack us, because their target is the Lake. With that said, it doesn't mean that they won't attack on sight if we approach them, just because we are there. We need to make sure we avoid being spotted when they clash," Leffer reasoned. It was true, the two insect armies would most likely fight each other and they didn't want to get caught in the crossfire.

"As to the situation of Mottor and Ekem villages, they are currently without leaders. We might be able to take their lands, if we act quickly. We need to heal our forces, conscript two hundred more men and prepare to move out as soon as possible." Leffer saw an opportunity to increase his clan's power.

The previous Niti Village Elder, Notomen, had lost his power because he was too hesitant to act. Leffer did not wish to repeat the same mistake. "With that, this meeting is adjourned. Commands will be issued shortly. Spread the word that anyone who needs rest should take it now. God Steve, do you have any issues you would like to discuss?"

"No, that's all fine," Steve calmly replied. Being addressed suddenly, he didn't quite know how to respond. He hoped by just agreeing, they wouldn't notice that he hadn't been listening.

Suddenly, Bonnie spoke in a monotone voice again, "Congratulations, everyone has survived half of the beginner period. You now have two choices: You may either specialize in one evolution or choose to have more memories unlocked!"

**

I...Do I get more information? Steve sent mentally. That couldn't be it, could it?

"Ordinarily not. But you are a special case, because of the consequence of Greater Mind," Bonnie replied robotically. "Specialization allows you to choose one evolution and receive tips from your helper to achieve the best route to success with it. The other option will unlock many more memories. Which will you choose?"

Steve considered for about two seconds, then made the obvious choice. "Specialization – Changeling." Having more memories might be helpful, but right now he wasn't even sure that they were his memories. Bonnie hadn't specified that they were his, and the wording didn't even give him any hints.

From what he'd seen though, the technology in the visions was incredibly complex. Considering all the possibilities, he couldn't even be sure that he wouldn't wake up one day in his own bed back home. Or maybe this was some elaborate prank. Who knew, maybe this was all a dream? One big, completely fucked-up dream.

Steve had taken everything at face value until the despairing flashback. Only then had it really hit him how scary this world and the situation he found himself in was. Now he'd just witnessed hundreds of human beings die violently. That hadn't improved his opinion of this place, at all.

There were so many things he didn't understand. He needed to get out of Niti Village and explore the world. Bonnie had said specializing would help get some answers, at least in relation to his evolution.

"You are the second one to select Specialization," Bonnie said, still speaking in a monotone voice. Then, she switched back to happy Bonnie. "Go to the Mana Lake, right now! Absorb the Crystal inside of it. The Water attribute will greatly benefit your Changeling evolution!"

So, it was like that. It was nice to get such direct advice and information. Steve found it interesting that he was the second one to select Specialization, though.

Bonnie made it sound urgent, so Steve left immediately. He had seen Ash and Azra milling about, as if they wanted to ask him a question, but they looked practically asleep on their feet, so he wasn't going to take them with him. This was his third time heading over to the Mana Lake. He remembered the way.

Steve checked his energy as he was heading out.

Current Energy – 10,328

Max Energy – 14,350

Steve burned energy to speed himself towards the Mana Lake; after that long fight, he had gained a lot. Draining from mages and warriors seemed to be much more efficient than draining from livestock or Crystals.

He guessed that absorbing the huge Crystal on the bottom of the lake would probably increase his energy by ten thousand or more, but he needed to be quick. Night was falling, and the creatures of the forest were probably going to be fighting for control of the Mana Lake.

Steve wondered if the ant and centipede armies really would clash. He could probably get a lot of free energy from that, if he was careful, but it was better to focus on the task at hand. He may never have this opportunity again if truly powerful creatures arrived at the Mana Lake. Plus, it would be a good idea to figure out whether Bonnie was omniscient, or if she were just well informed, compared to himself. Ifhe got there and saw the Mana Lake was dried up, or otherwise inaccessible to him, then he would know that Bonnie's guidance was only based on limited knowledge.

He was still wondering if the information about the best path to his desired evolution had come from Bonnie, or was provided by some third party. The voice had changed when it had given him the suggestion, but Steve still knew better than to trust it blindly. He eventually decided that such a detail was irrelevant at the moment. He would have to absorb that Crystal anyways, so better sooner than later, judging by the circumstances that had already arisen in the short period of time since he killed the fish in the lake.

Steve had passed the inner village wall and kept on going. He didn't see anything unusual in the outer village, other than tracks of the ants, who had been forced to detour around the wall. They were heading to the Mana Lake as well; that much was obvious from the direction of the tracks.

Steve had ignored most of the conversation in the meeting, but he got the gist of it. The creatures that were now contesting the Mana Lake weren't always this large or aggressive. They used to be several orders of magnitude smaller, but had become larger and larger due to the amount of mana they had absorbed. The amount of food they needed to survive also decreased as a result of the mana infusion making their bodies more efficient.

Steve traveled as fast as his energy allowed him to. If he focused completely on traveling, then he would be able to get there in around twenty minutes. Just as he was about to reach the Mana Lake, he saw remnants of the bug battle between the ants and the centipedes. Judging from the bodies on the forest ground, the centipedes had won.

It looked to have been a close battle though; they seemed to have exchanged casualties at a near one-to-one ratio. Nearby, Steve saw a scorch mark on a tree, that appeared from the shape of it to have been caused by magic.

Steve stopped to look at the mark a little more closely. He contemplated the implications. If all, or even some of them can use magic, I need to be more careful than I had first thought. If that's the case…then maybe I shouldn't go in directly.

Even as he had that thought, he saw something fly at him out of his peripheral vision. It was a fireball, streaking from the nearby underbrush. Steve couldn't activate Blink quickly enough, so the fireball hit him straight on.

Steve didn't feel any pain—in fact he didn't feel anything—but the fireball turned half of his field of view black as it went on through his side and continued on, into the forest. Steve's vision returned slowly, as his light body recovered from having half of it blasted away. Steve could feel that his light body had become smaller. He wondered if there was a point of no return. That would be disastrous.

The spell had come from an ant that was twice the size of the others he had seen, almost two feet long and bright red, with shiny wings on its back.

In the time it had taken to make that observation, Steve readied his Shock spell in his mind and fired. It struck the large red ant in the thorax, the heat of the lightning making its chitin shell crack and char around the impact. Steve readied another blast, intent on killing his attacker.

"Wait!" a distinctly female voice screeched in his mind. "Don't!"

Steve was confused. It sounded like someone was trying to talk to him.

"Who's there!" Steve shouted.

"Queen Tolma, hive mind of the fire ants. We deeply apologize for giving offense, we just sensed a large amount of energy," the red ant said. Steve was shocked that the ant that attacked him was speaking to him telepathically. A few other smaller, brown ants appeared and took up defensive positions around the large winged ant. "Please forgive our transgressions."

I think I should gather whatever information I can from this ant. It seems to be the leader of the smaller ants, Steve thought. Besides, without the element of surprise on its side…I can kill it easily if I need to.

"I accept your apology. How are you talking to me mentally like that, though?" Steve said aloud. Even though it was communicating mentally with him, he wasn't sure how to return the message in kind.

"We believe you should be capable of this…" Tolma replied. From the tone of the voice in his mind, it sounded like the ant didn't believe he was asking a serious question.

Steve tried it. He focused his attention on Tolma and tried to speak to it from his mind. It didn't work. He then imagined a box space in his mind, labeled it Tolma, and spoke to it.

Ah, I see, Steve sent mentally. This time, there was a definite sensation that the message had gone through, so he moved on to the important topic. Why did you attack me?

He wouldn't spend more than a few minutes on this and he was already near to his destination. Maybe he could get some insight on what to expect to run into at the Mana Lake.

"We just lost the war against the centipedes. Needed energy to recuperate. You were a large source of energy passing by," Tolma answered quite honestly. Likely it understood that if it didn't, then Steve could kill it on the spot.

How many races are at the Mana Lake right now? Steve asked directly. He needed to know this most of all.

"The surviving centipedes are in combat with something, though we can't sense what it is," Tolma told him.

Can you fight? How many of your number are left? Steve asked. He was planning on taking these ants and contesting the Mana Lake.

"We number only in the tens. We will have reinforcements soon. Another of our armies is coming. We will take the Mana Lake then," Tolma replied. That didn't exactly answer the question, so Steve pressed on.

Help me take the Mana Lake. I will compensate you. There's no time to discuss it right now, figure out the details later. I just need a distraction when I go in, Steve confidently stated. He didn't know what other race was fighting with the centipedes, but in case they could use magic, it would definitely be better to go in with an ally.

There was a pause, the queen ant shifted its head to the side...then was motionless even longer. It seemed to be calculating something.

"We will go, lead the way," Tolma declared. Even more ants then scuttled out of the underbrush to form their neat double column formation near Tolma once more. Though now, instead of the massive line stretching toward the horizon he had seen from Niti, it was only around fifty feet long.

It's hard to believe this is all that's left, they must have started out with hundreds, maybe even a thousand! Steve boggled at the carnage.

He then led the way toward the Mana Lake, with the several dozen ants behind him. Steve was certain that they would betray him if he showed that he was incapable of upholding his end of the deal, but for now, they seemed to trust him. Perhaps claiming they had reinforcements coming had just been a bluff, meant to increase their bargaining power, but it did seem plausible.

Draining the massive Crystal took priority over everything else.

He just needed to use them to serve as a distraction. He would deal with the consequences later. Everything depended on what he encountered when he got to the lake, so Steve worked to form a few contingency plans as he covered the last bit of distance.

Chapter 20

Steve's plan to take the Mana Lake hinged on surprise. Steve had to assume that the other races also knew magic. If even some ants had magical abilities, then it seemed likely that every race could use magic in some way—it was an integral part of this world.

Steve knew the centipede army would be here, battling for control of the Mana Lake, but he hadn't expected two other races contesting the territory, one of which was aerial. Some sort of large birds were swooping down and feeding on the centipede and other bug armies.

"What are those?" Steve asked Tolma. It was better to know what he was dealing with before he jumped in.

"Grasshopper clan," Tolma said. She gestured with her antennae in the direction of the large green insect. "We believe the head of that clan uses only nature magic. The ones flying above are birds known as falcons. The leader of their flock uses air magic."

After Steve heard this, he moved into position. He would need to be a bit farther away from Tolma and the ant army.

The centipedes weren't nearly as numerous as the last time Steve had seen them. They were now roughly equal with Tolma's ants and losing another of their number every few seconds. It was a chaotic fight, as centipedes grappled on the forest floor with grasshoppers twice their size and both sides were being picked off by the falcons in the air. The falcons in turn took losses, when one would occasionally get caught by a grasshopper or be shot down with magic by the largest centipede Steve had ever seen.

Steve was currently two hundred feet from the water. He needed to get closer; right now a couple Blink spells would only get him about halfway. They would need to act fast in order to make sure no other races would come to contest the Mana Lake. Steve observed for a few more moments, then when the time looked right, he gave the command.

Now, Tolma! Steve sent mentally.

Ten ants pushed their way out of the ground near the Lake, on the opposite side of the fight from Steve. They immediately moved toward the three-way battle unfolding on the lake shore. A small group of centipedes split off to challenge the ants. The ten ants formed two ranks of five each, with a small gap in the middle, and charged.

As the centipedes converged on the charging ants, a fireball shot through the hole in the ant's ranks and blasted into the centipede army. The display of magic caused more of the centipedes and a falcon to go for the ants.

More ants tore themselves free of the ground around their brethren, making the threat clear to the other creatures contesting the Mana Lake. The focus of the battle slowly shifted towards this new challenger, until Steve finally judged that he had the space he needed.

By now, the sun had almost dipped below the horizon and the light was getting weak, though thankfully it wasn't yet fully dark. Steve turned his light down as much as he could and went for it.

Steve estimated that he could travel ten feet a second when he pushed as hard as possible. He couldn't afford to do that here though, as it would require putting out a lot of light, making him nothing but a glowing target to the assembled animal combatants.

He moved as quickly as he was able, while maintaining minimum luminescence, and took in the battle. The ten ants that had led the distraction force were already in bad shape. As Steve watched, a wind blade from a falcon decimated the ants' formation. Centipedes took advantage of the opening and moved to flank them. The grasshoppers weren't faring any better though. It seemed like centipedes were still the strongest of the three landbound forces, despite being less numerous now.

Steve was about halfway to the water when he noticed two spells coming at him out of his peripherals. One was shot by a large centipede in the middle of the fight. The other was created by a grasshopper. Not having any interest in being hit by a second spell today, he Blinked out of the way and moved at maximum speed towards the lake. There was no chance to be stealthy anymore.

A wind blade came from above, narrowly missing Steve as he slowed to avoid it. The spell slammed into the ground and blasted a shower of dirt into the air as two falcons swooped at him from above. Steve narrowly managed to avoid their coordinated attack by quickly dodging to the side. He continued towards the Mana Lake; this was getting a lot more hectic than he'd hoped, but just a few dozen feet remained until he reached the safety of the water.

At that moment, a roar came from the forest behind him, followed by a screech, different from the falcons above. They were loud and ferocious. Steve was sure that more powerful beings had arrived for the Mana Lake. He couldn't spare the time to worry about what exactly they were and continued full speed ahead.

Steve made it to the Mana Lake without any more close calls and dove down into the water without hesitation. This part at least seemed to be going according to plan.

I hope Tolma is okay, Steve thought. Its distraction had been a great help. Without it sacrificing some of its remaining forces for him, the other combatants may have been able to fire more than one rotation of spells or had more time to gather their magic for a stronger effect. He didn't want to think about how badly that might have gone for him.

Now there was a new issue Steve hadn't anticipated; the Mana Lake itself was very murky, especially after having been churned up by his earlier attack on the fishmen. Even with Steve's quality omnidirectional vision, and being a living light source, he could still barely see through five feet of water around him.

Bonnie, what do I do? Steve asked.

"Imagine yourself as a box in your mind, then direct your Energy to suffuse and strengthen that box," Bonnie carefully instructed him. "Then dive down."

He did as instructed, then dove down into the deeper water. Pressure built around his little energy field as he dove ever deeper. At one point, he worried that the pressure would overcome his protection, so he paused a little and tried to get used to it. In a few minutes, he felt confident enough to dive down once more.

All this time, Steve couldn't see anything. His only method of navigation was to make sure he was headed in the direction of the densest energy, which he could vaguely sense. The Crystal's energies were diffused rather evenly throughout the water now and had begun leaking out into the surrounding atmosphere, drawing all the creatures who coveted the mana for themselves.

Now that I think about it, why did it take an entire day to become like this? Steve wondered. *Shouldn't the mana have immediately spread?*

The answer became clear when he reached the lake floor. He noticed the reflection of his own light off of the blue Crystal first, then was able to make out the outline of a massive, eight-tentacled creature looming near it. It was hard to judge with the tentacles coiled around the crystal, but Steve guessed they may be nearly a hundred feet long. The Crystal was almost totally enveloped by the immense body and many coils of tentacles. Whatever this creature had been, it looked to have been crushed, along with everything else on the floor.

It must not have died immediately... Steve thought. He had dropped millions of gallons of water onto the creatures, but something this size may have been able to create a barrier or something that prevented it from being killed outright. Steve felt sure that nothing could have survived the hit directly.

Aside from that large eight-limbed creature, there were a lot of other elongated, flat fish strewn around the lake floor. They were many different colors, but Steve could only make out any detail when he passed directly above them. The range of his vision was even worse at the bottom of the lake.

Finally, he reached the Crystal.

The variety and density of the fish population here is really something, Steve thought to himself. There must have been at least a couple hundred different species in this lake. *What now, Bonnie?*

Steve checked his energy levels and found he was running low. It read:

Current Energy – 3,509

Max Energy – 15,050

"Start absorbing the energy by touching the tip of the Crystal," Bonnie commanded. It seemed like this was an important part. "You'll gain a strong affinity for water this way."

He moved to do so. As a part of the Crystal entered his light body, all of the mana accumulated in the water started moving towards him rapidly, drawn in by his absorption of the Crystal. Steve's energy filled up and his light body became hot. It felt like being swept along by a river of pure mana.

As Steve began to absorb the Crystal, he had a feeling it was giving him much more than just energy. It was a deep-blue Crystal, the deepest shade he had ever seen. Only now, could he fully appreciate the beauty and majesty of it.

As with the other times that he had absorbed energy on an unprecedented level, it felt better than anything he'd ever experienced or even imagined. But it was starting to overwhelm him, the energy didn't seem to be stopping, and Steve didn't know if he even could stop it safely.

Bonnie? Steve queried nervously. He could try to stop right now by moving away from the Crystal, but he wasn't sure what Bonnie intended and she conveniently hadn't told him what would happen.

"Keep going!" Bonnie said happily.

Steve kept at it. She hadn't led him wrong before. Even if it started to go badly he could just burn off the excess energy by repeated spell casting…he hoped.

His energy rose until it surpassed the maximum and even then the Crystal had a long way to go until it ran out. He was trying to absorb a whole lake's worth of mana, after all.

The sensation of heat was becoming unbearable and Steve became dizzy. His mind felt like it was being drawn out of his body. Everything became surreal for a moment, and then he blacked out once more.

***

He came to in a white room that seemed endless, though only when he tried to focus on a wall. Steve still had his omnidirectional vision, but it felt somehow out of place, here, in a way he couldn't quite pinpoint.

A symbol he didn't recognize suddenly appeared on the wall.

What was this place? Why was he here? Other questions Steve couldn't answer floated through his mind as he was launched back out of the strange white void.

***

Steve was still underwater at the bottom of the lake. Only now, the Crystal had lost its deep-blue hue and was dull gray, just like the other absorbed Crystals. Steve immediately checked his energy storage. It read:

Current Energy – 23,000

Max Energy – 24,000

It seemed strange that he wasn't at max energy, even after all that had occurred. Still, absorbing this Crystal had helped both his current and max energy immensely. Steve wondered what that vision had been about; it didn't seem that it could be related to the countdown, since he wasn't anywhere close to a memory point. Also,

Steve had a feeling that since he chose Specialization, he wouldn't be experiencing any more memories.

Well, time to go check up with Tolma, Steve thought, after inspecting his body. It was hard for him to observe himself, but there hadn't been any noticeable changes. *I wonder if they're okay.*

The journey up was far easier for Steve. There wasn't a need to put up an energy barrier this time. Steve just needed to find out whether the Mana Lake was still being contested. If it was, then he would drain the mana still remaining in the water, leaving nothing behind.

To his surprise, there was nothing to be seen on the surface when he emerged. There wasn't anything at all; the combatants and the dead bodies were gone. There were traces of gore and craters in the ground, but other than that, one wouldn't have known that a massive multi-species battle royale had occurred.

How were the bodies cleared away so fast? Steve wondered. After considering it for a moment, he realized the truth. *The bodies weren't cleared away rapidly…I was submerged for quite a while. How long was I down there? What did the Crystal give me?*

After another moment, he put those questions aside; there was no point worrying any more about it.

Bonnie, what next? Steve asked. He would have to make the most of the Specialization perk he had chosen. The sun was already rising above the horizon, meaning he had been out all night. Steve was a bit irritated at the loss of time; he needed to take every opportunity to shape his evolution.

Bonnie led him around to various areas near the lake. They made sure to never go beyond the ten-mile radius allowed by the rules; Steve didn't need another penalty. He did what Bonnie suggested, as he tried to make up for the two days he hadn't had her to advise him.

The next few days were spent in Niti Village. The Nitians were all in mourning as they slowly worked to rebuild what had been lost. Plans were made to send a scouting expedition to see how the Mottor clan was handling their loss. They hadn't seen the Mottor's Right in the prisoners or corpses they had, so Leffer assumed he was still alive and had probably informed them of what had happened. That was fine, though; Niti Village had time to prepare and new options on the table.

Leeroy hadn't survived the surprise attack that had been launched at the moment of surrender. Loop was sad at the loss but there was also another air about him. The boy was calm, almost frighteningly so, during the funeral ceremony.

Joffrey had survived—after the battle, he was found in a bush, unconscious. His mana had been entirely spent and he broke an arm and a leg. Thankfully, with the dregs of his mana, he had been able to prevent most of the damage from the lightning itself.

Ash's hair was now yellow, apparently from the bolt of lightning which had charged him after the naming ceremony. He acquired a lightning affinity in his naming, so Leffer and Amon had agreed to send Ash to the Capital to learn about his affinity in their academies.

The rest of the goings on didn't interest Steve, who was mainly focused on acquiring the correct types of energy and increasing his max energy storage. The big moment was drawing near.

Finally, the countdown reached:

0 Days 0 Hours 0 Minutes 0 Seconds

It was time to evolve.

***

"Steve! Countdown has reached zero," Bonnie said happily. "Restrictions on my thoughts have been lifted somewhat. Let me show you the rules for this next stage."

At that moment the rules appeared in Steve's mind, almost as if they were floating directly before him. Even if he tried to shift his focus, they moved with it.

1) Don't die.

2) The first evolution must be completed within an hour of the beginner countdown ending.

3) Don't wander outside of your starting continent.

4) Don't evolve to highest evolution.

5) Locked

6) Locked

"As always, breaking the rules involves consequences!" Bonnie finished up. "You have an hour to evolve to your specified evolution – Changeling. The next stage has officially started!"

Another image appeared in his mind at this point. This one was a handful of dots, spread across a flat white sheet.

"What am I seeing?" Steve asked. The rules and whatever this was, were overlapping and interfering with one another. It was annoying and he couldn't seem to get rid of either of them.

"Those are the other members of your generation of balls of light!" Bonnie said. "You get this information for being the first one to break a rule, when you killed that chicken."

Steve remembered. That hadn't been the smartest move, looking back on it. Though, it did seem to still be giving him some benefits. Steve wanted to know what he was supposed to do with this information so he asked, "How do I use this, Bonnie?"

"Just focus in one direction and you'll see the dots move," Bonnie instructed. She had always been very helpful when it came to instructing him to perform tasks like this. Steve focused on a random direction and found that the six dots were scattered around on the sheet. He tried to grasp their locations, relative to his own position, but realized he had no scale to work from.

As he manipulated the map some more, he found that one of the dots was above the sheet. The dot's position was odd, because if he was understanding this, the white sheet represented ground level. Steve wasn't sure what to make of this featureless map, that seemed to only contain the direction and location of other balls of light like him.

The closest dot was to the East—according to Ash, that land was called Mudda. Steve remembered that Ash said it contained various Beast-man tribes and monster races. The distribution of the dots was interesting; it seemed likely that most of them were in different countries, spread around the continent.

There were four dots clustered around him; that included the one that seemed to be high above the rest. Though, there were also two dots which seemed to be a lot farther off than the others. Judging from to the direction they were in, Steve guessed they were across the Great Ocean Lovoth. He assumed them being so distant had something to do with rule number three, which forbade him from leaving this continent during this stage.

What are these rules? What is even the point? Steve thought to himself. It was obvious that whatever had brought him here was restricting his freedom, but why? After pondering for a moment, Steve let it go, as he'd had to with so many other mysteries in the last few days. There wasn't time to analyze it anyway—he had to prepare, as he only had around forty-five minutes left to evolve or risk another penalty.

How do I evolve? Steve asked Bonnie. It was finally time. The last two days had been extremely productive; they had journeyed all over the place collecting energy. He had even unlocked the third question-marked evolution, though it wasn't anything noteworthy and was made further irrelevant, as he had already focused on Changeling.

"Well, you have to put your mind to it, as always," Bonnie said. "Just try it first, I'll advise you if it doesn't work."

Steve imagined his body changing, and it reacted. It was strange to know his body was changing into something that he only knew by name; he didn't know what to expect. His vision warped as he fed the change with his energy. Bonnie had taught him during the prior two days of instruction that he could use his energy in all kinds of different ways. Even charging his own mind wasn't out of the question.

Steve's vision went black, though this time he didn't lose consciousness. Something told him that his body was still changing, even though there was no sensation.

After few more minutes, he definitely felt the change as his body gained flesh and bone. He found that the Energy storage he had accumulated was flowing on its own into his new body, strengthening it. Eventually there was an unpleasant tingling sensation in his newly forming body. There was nothing to do about it though, so Steve prepared himself to endure the feeling.

Then he passed out from a wave of pain.

Chapter 21

Mika flew with all her might. She was almost through the gate.

Fuck these Lesser Satans, Mika thought to herself. Cursing her pursuers helped her deal with the stress of the chase. *Sons of bitches, all of them.*

When the countdown had ended, she had evolved immediately. It had been hell being trapped in the Satan's residence.

"Duck left," Steve mentally told her. Mika narrowly avoided an ice lance that would have disemboweled her.

Steve had been indispensable lately; it was irritating that he hadn't been more helpful earlier. Maybe then, she wouldn't have been caught in the first place. She was grateful he'd probably just saved her life, but still blamed him for this entire situation at the same time.

Fuck! That was too close, Mika thought as she continued running. She was at the gate now. It had been closing, but they had stopped, apparently realizing that she would make it anyway and not wanting to instead cut off her pursuers.

Just as escape seemed imminent, an arrow pierced her arm and pinned her to the wall just shy of the gate. The pain of being yanked to a stop by the arrow stunned her.

Despair welled up as the gate closed right before her eyes; her escape had failed. Mika let out a cry of pain and defeat, then closed her eyes and sighed deeply. She was never getting out.

With that sigh, her mana was released as she unknowingly cast a spell. Her body phased out, freeing her from the arrow, and she passed through the gate bars as if they were nothing, just as the Lesser Satans closed in on her location.

***

Xander sighed. It had been five days since he was brought to this place, with strange rules and creatures unlike any he had ever seen in his memories. Now it was getting ridiculous. Why did she want him to evolve within the hour?

Why? Xander questioned Mika.

"Because I fucking said so," Mika replied, her tone harsh. The voice was headstrong and confident as she continued to berate him.

"Do it or suffer the consequences, you little—"

It was always like this. Xander had the unmistakable urge to bury his head in his hands, despite the fact that he didn't have hands, nor a head really. He had a light body, which was useless.

"Fine, mom," Xander agreed. He couldn't argue with the rules, it seemed. Xander had tried to find loopholes over the last few days as well, but there didn't seem to be any. "I guess it's time to transform. Woo, so fun!" he cheered sarcastically.

***

Todd was confused. Where was he again?

"For the last time, you're at the pyramid, dude," Xander mentally sent. "This place is kinda shifty, I get it, man."

Todd was grateful. He was glad that his helper always enjoyed helping him.

"I don't," Xander replied, instantly correcting him.

Oops! He had meant to keep that one to himself.

"You never do," Xander said exasperatedly.

"Listen up, dude. I got something to tell you," Xander continued. "You're gonna love this."

***

"I have something to share!" Todd announced into Ray's mind.

"Holy shit!" Ray startled badly. He had been experimenting with a powerful spell and almost lost his concentration. It would have destroyed half the island.

"Why, Todd, why?" Ray repeated what had become his favorite expression during the five days of countdown.

"Sorry!" Todd was his helper. Too bad he acted like he was mentally handicapped. "Hey! I heard that, you're mean…"

Ray ignored him as he focused on safely canceling the spell. It took a while to undo but he ended it, then turned his attention back to Todd. "What is it this time?" he asked tiredly. He wished he didn't have this kind of useless help. Todd had seemed alright at the beginning, but as Ray regained his memories, he'd realized that Todd's 'help' was a farce. His helper was retarded, though he meant that in the nicest way possible.

"New rules!" Todd resumed his announcer voice. "It's time to evolve!"

***

Chang was in the middle of a school of sharks, but didn't care. They were a hundred feet long and obviously deadly. It didn't matter to him; they were energy. He had prepared his spells beforehand. He engaged his protection and began the assault.

"Greater Air Manipulation," Chang called out. A tornado whirled around him, picked up the sharks, and threw them high into the air. The flying sharks were literally fish out of water and at his mercy.

"You know, you don't have to say that," Raymond commented on the matter.

Chang knew this was true; his helper was extremely clever. Nevertheless, he replied, "I have to. It sounds too cool. It never gets old."

Chang activated his drain and began absorbing the energies from the sharks in the air.

"Received new information," Raymond interrupted. "You should hear this."

***

Bonnie was tired. It seemed she was always tired. The last five days had been mentally exhausting for her. Why had she been brought here and paired up with a buffoon?

"Say it," Chang commanded. "You have to say it, or it won't be as cool, I mean effective."

"Greater Lightning Storm..." Bonnie had learned to go along with it. When she tried to resist, that only meant that the voice in her mind would never shut up. She watched as her energy flowed out of her light body, forming the spell which dropped the two trolls.

They lay on the ground, paralyzed as she started draining them.

"Say it…" Chang warned again.

Bonnie sighed mentally.

Chapter 22

"Steve! Wake up!" a voice shouted in his ear. It sounded pleasant, female, and maybe a bit familiar. "Steve?"

Steve awoke with a start. Everything was dark. He tried to focus his vision to no effect.

Another vision? Steve thought immediately. Then he remembered his evolution. What had happened?

Bonnie, I can't see, Steve sent. *What happened?*

"Try opening your eyes!" Bonnie unhelpfully replied.

Or maybe she had a point…

Steve tried opening his eyes. It worked!

It was disorienting; he was so used to just being able to see everything around him. Now, his vision was limited to two eyes; it was a severe handicap. He was in his residence, but everything seemed a lot bigger than he remembered. Maybe it was the height difference?

Steve walked over to a vanity mirror. His original guest house had been upgraded with the addition of better furnishings when he had transitioned from a guest to an honorary part of Niti Village, after his aid in the battle against the Mottor. He now had status on par with a Left or Right in the village hierarchy.

Steve looked into the mirror and saw a black humanoid of childlike proportions staring back at him. He was about three feet tall, thin, and had no mouth or nose. The only distinguishing features on his face were two eyes that could barely be seen, as they were hardly more than slits on his face.

There was a problem. The issue wasn't that his appearance was ugly to him or aesthetically displeasing. Or rather, there was that too, but the bigger issue was that he felt exactly the same as he had as a ball of light, despite his fully transformed appearance. Logically, it seemed he shouldn't be feeling that way.

Did anything change, Bonnie? Steve asked, hoping to hear good news.

"You're black now!" Bonnie cheerily answered. This was beginning to irk Steve, even though she was technically right. "Aside from the color, you have a fleshly body!"

"You're right, Bonnie," Steve said patiently. He went on, "Did any of my abilities change?"

"Yes! They're all erased, besides the Mastery of Languages one," Bonnie replied, this time a bit more serious.

As soon as Bonnie said this, Steve's patience ran out. Had he been tricked?

"Though, you get to keep your Energy system!" Bonnie declared. Then she giggled before continuing, "And you gained one new spell. You can change forms using your Energy! You should have seen the look in your eyes. Absolutely murderous!"

Steve almost spit out a sarcastic retort, but then thought of something.

Was it just his imagination, or was Bonnie acting out more than usual? In the last few days she had seemed to talk back a lot more. Maybe it had something to do with her restrictions being lifted.

So, I can become whatever I want now? Steve asked. This was important to understand. If he could copy whatever he wanted, then he could just become a bird and fly over to the first dot on his mental map. Or maybe even hitch a ride on a bird by becoming one of its feathers.

"Nope! You're limited," Bonnie clarified. "You can only become a living organism that you've seen before. Also, it can't be too complicated for you to hold in your mind. As you're keeping your Energy system, you should try to think of ways to manipulate your energy to your advantage!"

Steve tried willing his energy to become Ash. He remembered the boy, blond-haired and tall. He watched himself in the mirror as the energy that made up his fleshly body rearranged itself. Was it even accurate to call his body flesh at this point?

He watched as his short black frame stretched and spread out. Steve grew into a slightly taller and skinnier version of Ash, though the color was completely wrong. Every part of him was still black.

That's underwhelming, Steve thought, a bit depressed. *Why did I have to lose my strong and useful abilities?*

After struggling for another half an hour, he finally succeeded in becoming a passable version of Ash. Though he still wasn't happy with the result. If anyone looked closely enough, they would be able to tell that he wasn't actually human. Steve adjusted his body a little more until suddenly it felt right. The lingering imperfections disappeared, leaving him a perfect copy.

At that moment, energy began flowing through his body. Something had shifted inside of him and let loose a torrent of power. Was this the mana he kept hearing about? Steve walked outside to test his new power. Pointing at a rock, he tried to recall the chant Ash had used when casting a spell. After uttering some nonsense, he became embarrassed and gave up. This was too difficult, so he tried doing it the way he always had before, instead.

He thought of his Shock spell and tried to trigger it. After ten minutes of fruitless attempts, a small lightning bolt was formed with his mana, struck the rock, and left a small black dimple in the surface of the stone. Why was it so weak? Mana seemed to be an even bigger disappointment than his Changeling evolution had been.

He had seen others cast spells through chanting and motions but it was another thing to try it himself. To Steve, the system seemed extremely inefficient, wasting a lot of time. Steve hadn't experienced using mana like this, so he didn't understand. Of course, if the users of mana suddenly switched to pure energy like Steve, casting would be a lot easier for them.

So, I'll just continue to cast using only energy. Mana is useless, Steve analyzed. *By using energy, I should be able to recreate a few of the spells that I practiced the most.*

Casting spells in this form was harder, for sure. Instead of imagining the spell and it taking form from his energy, he needed to envision the energy taking a route through his body. Achieving even basic competency at this took a lot more time and effort than he expected. The magic system he'd enjoyed as a ball of light had been perhaps too simple, compared to this. Steve hadn't expected this new difficulty; it was going to take a lot of time to learn the ins and outs of this new evolution.

Alright, I think I have the basics down, which is fine for now, Steve thought as he concluded his training session. He felt better about this evolution now that he was confident he would regain at least most of his ability with magic. Hopefully being able to turn into anything living that he knew about would become a massive advantage if he used it properly. At the very least, he could already imagine some good uses for it when it came to defense and utility. He headed to Ash's house, still in the guise of Ash himself. He needed to inform the villagers of his evolution, before there was some misunderstanding. If they didn't realize who he was, they just might group together and try to oust him from the village.

Steve passed a few villagers on the way, who all waved in greeting to him. He waved back. Perception was simpler having only two eyes. He noticed that he didn't really miss his omnidirectional field of view. Before, he was constantly distracted by the slightest movement anywhere around him, so this form simplified that aspect of life a lot.

Steve reached the residence and pushed the flap aside to get in awkwardly with his hand. After five days of being a ball of light, it seemed he was still getting used to a humanoid body...or any physical body really. The way he moved wasn't natural, even though he had been human in his memories. It made sense though; a few mere memories wouldn't replace a lifetime of experience.

"Hi! Don't worry, it's me, Steve," he said before Ash could even process what he was seeing. He realized his current appearance might be a bit overwhelming for the young man, so he wanted to avert any extreme reactions.

In fact, Ash's reaction was the exact opposite of what he'd been concerned about. He returned Steve's greeting and took the situation in stride. Apparently, the villagers sincerely believed there was nothing Steve couldn't do.

During his last two days at the village, he had noticed more and more villagers bowing down to him when he passed by. Steve knew now that he wasn't a god; in fact, far from it. Someone or something far more powerful than he could imagine had placed him in an energy-powered light body in this world. The rules they placed on him seemed to hint that there was some reason behind it, even if he had no grasp on it for now. That said, he wasn't in a hurry to change the villagers' minds. There were benefits to being thought of as a god.

The village was now on track to becoming an official town of the Empire, though nothing was set in stone. Niti still had quite a way to go to becoming a town. First, they needed to sell off the remaining

Crystals and Elemental Bark to nearby cities and the Capital. If he remained a revered figure in Niti, there was no telling what benefits that might provide him in the future.

Steve spent some time with Ash. The boy still wanted to learn from him, but Steve had deflected, telling Ash he would come back around for him. Steve was confident that the correct path going forward was to leave and seek answers elsewhere. Once he understood his place in this world a little better, he would revisit his starting area with new eyes. The few days he had spent in Niti Village had made a significant impression on him.

Niti was a large, peaceful village that gave Steve a warm feeling. Of course, over the last few days, he'd learned that the Nitians' love of a simple lifestyle didn't mean that they were completely weak. Steve understood enough of their way of magic now to know that if they had been enemies from the start, he wouldn't be alive right now.

Their dislike for conflict did not imply weakness, though many misunderstood this, including the Mottor clan. They had thrived on conflict, but in the end had been destroyed by a conflict they had sought out.

Steve had discovered that Leffer was preparing to sue the Mottor for damages. That would likely result in their clan being disbanded and any survivors of their ruling class being executed. The Empire granted no mercy to those who so flagrantly violated their laws. That iron-fisted justice was the foundation that their society was built upon.

Steve had enjoyed his time in Niti Village, but now needed to move on after he made his final preparations. As he left Ash's house, he felt an eerie rumbling in his lower torso. It was familiar, but also completely novel at the same time.

Was he hungry?

"Wow," he said out loud. "Things change."

***

This is the end of Ball of Light: Evolution

Steve's adventures will continue.

End of Ball of Light: Evolution,

—The first published book by AR Chen!

The author intends to continue Steve's adventures in the next book of the series!

Please read on for a note by the author...

...And don't forget to review this novel!

(Even a simple review will help!)

To check out more GameLit and LitRPG stories, and join a couple large communities, feel free to check out:

GameLit Society

and

LitRPG Books

And for a trashy (but large) meme group around GameLit, Eastern novels, LitRPG, etc, check out the **GameLit, LitRPG, Xianxia, and Wuxia -- fun group** (it's a silly place.)

About the Author

AR Chen is a serious gamer.

When he first started writing this story as a web serial on the internet, he never imagined to one day actually hold this book in his hands.

A fan of comics, games, RPGs, and LitRPG stories, it seems appropriate that Ball of Light would be his first published story.

A Note by AR Chen:

And here we are. At the final page.

I would like to take a moment to thank Blaise Corvin for helping me put the book together. It would not have come together so nicely if he hadn't reached out to me.

A fantastic journey awaits Steve and his companions in book 2 as we explore the world past Niti Village.

I hope you are all excited for the journey ahead of us!

-AR Chen

You can reach me at: https://www.facebook.com/AR-Chen-108628970477547/

www.ingramcontent.com/pod-product-compliance
Lightning Source LLC
Chambersburg PA
CBHW051326250626
47155CB00007B/2468